hurt you—which is something I'm still working on myself, even to this day.

Writing Summer as she regains her agency and falls in love was healing in and of itself. The romance between her and Jules is one that is kind and patient—a love that allows for breathing room and sparks bravery. And, of course, building their romance was *fun*. As someone who studied public relations in college, I figured it was inevitable that I would one day write a book centered around a PR stunt. After *Counting Down with You*, I wasn't sure if I would be inspired to write the fake dating trope again—but the context was so different this time around that it felt entirely new. Pretending to date around your friends and family is nothing like pretending to date in front of the whole world, and it was so delightful to explore the trope through a new lens.

I will *also* say I was heavily inspired by pop culture while writing this story. Again, as a PR major, how could I not be? I loved exploring the idea of how our reputations can precede us—and how sometimes we pretend to be people we're not because that's what the world expects of us. As you'll soon discover, I decided to frame this narrative using playlists to show the interior of Summer's mind and headlines to show the exterior of how she's being perceived. There's a lot to be said about performing for an audience—but I'll let you find that out for yourself as you read on.

Thank you for giving this story a chance. I hope you come out of it with a sense of hope and a sense of belonging. And, like Summer, I hope you choose to be true to who you are, even if it's only in the safety of your own heart.

All the love,

Tashie

Dear Reader,

I honestly don't even know how to write this author's note. It's difficult to put into words what this story means to me without revealing almost too much about who I am. This story follows a girl named Summer Ali as she grapples with her identity and who she is—and it's very personal to me. I see myself in her more than I've ever seen myself in my previous books. Her journey to figuring out who she is, what she wants, and what she's willing to sacrifice was simultaneously the most difficult and the most easy thing I've ever had to write. I'm so excited for you to meet her because she's so deeply beloved by me, and I will always cherish her and this story.

On a different note, this book follows in the footsteps of my previous books in the way it tackles mental health and complicated familial relationships. Despite the fact that Summer is an internationally famous popstar, she's still a teenager, and she's going through things any eighteen-year-old might go through, up to and including having several mental breakdowns. In writing this story, I really wanted to explore the aftermath of cutting off toxic relationships and what that healing process is like—and how freeing yourself doesn't necessarily mean you're *free*. How the pain can linger and affect you weeks, months, even years after you sever ties. How much of a struggle it is to unlearn everything that's been taught to you, especially when you're still a kid and don't really know how to function in the world on your own. How unbelievably hard it becomes to maintain boundaries with people who have

# I'LL PRETEND YOU'RE MINE

Also by Tashie Bhuiyan
*Counting Down with You*
*A Show for Two*
*Stay with My Heart*

# I'LL PRETEND YOU'RE MINE

**TASHIE BHUIYAN**

**HARPER**
*An Imprint of HarperCollinsPublishers*

I'll Pretend You're Mine
Copyright © 2025 by Tashie Bhuiyan
All rights reserved. Manufactured in Harrisonburg, VA, United States of America. No part of this book may be used or reproduced in any manner whatsoever without written permission except in the case of brief quotations embodied in critical articles and reviews. For information, address HarperCollins Children's Books, a division of HarperCollins Publishers, 195 Broadway, New York, NY 10007.
www.epicreads.com
Library of Congress Control Number: 2024952994
ISBN 978-1-335-01392-7
Typography by David DeWitt

First Edition

*To Rachel Koltsov,*
*for always keeping my secrets safe.*

# PART ONE: WINTER

## SUMMER ALI'S WINTER-ISH PLAYLIST
**December to February**—*wet lashes and black snow*

1. "decode" —Sabrina Carpenter
2. "Family Line" —Conan Gray
3. "I miss you, I'm sorry" —Gracie Abrams
4. "mirrorball" —Taylor Swift
5. "i hate to admit" —Bang Chan
6. "Pink Pony Club" —Chappell Roan
7. "i wish i hated you" —Ariana Grande
8. "making the bed" —Olivia Rodrigo
9. "Your Power" —Billie Eilish

## CHAPTER ONE

## TEENAGE POP SENSATION SUMMER ALI SEEN ENTERING FIREBRAND STUDIOS SHORTLY AFTER FIRING HER PARENTS AS HER MANAGERS

Since my eighteenth birthday last month, I've had one cardinal rule: do not speak to my parents.

Every single day, I've been tempted to break the rule.

My best friend, Barbara Li, walks into the living room and takes one look at me gazing longingly at my phone and immediately snatches it away from me. "Absolutely not, Summer," Barbie says, a note of warning in her voice.

I sigh, thunking my head against the back of the couch. "I know. I know."

"I don't think you do," Barbie says with narrowed eyes. "What's the rule?"

"Do not speak to my parents," I mutter under my breath.

"Louder," she says. "Don't make me call Zach."

I glare at her, all too aware that she really will call our other best friend, Zach Murphy, for backup. Barbie only makes threats she's willing to follow through on.

"*Do not speak to my parents,*" I say again.

Barbie nods, satisfied, before handing me back my phone. "Come on, I made breakfast."

I follow her into the kitchen, trying my best not to twiddle my thumbs out of pure anxiety. If someone told me ten years ago that I'd spend the month after my eighteenth birthday couch surfing, I probably would've scoffed, but there's no other way to describe the predicament I've found myself in.

For what it's worth, Barbie *did* offer me her guest room to sleep in, so at least my back isn't suffering from tossing and turning on her fancy couch.

But still, as I wander around her apartment, there's something that feels distinctly off—something in my brain that buzzes insistently: *you don't belong here.*

"Stop with the puppy dog eyes," Barbie says, coming up from behind me to tug on my ponytail. "It's not like I burned it or anything."

I look down at the breakfast she made for us this morning. Two pieces of toast and half an omelet. It's a decent meal—a good meal, even—but I can't really find it in myself to eat. My stomach has been in knots since yesterday, too nervous to really sit still. It doesn't help that I'm so used to my parents standing over my shoulder, counting my calories.

"Sorry, it's not that. It looks delicious," I say, patting her on the arm as she passes. "I'm just not that hungry."

Barbie sighs, sitting down across from me. "Summer, it's going to be fine. I promise Ariana doesn't bite."

I make a face, my thick eyebrows drawing together at the mention of her manager—*our* manager now, which is strange to think about. "Of course you're gonna say that, you've worked with her for *years*. She likes you already!"

"She likes you too!" Barbie says, exasperated. "Why else would she have taken you on as a new client?"

"Yeah, but last week she had to talk me down from an anxiety attack because I was afraid my parents would jump out from behind the bushes outside her office while I was signing our contract. That's not exactly dream client behavior!"

It's hard to believe that it's only been a month since I switched management teams—and subsequently, a month since I fired my parents and moved out. Despite Ariana Carter being Barbie's manager of three years, I'm still nervous when it comes to working with her. It has less to do with her and more to do with the fact that I've spent five years having my parents oversee every move of my singing career, and it's terrifying to put it all in the hands of someone I barely know and to trust them to handle it for me instead, even if it's the right choice.

"It'll be good," Barbie says softly, her brown eyes warm as they meet mine. She has a lovely heart-shaped face, framed by dark brown hair, and every time I look at her, I'm even more certain that she was born for the stage. I wonder if people feel the same way when they look at me. "I promise, Ariana's the best there is, and she'll never judge you for mental health stuff. I wouldn't have recommended her to you otherwise."

I shrug, tugging at the sleeve of my sweatshirt. "I know, but . . ."

"But you're anxious," Barbie finishes, and finally abandons her food entirely to come back around and give me a hug. She knows physical touch tends to calm me down, and unsurprisingly, the moment her arms slip around me, some of the tension falls off me like a second skin. "I've got you, Summer."

I hold her tightly, breathing in the familiar scent of her citrus perfume, before letting go and centering myself. She's right. It'll be okay. Every time I've met with Ariana so far, she's been super friendly and down to answer my questions, so this time should be no different.

Except today I have to tell her I have an awful case of writer's block that might delay my sophomore album even longer. I've been holding off on mentioning it in case my brain decided to give me a break and actually *work*, but it's almost January now, and six months of no writing is a few too many.

I've already pushed back my deadline twice, and I'm terrified I'm going to strike out if I ask for a third time. It's a miracle my record label hasn't dropped me already. At least I'm spared from having to ask them directly—that's Ariana's job—not that it makes it any easier.

"What if she gets mad at me?" I ask once we've cleared off breakfast, setting my almost entirely untouched plate in the fridge. "We've only been working together for a few weeks, and I'm already causing so many problems."

Barbie finishes washing the last dish in the sink before she says, "Summer, as kindly as possible, Ariana is not your mother. She's not going to yell at you for being in a rut. This is a business, and she's going to help you handle it in the best way possible to maintain your career long-term. That's her *job*."

"I don't want to be a problem child, though," I say quietly, fidgeting with the end of my sleeve.

"You're hardly a problem child, Summer." Barbie reaches under the counter to grab a stack of magazines from a basket near our feet, then slaps one down in front of me. "*That* is what a problem child looks like."

It's an old magazine, from over a year ago, but the words are still familiar.

---
## JULES MORADI INVITES MULTIPLE GIRLS TO HOTEL ROOM AFTER MOVIE PREMIERE
---

"Okay, but this is just Hollywood being Hollywood and slut shaming people for no reason," I say, rolling my eyes and shoving the magazine back at her. "Why do you even have these?"

"It was still a PR nightmare," Barbie says, shaking her head. "And I like to keep magazines with my interviews. I'm on page twenty-two."

I go to grab the magazine again but she snatches it up, depositing it back in the basket, and I stick my tongue out at her.

She shrugs, leaning against the counter. "Like I was saying, as long as you don't have headlines like this, I promise you're not a problem child."

"Well, it's not like Ariana has to deal with him," I mumble. "She *does* have to deal with me."

Barbie's eyes light up. "Actually . . ."

I squint at her. "You're lying. I thought he retired early."

I don't know much about Jules Moradi, but I do know that it's been months since he was last seen in the public eye—maybe a year, even—as if he dropped off the face of the planet after his infamous bender following his last film release.

I've seen countless headlines theorizing on his absence, everything from him having a falling out with his film agent to growing so ill that he needed to be hospitalized for weeks on end. I personally thought retirement made the most sense, given the fact he's been working in Hollywood since he was in diapers, but from the look on Barbie's face I couldn't have been more wrong.

She scoffs. "He's like a year older than us. He doesn't have enough money to retire early."

"So then where is he?" I throw back.

"Fuck if I know," Barbie says with a sniff. "But Ariana offhandedly mentioned she signed him a few weeks back. If she can handle working with someone like *Jules Moradi*, you're light work, babe."

"Don't sound so reasonable," I complain. Her words help to some degree, but not enough to completely absolve me of any worries.

Barbie's unwavering faith in Ariana isn't unexpected, but it is strange after having my parents as the only people in my corner for years. I've never relied on them the way Barbie relies on Ariana.

Then again, Ariana helped Barbie secure a place as the opening act for Third Eye's first US tour, which in turn launched her career in a huge way. If Ariana did that for me, I probably wouldn't doubt her either.

Slowly, my body relaxes, my shoulders dropping. This is part of why I left my parents behind, after all. I'm tired of doing the same old thing and pretending to be some version of myself that never felt real. I want to be more than the nice girl from that one music competition who had a one-hit wonder.

And attending this meeting is the first step to making that happen.

By the time we're in a car and halfway to Firebrand Management, I've successfully compartmentalized most of my thoughts, and I'm as ready to see Ariana as I ever will be. Barbie still holds my hand the entire car ride, which I'm more grateful for than I can put into words, so I settle for squeezing her fingers as tightly as I can. By the way she hides a smile, I'm certain that she knows.

"Look," Barbie says suddenly, pushing me closer to the tinted windows in a bid to see for herself. "There's a bunch of paparazzi."

I lean forward, trying to see what she's looking at. It takes a moment, but eventually my eyes land on all the photographers standing outside of the Firebrand Management offices, watching the door.

"That's not for us, right?" I say, a little bewildered.

Barbie is too busy adjusting her hair using the rearview mirror. In the back seat behind us, Barbie's bodyguard, Spencer, is watching her with a fond expression, while my bodyguard, Damon, is eyeing the group of paparazzi with a look of distaste on his face. To be fair, I think Spencer is barely older than us and newer to working security, while Damon is a middle-aged father of two who's been in this industry for decades, so he probably has a lot more experience that leads him to be wary of the paparazzi.

"Barbie, did you call the paps?" I ask, nudging her with an elbow.

She makes a face at me in the mirror as she reapplies her lip gloss. "You think I would've worn *this* if I had?"

I roll my eyes. She looks gorgeous as always, in a comfy lavender sweater and mom jeans. I'm not dressed much differently in a huge hoodie that falls to mid-thigh and leggings. In my off time, I don't put too much effort into my outfits, but I recently hired a brand-new team of stylists in case the opportunity for a photo op arrives in the near future.

I try not to itch at the thought of how many people I've started to employ since leaving my parents, from my bodyguard to my stylists to an entire PR team. Most of them were already around, but they worked with my parents and not me, so it still feels like a huge change.

I can afford all of it thanks to the royalties that continue to pour in from my first—and only—album, but it still makes me want to scratch at my skin every time I see money taken out of my bank account.

Following Barbie's lead, I give myself a brief look over using the front camera of my phone and immediately wish I had thought to put on mascara before I left Barbie's apartment, but there's nothing to be done about that now.

"If they're not here for us, who *are* they here for?" I wonder, glancing out the window again as the car comes to a standstill.

"Someone who wants to be seen," Barbie says thoughtfully before gesturing to the other door. "Let's get out the other way so the car will block us. I need to fix my sweater."

I nod and pull the door of the Escalade open, hopping out of the car with a curl of anxiety tugging at my heartstrings. Barbie comes out after me, followed by our bodyguards. My eyes catch on the way Spencer whispers to Barbie quietly before taking up his spot at her side, and I make a mental note to ask her about it once we get back to her place.

Barbie finishes adjusting her sweater and gestures for me to go ahead. With a deep breath, I brace myself for an onslaught of paparazzi and hope to God they deem us unimportant so we can get in and out of the building without a fuss.

It's obvious that it's a lost cause the moment they see us, their cameras already flashing, loud clicks filling the air. I keep my gaze trained on the ground, shielding my eyes from the light, intent on getting into the office as soon as possible.

One of the paps gets too close, and Damon immediately pushes him away from me. I give my bodyguard a grateful smile before I keep walking, counting down from ten in my head to keep myself calm.

Not even two paces later, I regret keeping my gaze on the pavement rather than in front of me, because I knock into someone, almost sending us both sprawling onto the ground.

"Oh my God," I say, halfway to falling over before the person reaches out and steadies me.

I look up to unfamiliar brown eyes. Vaguely, somewhere behind me, Barbie says, "Oh, shit." I understand why soon enough, when I have a second to process the boy's entire face and match it to one in my memory.

Jules Moradi is standing in front of me, and he's somehow more handsome in person than he is on the big screen. His dark hair is slicked back, out of his face except for one lone strand that falls onto his forehead, and he's dressed head to toe in designer clothing, including a hole-knit sweater that's currently caught on one of my necklaces, tying us together. On one side of him is a bodyguard, and on the other side is another boy that must be a friend, though not one I recognize.

Barbie and I must've jinxed it. I don't know how, but it's obvious the fates colluded to make this entire situation as ironic as possible.

It clicks then that all the paparazzi must be here because of him, desperate to get a glimpse of him after months and months of radio silence.

And now I'm being photographed with him because my jewelry is refusing to come free from his clothes.

I reach out and try helplessly to untangle my necklace from the knots of his sweater. "Sorry, I'm doing my best," I whisper.

"Let me help you," he says, and his voice is deeper than I expect. The only clips I've seen of Jules in action are from *World of Tweens*, the show he was on through most of his childhood, and what launched his career as a child star. His voice was a lot squeakier on the show than it is now, which makes sense since he's nineteen now and not nine, but it still comes as a surprise.

I immediately drop my hands to my side and try not to blush as more and more flashes go off on either side of us. Damon has stepped up to try to shield us from most of it, and the same seems to be true of Jules' bodyguard.

His fingers are deft as they start to untangle us, but then one of the paps shouts, "Move out of the fucking way!" and everything goes a little sideways as the crowd presses up against us.

I widen my eyes, dragged along by my necklace as Jules shifts backward to get us out of harm's way.

I don't know which one of us trips, but suddenly we're hitting the ground, Jules' body taking the brunt of the impact underneath me. I hold my hands over my head, unintentionally burrowing closer to him to get away from all the noise and commotion around us.

"Shit," he whispers and his arms come around me, almost protectively, as people shout around us. "Are you okay?"

"You're the one who hit the ground," I say almost apologetically. Up close, he's even more gorgeous, a beauty mark dotting the side of his nose, his brown eyes warm like molasses.

Suddenly there are hands underneath my armpits, pulling me off the ground. I glance behind me in fear and relax only when I see it's Damon. My necklace stretches and then snaps, but I can't focus on it as my bodyguard herds me back into the car.

Ahead of me, Barbie is already inside, her expression frenzied, Spencer's hand on her shoulder.

"Get in, get in," she says to me quickly, voice tight with panic, and I hop inside, Damon shutting the Escalade door behind us.

The car shifts out of neutral, and the driver takes off down the New York City streets.

I struggle to catch my breath, looking around the car like it might explain what the fuck is going on. "What *happened*?"

"One of the paps got aggressive," Barbie says with a furious look on her face. "Are you all right? Did you get hurt?"

"No, I—" I glance over my shoulder, but the Firebrand Management offices are long out of sight. "That was Jules Moradi, wasn't it?"

"Yes," Barbie says, sounding as mystified. "We jinxed it."

"I had the exact same thought," I mutter. My brain is whirring, trying to piece together the puzzle in front of me. A year ago, Jules was in the media constantly for all kinds of things—underage drinking, lots of clubbing, a different girl on his arm every other day, some of them unknown, most of them his costars. But the boy I met ten minutes ago looked tired, a little rough around the edges, sure, but not the playboy I assumed he was.

I open my mouth to say as much when I realize we're headed back to Barbie's apartment instead of circling the block. "Wait, what about my meeting with Ariana? We have to go back."

"We're not going back," Damon says firmly behind me. "Your manager will understand."

I look to Barbie helplessly. "What if Ariana fires me?" I say, already knowing how irrational it sounds, but unable to stop myself. "What if she thinks I'm unreliable and can't keep to deadlines, and then—oh God, what if she reconsiders representing me at all? This might be the wake-up call she needs to realize she only signed me for your sake and I've peaked as an artist—or maybe she'll realize my music is shitty—or what if—"

Barbie claps a hand over my mouth before I can continue. "That's your anxiety talking. None of that is going to happen and you're psyching yourself out for no reason. Just *breathe*, Summer."

I force myself to inhale and exhale. It's okay. This is going to be fine. It has to be. It will be.

"You can reschedule the meeting," Barbie says gently.

It takes a while for my brain to process the words, but Barbie waits patiently as I figure it out. Eventually, I nod shortly. "Okay. You're sure it'll be all right?"

Barbie gives me a reassuring smile. "I'm sure."

## CHAPTER TWO

## ACTOR JULES MORADI IS OUT OF HIDING AND BACK TO HIS OLD WAYS: SINGER SUMMER ALI "FALLS" FOR HIM

Ariana closes her laptop slowly, but I'm unable to tear my eyes away from the screen, even as it disappears from sight. It's the first time I've had such ridiculous headlines run about me, and I can't help but wonder if this is a direct side effect of leaving behind my parents as my managers. I wouldn't have been in a position to be labeled one of Jules' many conquests if I hadn't been in front of the Firebrand offices in the first place. It's hard not to see this as the first sign of my impending doom, though I try to shove that thought down deep into the recesses of my mind.

"The whole encounter barely lasted a minute," I say in disbelief. I came in here to tell Ariana about my songwriting issue, but she waved that off entirely in favor of showing me *countless* articles about me and Jules. Both of our names have been trending on social media for three days straight.

"That's usually how these things go," Ariana says, shaking her head.

"It's not that big of a deal, though, right? It'll blow over?" I say, and I instinctively reach for my necklace to fiddle with it, but it's no longer there.

Ariana pulls a face that I don't like.

"What?" I ask, looking at the closed laptop again. "Am I missing something? It's not like anything actually happened. All I did was fall on top of him, not fall *for* him. Anyone could tell it was an accident. Right?"

"In theory, yes," Ariana allows, which isn't quite the answer I was hoping for. "But Jules has been out of the media for a long time, and everyone is hungry for scraps about him, so it might be weeks before this blows over."

I lean back in my seat, still staring at the laptop. "That's wild. Over something as small as this?"

"I know. But . . . there is a way to turn it around before then, if you're up for it."

I turn my gaze back to her. Her Afro from the last time I saw her is gone, tiny twists in their place instead, but otherwise she doesn't look any different from a few weeks ago, her face pleasant and neutral as if her last few words haven't dialed my anxiety up to a ten.

"Do we need to?" I ask. "I'm still two months out from tour. Who cares if there are fake headlines about me right now?"

"It's true that *you* don't need to care," Ariana says before sliding a folder across the table at me. "But I'm also Jules Moradi's manager, and he came to me immediately after what happened. He thinks there might be a quick fix that could benefit both of you."

I take the folder warily, flipping it open. Inside is a brief bio of Jules, an NDA, and a pitch for . . .

"You want me to do a PR stunt?" I ask, a little incredulous at the prospect. "With *him*? I don't even know him."

Ariana nods. "I know. But let's forget about Jules for a second, and talk about you. When you came to me from your parents, you said you wanted to take your career to new places and be the best version of yourself, but they were holding you back. Do you still feel that way?"

I shift in my seat, trying not to let too much of my discomfort show. "Well, yes."

"That's what I thought," Ariana says, tapping the folder again. "Jules is currently in the middle of auditioning for what is most likely going to be an Oscar-nominated film. He believes if he lands the role, he can get you a song on the soundtrack. I'm not sure how familiar you are with the Academy Awards, but there is an award for Best Original Song, and seeing as you write all your own songs . . . do you see where I'm going with this?"

My eyes bulge. Even in my wildest dreams, I never imagined something like this. "You think I could be nominated for an *Oscar*?"

"It's not out of the realm of possibility," she says. "I'll admit the odds of you winning are less likely, but even being nominated is a huge honor, and I believe it could take your career to new heights."

I look down at the folder, taking in the small photo of Jules in the corner. He's flashing a wide, dimpled smile, and he looks warm and approachable, though I don't know how much of that is an act and how much of it is real.

"I'm still not getting it. Why does *he* want to do this?" I ask, pointing at the photo. "You just agreed the headline will blow over in a few weeks."

"He can't afford to wait that long," Ariana says, but she looks a little uneasy for the first time since the meeting started. "I can tell you more, but you'll have to sign the NDA first, Summer. I can't give out confidential client information otherwise."

I resist the urge to pinch the bridge of my nose. "Do I need a lawyer to look it over first?"

Ariana considers this before nodding. "I understand we're still in a pretty new relationship, so I don't expect you to trust me blindly. Call your lawyer. I'll be outside."

Then she gets up and exits the room, leaving me alone with my thoughts. I take a moment and just breathe. When did my life get so needlessly complicated?

With a groan, I dial my lawyer's number. As it rings, I take pictures of the folder, all the while wondering if it might be easier to just climb into a manhole and disappear forever. A few months ago, my only responsibilities were writing my songs and performing them in front of other people, and now there are so many more things to juggle.

I guess I have to assume my parents were doing all of that on my behalf before—or actively ignoring all of it, causing me to lose out on who knows how many opportunities. Either way, with how they were managing me, it didn't look like I'd experience growth as an artist anytime soon, and they weren't eager to push for it. They would have rather controlled my entire career, kept me right under their thumb, so I could never be anything more than their daughter.

"Hello?" my lawyer says, and I fill her in, a deep sigh building in my chest. By the end of the call, she clears me to sign the NDA but tells me to immediately send along anything else Ariana asks me to sign for her to look over.

A headache starts to build between my temples as I text Ariana to come back in, waiting until she's in the doorway to pointedly sign the contract. I'm too young to be calling a *lawyer*. This is stuff adults deal with, not someone who doesn't even know how to cook rice.

"So what does he get out of it?" I ask again.

Ariana grins at me, taking the NDA back to look it over. "Fantastic. So essentially, Jules is auditioning for a movie called *Right as Rain*. It's currently in pre-production, but the previous lead actor had to drop out because of scheduling conflicts, so they're holding last-minute auditions. Due to the timing, we already know most of the names attached, and they're huge. Angelina Rodriguez has been cast as the main actress, and she's one of the youngest actresses to ever be nominated for an Oscar. Her father is played by Jorge Alvarez, who has nearly half a dozen Oscar nominations under his belt. The coproducers of the film are Brian Russell and Tiffany Lennox, known for hits like *Volume Up* and *Hidden Light*. As for the director, this is her film debut, but she's been up-and-coming in Hollywood for years. Everyone who's anyone in the film industry knows this movie is going to make a splash, and if Jules is cast in it, it'll be his big break."

I blink at all the names Ariana throws at me, most of them unfamiliar because I've never really dipped my toe into the film side of the entertainment industry, but I do know of Angelina Rodriguez.

Mostly because I had a brief crush on her after watching *Breakeven*. I've never actually met her, and the thought of doing so terrifies me for more than one reason, but I choose to brush past that to say, "But what does any of this have to do with *me*?"

Ariana purses her lips, like she's carefully choosing her words. "Jules . . . has a big reputation. One that does him no favors in Hollywood, especially when it comes to auditioning for serious films like this one. Right now, he can't afford to be seen that way, and given all the recent headlines, he's in between a rock and a hard place. The best way to offset it would be if he appeared to be in a long-term, committed relationship, and he knows that, which is why he proposed this solution."

"And this was his brilliant idea?" I ask, taken aback. "For us to fake date?"

"There's a lot at risk for him right now," Ariana says, her forehead wrinkling with lines. "His plan was to stay under the radar until after the auditions, but the paps must've caught wind of his comings and goings. If it hadn't been for the timing of the situation, we probably could've swept this under the rug, but . . . anyway, he knows it's a lot to ask, which is why he pitched the idea of getting you a potential song on the soundtrack to make it worth your while. I wouldn't bring this to you at all if I didn't think it could help your career, but I genuinely think it would. He's never dated anyone long-term before and you've never been in a public relationship, so the media will be all over this. Actor-singer combos are always a hit, and this would be no different."

My temples start to throb from the force of my headache. "Can I take some time to think about it?"

Ariana gets to her feet, already clearing off the table. "Of course, take the next few days and let me know if you have any questions or concerns. If you can, get an answer back to me by Friday."

I nod, though I have no idea how I'm going to make a decision before then.

In the end, it turns out to be easy. I might not allow myself to contact my parents, but that doesn't mean they aren't allowed to contact *me*. My call log is almost primarily made up of missed calls from them, accompanied by angry voicemails and even angrier text messages.

Barbie tries to delete them when I'm not looking, but I still see enough of them to know my parents are *incensed* about everything I've done in the last month.

I'd block them, but I'd never forgive myself if something happened to my younger sisters, Sanjana and Safina, and I missed it because I was too petty to allow my parents' messages through.

Instead, I try my best to scroll past their messages, so long as they don't pertain to my sisters, but I stop short when I see a message from my mother in all caps in the family group chat.

> **Mother Figure:** WHY IS JULES MORADI'S TEAM CONTACTING US LOOKING FOR YOU? WHAT DID YOU DO?

> **Father Figure:** Sumaira, you need to call us right this instant. These headlines are incredibly inappropriate. Do you have no shame? Is this how we raised you?

> **Mother Figure:** CALL US BACK SUMAIRA

> **Father Figure:** You need to stay away from this Jules character, Sumaira. He will ruin all the hard work we've put into your career. You know better than to get involved with someone so distasteful.

> **Mother Figure:** SUMAIRA PICK UP THE PHONE

> **Father Figure:** Think about what you're doing. Is this silly rebellion worth losing everything we've built?

I make a face at my phone, scrolling out of my notifications. Someone on Jules' team must've found the wrong contact information for me, which isn't that surprising given I deal with this a couple of times a week as I try to reconfigure my life and my career without my parents' involvement, but it does make for an additional headache.

A buzzer from the lobby rings through Barbie's apartment, and I look up from the blank pages of my journal. With a grunt, I get to my feet and check the camera to see who's outside. Maybe Barbie forgot her keys?

A delivery man carrying flowers and a gift basket waves back on the screen. My brows raise but I buzz him in, going over to open the front door.

"Is this for Barbie?" I ask when the man approaches from the elevator moments later.

He shrugs, handing the stuff off to me. I stumble a little under the weight but mumble a thanks before shutting the door behind me. I manage to get to the counter, where I set it all down and check the note.

*To Summer Ali,*

*Sorry for breaking your necklace. I owe you a new one.*
*And thank you for considering my proposal.*
*I look forward to your response.*

*Gratefully,*
*Jules Moradi*

I gape at the note for a solid two minutes before rifling through the gift basket, filled with cheeses and chocolates and champagnes. The flowers are my favorites, lilies. He must've looked up one of my interviews to find that out—or more likely, someone on his team did. But still, it's way more than I was expecting, and I'm completely taken aback.

**You need to stay away from this Jules character**, Baba had written, and I almost hear the vehement disapproval in his voice through the text. Initially, I wanted to flinch at how displeased they were, but now the rest of me feels a wicked sense of vindication.

They don't get to decide this for me. Not this time. It's up to *me*. It's *my* decision.

Pretending to date Jules will probably be a little annoying, but it's hardly the worst thing in the world. Most of what I know about PR stunts comes from Zach, since he had one for half a year, back when he hadn't come out yet and needed a beard. I briefly consider calling him, before I remember he's finishing up the Australian leg of his world tour. With the time difference, he's definitely asleep.

I rack my brain as I try to remember if he had anything bad to say about the experience, but from what I recall, all he really had to do was show up for pap walks. I can do that, surely?

Putting aside my parents, there's a part of me that's been thinking of saying yes anyway, for a similar reason to Zach's, though not quite exactly the same.

For two years now, I've struggled with my sexuality. I've always been prone to mini-crushes, but the first time I had one on a girl, I thought I was losing my mind. Except it happened again, and again, and then continued to happen with every and any gender under the sun.

In theory, this shouldn't be a problem, but I saw the way the world reacted when Zach came out. As much as there was support, there were also people who were absolutely horrid to him in the aftermath, and I don't know if I'm strong enough to go through something like that.

But even scarier is the thought of my *parents* knowing. They've never hidden the fact that they're homophobic, going as far as trying to ban me from hanging out with Zach. That was the first time I put my foot down and showed any level of defiance in the face of their rules.

I already had so few friends because of their strict regulations, stuck with only my labelmates for company. If Barbie and Zach hadn't also been under Ripple Records, I probably wouldn't have a single friend in this whole industry.

In a lot of ways, they've been my true north through this whole situation. And even then, *knowing* my friends would fully support and accept me, it was still terrifying to come out to them as queer.

I can't even fathom coming out to Ma and Baba. It would be akin to signing my death certificate, and I'm too young to die.

With all that in mind, the situation with Jules is starting to seem like more and more of a compelling idea. I lean in closer to the lilies and take a deep breath, something in my heart settling at the comforting smell.

Then I pull out my phone, ignoring Ma and Baba's messages to find my text thread with Ariana. I open it and I send a message entirely too simple for the fact it's likely to change the trajectory of my entire career.

I'll do it.

## CHAPTER THREE

## NEW COUPLE ALERT? JULES MORADI AND SUMMER ALI SEEN WALKING THROUGH GANTRY PLAZA STATE PARK ONLY A WEEK AFTER "ENTANGLEMENT"

The barista behind the counter is staring at me. I can't tell if it's because she recognizes me or because I've yet to order anything. I give her an awkward smile and mess with my bangs for something to do as I sit at a table near the back.

I've been simmering with tension all morning, which is what led to my decision to arrive at the designated Dunkin' Donuts nearly half an hour early. I was afraid that the subway might be delayed, and I can't stand the idea of being late and forcing someone to wait on me.

But this isn't much better. I'm still anxious, but now I'm in public instead of the safety of Barbie's home. Coffee will likely make the jitters worse, which was my rationale for initially skipping out on ordering something, but now I'm wondering if I should've just bitten the bullet and bought a muffin or something.

I glance out the windows, trying to see if Jules is here yet, but it proves to be fruitless. In his defense, the agreed-upon time was noon, and there are still a few minutes to go, but I feel like I might vibrate out of my skin at this rate.

At least the Dunkin' Donuts is mostly empty—which is awful in that the barista's attention is solely on me, but wonderful in that no one else will be around to see Jules and me humiliate ourselves in front of the paparazzi.

It's bad enough that Damon is here, giving me a sympathetic look as he eats a donut.

I sigh and reach inside the Versace bag my stylists instructed me to bring, digging around until I find a stress ball shaped like a tiger. I squeeze it in between my fingers and will myself to *breathe*. I focus on inhaling and exhaling until the door opens, the bell above it dinging.

I look up, and there he is. Jules Moradi. His dark hair is pushed back, but this time more strands are loose, as if he ran his ringed fingers through it a few too many times. Like me, he's dressed entirely in designer clothes, from his white turtleneck to his long black trench coat to his slim-fit jeans. I check for a brand and find YSL on his belt buckle. I wonder if he paid for any of it. I know *I* didn't pay for this black satin dress or the varsity jacket on top of it. Not even the leather boots are truly mine.

But if I'm being papped, then it's better to wear all of this than the ratty old T-shirt or hoodie I have tucked away in the duffle bags in Barbie's guest room.

Jules' eyes wander around the Dunkin' Donuts until they land on me, and I expect him to smile, but he only nods coolly and heads for the counter. I sag in my seat, simultaneously relieved and dismayed. A nod? That's it? Not even a little wave?

This is going to be a long day.

Jules returns a minute later, holding a drink. He looks effortlessly handsome, and I have no idea how he does it. "Hi, Summer." His gaze lands on the empty table, and he looks a little uncertain, glancing back at the counter. The barista is having a furious, whispered discussion with her coworker, both of them staring at us. "Did you want me to get you anything?"

"No, I'm fine," I say, getting to my feet. "Hi, Jules."

Again, I wait for a smile. Some sign of life behind those dark eyes. Something. *Anything.* But he keeps staring at me evenly, taking a sip of his coffee.

"So," I say, shifting my weight from my heels to my toes, back and forth, back and forth. "I think the paps will be here in about five minutes. That's what Ariana said."

Jules glances at the watch on his wrist. "Yeah, probably." An indent forms between his brows. "Have you been waiting for long?"

"No," I lie, reaching up to brush my hair off my shoulder. There's something fluttering in my stomach, but it's not butterflies—it's vicious in nature and more likely to make me hurl my breakfast back up. "I got here right before you did."

> *Something flutters in my belly*
> *Not quite butterflies*
> *Something older, wiser*
> *That knows to be afraid of*
> *Whatever lies in the space between us*

The lyrics float through my head before I discard them to the side. I don't even know what kind of song that would be.

Meanwhile Jules is nodding slowly, though I have a feeling he doesn't believe me. "Well, thanks again for agreeing to do this. I really appreciate it."

"Yeah, of course," I say, and we fall back into an awkward silence. He seems content to keep sipping his coffee quietly, but the longer neither of us speaks, the more my anxiety builds.

This is a transaction. I need to remember that. Jules isn't my friend—we're coworkers at best, and I shouldn't expect anything more from him.

But it's hard not to try to bridge the gap between us.

"So!" I say again, a little more brightly. "Have you done this before?"

"This?" he repeats.

I nod, trying to channel the Summer that comes to life in front of a crowd. "Y'know. Getting papped and all that. On purpose, I mean."

He raises an eyebrow, looking slightly amused, though likely at my expense. I'll still take that over not really acknowledging me at all. "What do you think?"

Why does that feel like a trap?

"I have exactly zero thoughts on the matter," I say with a smile. "Hence why I asked you the question."

"No comment," Jules says, blowing at the steam unfurling from his coffee cup.

*This isn't an interview, dude*, is what I would say if we *were* friends. Instead, cheerfully, I say, "That's fine! It's my first time, if you were wondering. The paps wait outside my favorite recording studio sometimes, but I think it's probably because they're hoping someone like Taylor Swift will show up. Other than that, I really only see them at events. You know, when I was younger I used to wonder how they knew where celebrities were all the time, but it's because they're *called*. Who would've thought? It's actually kind of wild that so much of what we see in the media is curated and—"

Jules catches sight of something over my shoulder. "They're here," he says, walking away from me, toward the door.

"Right," I say, deflating. It's probably better this way. If my anxiety had its way, I probably would've kept running my mouth until I ran out of breath.

I follow him to the door and pretend not to notice when one of the baristas snaps a photo of us on her phone. If they didn't recognize me earlier, they definitely do with Jules by my side.

"Ready?" he asks, pulling sunglasses out of seemingly nowhere and sliding them onto his face. "My car's right outside, and it'll take us straight to the park."

"Uh, kinda?" I say, tugging the handle of my purse further up my arm. "What are we supposed to do when we're there? Hold hands? Laugh at each other's jokes?"

I can't see his eyes, but I imagine he's giving me an exasperated look. But when he speaks, his words are surprisingly gentle. "Just be normal. Pretend we're two friends taking a stroll. It doesn't have to be anything more than that right now."

I nod, fixing my bangs again. "Okay. Are they going to follow us from here to the park?"

"Yeah, they have their vans," Jules says, pointing them out through the windows. "Your PR team didn't prep you before this?"

"I'm having a bit of a situation with them right now," I admit sheepishly. "Haven't gotten around to talking to them about you yet."

What I don't tell him is that I have no idea *how* to broach the subject with my PR team. Even if I knew them tangentially before, they're still strangers to me, like everyone else in my professional life. Resigned, I realize I'll have to call them after this. Better they find out from me rather than the media.

The corner of Jules' mouth twitches like he wants to ask, but then he shakes his head, almost to himself. "I guess this will be a learning experience then. Shall we?"

I nod and let him lead the way out. As soon as he pushes the door open, flashes start going off. I force myself to keep my eyes on the ground to make sure I don't trip over anything, trusting that this time there won't be anyone to bump into, since Jules is right in front of me. I follow his loafers as they lead the way to the car. I look up only when he gets inside, and he holds out a hand, offering it to me.

I take it in mine, climbing inside the SUV, and the door falls shut behind me. I force out a breath and glance through the tinted windows to see the paparazzi moving toward their vans, ready to follow us.

Damon gets in from the other side of the car, slipping into the back to join Jules' bodyguard.

"That wasn't so bad," I say, but my voice is a little weak. I'm still holding Jules' hand, and I immediately pull it back, embarrassed. He doesn't comment on it, taking another sip of coffee.

"It'll be better when we're walking," he says, before shifting forward to talk to the driver. "We're ready when you are."

That's one way to put it. I lean back in my seat and take a deep breath.

## CHAPTER FOUR

# WILL SUMMER ALI BE THE ONE TO BREAK JULES MORADI'S NO-SECOND-DATES RULE?

The park is beautiful, with a view of the East River and the Manhattan skyline. Even now, years later, it's strange to see it from this side. I'm so used to viewing it from across the Hudson, from New Jersey, and five years hasn't changed that.

"Where are you from?" I ask Jules as we walk down the stone path. There are three men following us, taking photos of us, while Damon and Jules' bodyguard linger out of sight. It draws the attention of more than a few people, but I manage to ignore it by focusing on Jules.

He glances at me. His sunglasses are tucked into his hair now, above his head, though the sun is still shining high in the sky. "I'm not white, if that's what you're asking. I'm Persian, my family's from Iran—"

I scrunch my nose. "No, not—like what *state* are you from?"

In the back of my head, I don't even think he looks that white. Sure, he's wearing makeup several shades too light for his actual skin tone, so he could probably pass if he wanted to, but with a last name like Moradi, I'd be hard-pressed to assume he's white before anything else.

"Oh," he says, a little surprised. "Sorry. I guess I'm . . ." He trails off, before offering me a shadow of a smile. "I'm from Philly, but I moved to California when I was five? Six? Something like that. My parents live in rural Pennsylvania these days, though, so I try to visit every now and then."

"Boooo!" I say, cupping my hands around my mouth to elevate my voice. *"Philly?"*

Jules gives me a knowing look. "Are you a native New Yorker then?"

"Worse," I say, leaning in like it's a secret. "I'm from New Jersey."

"I guess that makes us mortal enemies," he says dryly. "I bet you still support the Eagles, though, don't you?"

"Are you talking about a sport?" I ask with a laugh. "Because I support the Eagles, the *band*."

"You can't be serious," he says, a little aghast. "You don't know who the Eagles are?"

"What sport is this? Baseball? Football? Hockey?"

"Summer," Jules says, eyes wide. His face is suddenly so expressive, and I'm reminded that he's an actor for a living. Is this for the cameras? Is that why he's playing it up so much? "Are you *joking*?"

"I am not," I say, trying my best to match my expression to his, even though my smile feels a little too fake. "Sorry to offend your delicate sensibilities."

"My delicate—" He splutters and reaches out a hand to stop me in my tracks. "Summer, look me in the eyes. You know who the Eagles are."

I meet his gaze without flinching. "Yes. I'm a huge fan of the song 'Hotel California,' but who isn't, right?"

He groans, shaking his head. "I'm calling this entire thing off. I can't live like this."

"Wow, you really are an actor," I say, raising an eyebrow before turning around, continuing my walk even though he remains frozen in what must be fake surprise. "I've heard you guys can be dramatic, but this is a lot."

"I genuinely can't believe my ears right now," Jules says, but he jogs to catch up to me. "You seriously don't know who the Eagles are?"

"Jules, darling, I really don't know how much clearer I can be," I say, and watch with glee as that finally seems to break through his mask, the apples of his high cheekbones turning red. "So what sport *is* it?"

"Football," he says with a heavy sigh.

"Oh." I nod sagely. "I know the Giants."

"*Summer.*"

I burst into laughter. "Sorry, I—" I can't find it in myself to stop when I realize even the tips of his ears are burning now. "I—I didn't realize football was this important to you."

"I'm going to drag you to a game," he mutters, crossing his arms across his chest. "Then you'll realize."

"No amount of PR could convince me to sit through a sports game," I say as the last of my laughter dies down.

We fall into an awkward silence then, the reminder of this being PR crushing whatever levity we've found.

I tuck my hands into the pockets of my varsity jacket for something to do. "So, football, then. Are you into anything else?"

Jules licks his lips, glancing at the paparazzi behind us discreetly before turning his whole attention toward me. "Uh, I recently learned chess for a role. I was actually speaking to Marian Yu about it—well, I was talking to her boyfriend, Robin, because he's a former chess prodigy and I thought it'd be good research. Do you know them?"

"No," I say, a little wistful. I love Marian Yu's music, but we don't run in the same circles. It's strange thinking about the fact that if Jules and I hadn't been photographed together, I'd say something similar about him. "She seems lovely."

"She is," Jules agrees, and then with a thin smile, "And we can actually be friends without anyone assuming we're dating thanks to Robin."

I tilt my head. "I seriously don't get it. They really assume you're dating any girl you're near?"

"I mean, considering the fact we knew each other for all of two seconds before the media labeled you one of my 'conquests,'" he says, holding his hands up to make air quotations, "it definitely seems to be a reoccurring theme."

"Point taken," I say, and steal my own glance backward. The paparazzi are walking at a respectable distance behind us, but it's still a little close for comfort. "So how many of your so-called conquests did you actually date? Your reputation precedes you a tiny bit."

Jules' expression screws up slightly and he refuses to meet my eyes. "Well. Depends on your definition of date."

I raise my eyebrows. "All right. How many did you hook up with?"

A bitter laugh escapes him. "Most of them," he admits, rubbing the back of his neck, "but it was all in good fun."

I nudge him with my elbow. "Nobody's heart was broken?"

"No," he says, looking down at my arm like it's a foreign object. I pull away immediately, a little embarrassed. "We all knew what it was. I know the media makes it out to be this sleazy thing, but it—it's not like that."

"So what *is* it like?" I ask, trying and failing to temper my curiosity. Were these girls like me, caught up in a PR stunt?

"I . . ." Jules runs a hand through his hair, shaking loose a few more dark strands. "I'll tell you some other time. When we're not in public."

I glance over my shoulder again. "I don't think they can hear us."

"You never know," he says, a sour expression passing across his face. "But enough about me. What are *you* into, if not the Eagles?"

"Music," I say with a shrug. "If it wasn't obvious."

"But what else?"

"My favorite color is pink?"

"All right, mine is red. What else?"

I purse my lips, considering the question a little more seriously. "I'm . . . growing a plant?"

Jules looks at me. "As in *only* one plant?"

"It's hard being a single mother," I say, turning up my nose. "I'm doing my best to keep it alive, but with the father out of the picture . . ."

One corner of his mouth turns up. "I suppose it's my responsibility to step up as its new father then?"

"I don't know if Jacqueline approves of PR stunts," I say, shrugging. The more I mention it, the less impact it'll have. I hope.

This time there's only one awkward beat of silence before Jules says, "I'll have to win her over then. What kind of plant is she?"

"Well, she's technically a strawberry plant," I say, wincing a little. "But I'm kind of in between places right now, so she's . . . not growing any strawberries. I don't think she's getting enough sunlight."

Jules tilts his head to the side. "Where are you based right now? Ariana gave me an address in SoHo when I asked."

My cheeks start to flush. I don't know if there's a respectable way to say it, so I might as well just rip off the Band-Aid. "Yeah, that's not my place. I've been crashing on Barbie Li's couch."

"Barbie Li's couch," he repeats, as if the words will make more sense when he says them.

"Don't ask," I say, shaking my head. "It's a long story."

"Hey!" one of the paparazzi calls, making Jules turn half-heartedly. "We're all set! We have enough photos."

I blink, glancing back at them. How long has it been? Fifteen minutes? Twenty? Is that all it takes?

"Guess that's a wrap then," Jules says, taking a step away from me. "Thank you!" he calls back to them.

"That was fast," I say, more than a little surprised. "I didn't realize it would be that easy."

"It isn't always," he says, looking a little distant, but then he shakes his head. "Come on, my driver will drop you off."

I follow him back to the car. It's quite a trek from the water's edge and neither of us talks the entire time, but it's still more comfortable than at the start.

I don't think Jules and I are going to be best friends anytime soon, but maybe I'll get through this in one piece after all.

## CHAPTER FIVE

# FANS ARE SPECULATING WHETHER JULES MORADI WILL ATTEND SUMMER ALI'S "TRUE TO ME" TOUR

There are few things in the world I adore more than my younger sisters, but even they're testing my patience today.

There's absolutely no reason for Barbie's living room to be a *disaster* right now.

"Sanjana!" I say, reaching out to grab Jana's shoulder but she slips out of the way. "Safina!" I reach for Safi, but she's even more nimble.

I glower at the two of them, wondering how a thirteen-year-old and an eight-year-old can make *this* much of a mess in such little time.

"One hour. I was gone for *one hour*," I say, incredulous. "To get you cupcakes, mind you!"

"Thanks," Safi says, darting in to grab the paper bag from my hand before returning to her perch on top of the couch.

I pinch the bridge of my nose. How does she even *move* that fast? Are eight-year-olds magic? "I don't live here. You two can't come in and make a mess like this. It's *Barbie's* apartment."

That seems to break through to Jana, because she darts a look toward the door. "Well, is Barbie going to be home soon?"

"That doesn't matter!" I say, throwing my hands up. "You two need to start cleaning *now*."

Safi hums, leaning her head on her palm. "What if we don't want to?"

"Then I'm never sneaking you out of the house ever again," I say sweetly. "You can spend your Saturdays with Ma and Baba instead."

Safi blanches. "Are you being serious?"

"Do I look like I'm joking?" I ask.

Safi jumps off the couch, going to gather her art supplies off the floor. I turn a pointed look on Jana, who grumbles as she starts to deconstruct their pillow fort.

I sigh and go to Barbie's kitchen, grabbing paper towels and disinfectant to clean the coffee table, with all its questionable stains and crumbs.

Ten minutes into cleaning, Safi sidles up beside me, her brown eyes wide. "I'm sorry, Summy Apu."

I falter, setting a plastic bag of trash down on the floor so I can face her better. "It's okay, Safi. But you have to remember that just because Ma and Baba aren't here doesn't mean there are no rules."

Safi nods, but her lower lip is jutting out in a pout. "Jana Apu said it would be fine."

I do my best not to glare at Jana. "I'll speak to Jana about that, don't you worry."

Safi shrivels further. "Okay," she whispers, and goes back to picking up stuffed animals off the floor.

Jana comes up to me next, though it takes another ten minutes, and her expression is wrinkled with reluctance. "Sorry, Summy Apu."

I reach over to tug her ear. "What's wrong with you? I left you in charge of Safi, and this is what I come back to?"

"Ow," Jana complains, but I'm hardly putting any strength into my grip. "I'm sorry, okay? It's just . . ."

I raise an eyebrow. "It's just . . . ?"

Jana huffs, blowing a strand of hair out of her face. "We never see you anymore, and even when we do, you leave us by ourselves. It's not fair."

The words are like a blow, and my hand immediately drops to my side. "I'm right here, Jana."

My sister doesn't look at me, her eyes focused somewhere over my shoulder. "But you're not. And I know—I know Ma and Baba . . ." She pauses, unsure what to say, but I can fill in the blanks. "I understand why you left. But I wish we were here with you, instead of there with them."

Safi shoves her body in between us, staring up at us with a heavy chest of toys in her tiny arms. "I agree! Ma and Baba are so much meaner now that you're gone."

I wince and lean forward to help her with the chest, placing it down by the edge of the coffee table. Her words don't come as a shock, but they do settle in my gut like a stone, heavy and unyielding. "Are they taking their anger out on you?" I ask, the question directed at Jana.

"Not yet," Jana mutters, crossing her arms. "But it's inevitable, isn't it?"

"Big word," I say, trying to lighten the mood.

"Can we come on tour with you?" Safi asks without pause. "I don't wanna stay at home with them."

I sigh, sitting on the couch and pulling them with me. "It's not that simple, Safi. You know that."

"But it's *your* tour!" Safi insists, turning to Jana for backup. "You can make it that simple!"

Jana doesn't say anything, frowning at me.

"Just because it's my tour doesn't mean I can do whatever I want," I say, reaching forward to brush a black curl out of Safi's face. "But it's not the tour that's the problem. Ma and Baba would never let you come with me. And you both have *school*."

"School is dumb," Safi grumbles, kicking a Jenga block near her foot.

"Don't use words like that," I admonish, reaching down to pick up the Jenga block before placing it on the coffee table. "It's not nice."

Safi says something else under her breath that I can't make out. I eye her suspiciously, and she gets up, storming off toward the corner to gather the rest of her things.

I look at Jana. "You know it's not up to me. If I could pack you in my suitcase and take you all over the country with me, I would. But you're both just kids and I can't . . ."

"I know," Jana says. "But it still sucks."

"When I have my own place, it'll be a little easier," I say, scooting closer so I can tug my sister against my side. "You can come over whenever you want. Both of you. But give me a chance to land on my feet."

Jana closes her eyes, leaning her head against mine. "I don't want to be there anymore, Apu."

My eyes sting as I nod. "I know. But it's only five more years."

"And then another five for Safi," Jana whispers.

I don't have anything helpful to say to that, so I hold Jana closer, pressing a kiss to the top of her head.

Safi cries out suddenly, and both Jana and I rush over without a second thought, nearly falling off the couch in our haste.

My youngest sister is clutching her foot, and when I look at the ground, the offending red Lego is still lying there. "Apu, it hurts!" Safi shrieks, hopping on one foot.

Jana and I trade a look, a half smile crossing our faces.

Safi glares, still hopping. "This is serious!" she insists, and it's obvious she'd punch us both if her hands weren't occupied holding her foot.

"I know, Safi," I say, gently pushing away her hands to take her foot in between my palms. Safi wobbles, but Jana reaches out to steady her before she can fall. "Would you like a Band-Aid?"

Safi pauses a moment, considering her options. "Only if it's pink."

Jana rolls her eyes. "I'll get it," she says, heading for her bag.

As different as we all are, Safi obsessed with art, Jana obsessed with sports, and me with music, we all share a mutual love for the color pink. At least I can count on one thing to not change, even if I'm not around them as often as I used to be.

I help Safi sit back down on the couch, though at this point, the initial pain is probably gone. The living room is mostly clean now, with the exception of plastic plates and cups on the TV stand, so I breathe a little easier.

I doubt Barbie would've been mad at the mess my sisters made, but I'm already intruding enough as it is. There's no reason to make Barbie regret letting me stay here for the time being.

Jana comes back, putting the Band-Aid on Safi's foot, and I blow on it, like that'll help heal the invisible bruise. Safi tests her toes out, wiggling them to make sure they still work.

"It'll do," she says seriously, and I smile at her, squeezing her leg once before letting go.

Behind me, Jana finishes throwing away the rest of the trash, and I finally release the tension in my shoulders, working out the kinks in my neck with a head roll.

"Wait, I wanted to ask—what's going on with you and Jules Moradi?" Jana wonders when she comes back from the kitchen.

I ignore her, grabbing the paper bag with cupcakes in it from the couch. "So! Dessert?" I ask brightly. If everything goes right, my sisters will never need to learn about Jules Moradi.

## CHAPTER SIX

# HAS JULES MORADI FINALLY RETIRED FROM BEING A WOMANIZER?

Later that night, after taking hours to mull it over, I go to my contacts and scroll until I find Tina, who's probably the nicest person on my public relations team. I've been ignoring calls from all of them for two days now, unsure what to say, but I can't avoid it for much longer.

Tina picks up after two rings, and the first thing she says is "What the hell is going on, Summer?"

That's not exactly reassuring since she *really* is the nicest person on my team. I'm suddenly very glad I didn't call Charlie. I also feel a little bad, because the people on my public relations team have always been lovely to me, despite my parents' strict rules about what I was or wasn't allowed to do. Springing a PR stunt on them out of nowhere probably wasn't my best move.

"So hostile, Tina," I say dramatically, because I don't want to give away how nervous I really am.

I can almost hear Tina rolling her eyes over the phone. "Don't you start with me. Everyone has been worried sick and the press is having a field day. There are pictures of you and Jules Moradi *everywhere*, and we didn't even know the two of you knew each other until a week ago!"

The guilt on my shoulders only grows heavier. "I'm sorry, Tina," I mumble, picking at my bottom lip. "It's . . . Well, I'm sure you heard, but my parents are no longer managing me. And I wasn't sure which of their connections would be willing to work with me without them around."

Tina sighs. "Summer, you're the talent. We work for *you*. No one here cares who your manager is."

It's the exact opposite of what my parents have been saying to me, through insistent voicemails and aggressive text messages. They're adamant that I won't survive in this industry without them. That I *need* them if I want to keep being successful.

"Right," I say, and the weight of the world feels a little more manageable. "Well. I'm kind of fake dating Jules Moradi?"

There's a moment of silence before Tina says, her voice measured, "You're telling me over the phone that you've somehow gone ahead and agreed to a random PR stunt with child actor turned playboy Jules Moradi?"

I nod sheepishly before remembering she can't see me. "Er, yes? That's exactly what I'm saying. Actually, my new manager, Ariana, was the one to suggest it. So, not completely random."

Tina makes a choked noise on the other end. "Ariana Carter, who is *also* Jules Moradi's manager?"

"The very same. But in my defense, she's also Barbie's manager! Either way, you guys can spin this, right? You've done it before and you can do it again?"

I'm so in over my head here. More than ever, I feel like a child playing dress-up as an adult.

There's another beat of silence before Tina sighs quietly on the other end. "You're really going to make me explain this to Zoey, Charlie, and Rory, huh?"

I bite my bottom lip so hard it breaks through the skin. "I'm sorry. I—I thought I was making the right decision. Did I mess up?"

"No, no," Tina says, though she sounds tired. "It's okay. We'll figure it out. Can you come in for a meeting this week? We'll make some calls and get in touch with Jules' team so we can coordinate better for the future."

"Of course," I say, though I still feel like I made a mistake. My palms are so sweaty that my phone nearly slips out of my grasp. "You're not mad at me, right?"

"No, Summer," she reassures me, more gently this time. "Don't worry. We'll take care of this. You focus on yourself and your music, all right?"

"All right," I agree. "Still, I'm sorry."

Then I hang up before she can say anything else.

I sit there for a few minutes, forcing myself to focus on my breathing exercises.

Belatedly, I realize I never told her *why* I agreed to the PR stunt in the first place and what it might potentially mean for my career.

I groan, throwing my head back against the wall. Why can't I do anything right?

I get an email from my PR team the next day. This time, from Charlie, who's simultaneously my fiercest advocate and the one I fear might yell at me the most for making stupid decisions because of a boy.

I try to prepare for the worst, hesitating to open the email for a full ten minutes.

Jana is unimpressed. She stopped by Barbie's apartment after school, telling my parents she was busy with Robotics Club and wouldn't be home until later, when I'm pretty sure she's not even *in* the club.

Since then, she's been sprawled out on the couch beside me, doing her homework while I painstakingly deal with admin.

"Just open the stupid email," she finally says, reaching out to kick me in the thigh. "You're being ridiculous, Apu."

"I don't want to," I groan, pushing my laptop away from me.

Jana tosses her textbook on the table before turning to me with a bored expression. "If you're not going to do it, I will."

I shake my head furiously. I want her to know as little about my PR stunt as possible, and God forbid my *thirteen-year-old sister* sees my publicist telling me what a complete and utter idiot I am.

"Then do it yourself," Jana says, picking up a pillow from the couch and tossing it at my head. I lean back, just barely avoiding being smacked in the face.

"Sanjana!" I protest, but she's not listening to me. She's busy leaning across the couch, making a grab for my laptop. I automatically pull it toward my chest, wrapping my arms around it protectively. "Fine, fine, I'll do it."

My sister leans back, a smug grin on her lips. "Good. I was prepared to sit on you, but it looks like that won't be necessary."

"Rude," I mutter before taking a deep breath and opening the email.

I skim the first few lines and then sag with relief. I'm not being chewed out. Jules' team thankfully filled mine in on *why* we started doing this in the first place, and my team agrees that the long-term gain is worth a couple of weeks of having my name dragged through the mud for being the next girl in Jules' long line of conquests. Seeing it written out so succinctly makes me feel a little nauseous, but I push past that.

Jana is watching my face closely, and whatever she sees must be good enough for her to turn her attention away from me and back to her homework.

For a brief moment, I yearn to tell her the truth about everything instead of having to carry this weight by myself, before I gather my senses again. I decided a long time ago that I would keep my sisters as far away from the spotlight as possible, but I hate that it means I have to withhold parts of myself from them.

It's already strange enough only seeing my sisters in little bits and pieces these days. When I'm on tour, I expect their absence, but being in New York and not being able to see them is making me a little unhinged. It doesn't feel right, sneaking around like this behind my parents' backs, but what else am I supposed to do?

It's not like they've left me a lot of options.

## CHAPTER SEVEN

## BARBIE LI AND SUMMER ALI SPOTTED AT SILVER SPRINGS STUDIO! COULD THEY FINALLY BE WORKING ON A COLLAB AFTER YEARS OF FRIENDSHIP?

The next time I'm scheduled to see Jules is at the grocery store. I give my entire PR team an incredulous look when they tell me, but know better than to argue.

To Barbie, though, I say, "I don't get it. Who wants to see us shopping for *groceries*? Also, as if we wouldn't notice someone taking pictures of us in a store?"

We're sitting in her room, both of us getting ready for the day. My makeup is spread out across Barbie's floor, and I wish Jana weren't in school so I could call and ask her for her opinion. She's been obsessed with makeup since she was old enough to put it on, and definitely knows more about it than I could ever hope to. I've gleaned enough to get by from the makeup artists that do mine for interviews and concerts, but it doesn't compare to what Jana can do.

Barbie keeps her eyes fixed on her full-length mirror as she continues curling her hair. "Yeah, but it's domestic."

"Who's domestic on the second *date*?" I ask, rooting through my bag for my favorite mascara.

"The public doesn't know it's the second date," my best friend reminds me, picking up another lock of dark hair to curl.

I wish I were going out with Barbie today instead of meeting Jules. She's meeting up with Zach for lunch, and I'm busy pretending to buy milk with a guy I've met two times.

I finally find the mascara and glance at the vanity mirror beside me as I apply it. "Okay, but who's going to believe a random pap found us in a *grocery store*?"

"Don't worry so much about it," Barbie chides lightly. "Your job is to show up and look pretty and pretend to be in love. Nothing else."

"I resent that," I mutter as I reach for my color corrector and start padding it underneath my eyes, to hide the dark circles from being unable to fall asleep until six in the morning.

Barbie finishes her hair, running a comb through it to loosen the curls. Then she turns to me, crouching so we're on equal footing. "Summer, my darling, my love, you have to trust your new team to know what's best. I know it's hard because of your parents, but these people are professionals, and this is what they get paid to do."

I scowl. "Stop making sense."

When I first dipped my toe into the entertainment industry, I was terrified that I'd never make any friends. I wasn't exactly in any of the popular crowds in middle school, and then suddenly I was a contestant on *Stars of America* and *everyone* from back home wanted to be my friend. My parents forbade me from talking to any of them, certain they wanted to latch on to my newfound fame, and while they were probably right, it left me so *lonely*. My world had narrowed down to my parents and my sisters and the random music executives who were in control of my career.

Then one day when I was in the studio, trying and failing to write a song worthy of my debut album, and Barbie Li walked in.

We immediately hit it off, and from there came a whirlwind of friendship. Barbie eventually introduced me to Zach Murphy, and then the three of us became an inseparable trio.

It's a little terrifying to be known so well, but I also wouldn't trade it for the world.

"I know you're anxious," Barbie says gently, placing her hands on my shoulders, half for balance and half for comfort. "But it'll be okay. You said last time was a breeze, right? This time will be, too. Let your team worry about everything else."

I sigh. "It's easier said than done."

I haven't felt in control of my life for the last five years, and this is another thing beyond my reach. Is there ever going to be a point in my life when I actually feel like *I'm* the one in charge?

"I know," Barbie says, shifting forward to give me a brief hug. "But everything will go smoothly, I promise."

"And if it doesn't?"

"And if it doesn't, we watch old reruns of *World of Tweens* and make a drinking game out of it."

I smile faintly. "Promise?"

"Promise," Barbie says, smacking a kiss against the top of my head. "Now finish getting ready!"

## CHAPTER EIGHT

# HAS THE LION FINALLY BEEN TAMED? JULES MORADI SPOTTED GROCERY SHOPPING WITH SUMMER ALI!

This time around, Jules gets there before I do. I find him in the bread aisle, wearing some kind of half-assed disguise.

"Raj, I can't do this," he says into the phone, a little too loudly. An elderly woman on the other side of the aisle gives him a glare, and I stifle a giggle. He hasn't noticed me yet, too busy adjusting a ridiculous scarf. "I'm honestly going to die in this grocery store if you don't save me."

For some reason Jules has his phone on *speaker* in the middle of a grocery store, because I can hear the other person loud and clear, even from all the way down the aisle. "I know you're an actor, but do you have to be so dramatic?"

Jules is opening his mouth to snap back at him when he finally sees me. His brown eyes widen and he quickly mutters, "I have to go," and hangs up.

"Nice . . . sunglasses," I decide to say, refraining from making a comment on the cowboy hat.

"I didn't want to get papped by myself," Jules mumbles, and he starts to pull off the pieces of his disguise, tossing them into his grocery cart.

"Would it matter?" I ask, slightly amused. He's grumpier than he was last time, in a pouty way that makes him oddly more approachable. Maybe I can crack him yet.

I decide to make it my mission for the day. Better that than focusing on all the ways this can go wrong or how much I wish I were at lunch with Barbie and Zach instead.

Jules looks like he wants to make a snarky comment, but then I watch as he takes a careful breath and his expression smooths out. "Hello, Summer."

"Hello, Jules," I say with a smile before gesturing to his cart. "Is there a . . . reason for this?"

"For what?" Jules asks before looking down at his grocery cart. His cheeks immediately flush bright red, and I have to press my lips together to keep from laughing. "Oh. Yeah. I—yeah. I really like bread."

"Is that right?" I ask, picking out one of *four* loaves of breads. "I would've never guessed."

Jules' face somehow turns even redder.

I grin and drop the loaf in favor of picking up a brand of sourdough from the shelf in front of us. "This is my personal favorite."

"Might as well add it to the cart then," Jules says dryly.

"Might as well," I agree, dropping the bread into his cart. "You've checked the expiration dates on these, right?"

The look on Jules' face makes it clear that he absolutely did not. I finally give in and burst into laughter.

"Dude," I say, shaking my head. "Have you *ever* been grocery shopping?"

"Of course I've been grocery shopping," Jules says, reaching in and tossing the loaves of bread back on the shelf. "I was just biding my time until you got here."

"Well, I'm here now, so I think you can leave the poor bread alone," I say, giving one of the loaves a light pat.

Jules lets out a long-suffering sigh, and I'm hit with the odd realization that I'm enjoying myself. Poking fun at him is more entertaining than I thought it would be.

"How about you push the cart and I'll do the actual shopping?" I suggest, offering him an olive branch.

He sighs again, loud and dramatic. "Fine."

"You really are an actor, huh?" I say, grinning ruefully.

"That's what they tell me," Jules says, giving me a flimsy salute. "What are you planning to buy?"

"Depends," I say with a light shrug, and start wandering down the aisle, idly glancing at the shelves. "Are we running up your credit card or mine?"

What I don't say is that I have no idea how to handle my finances now that my parents are no longer in the picture, and that it makes me stressed enough that I regularly grind my teeth over it.

"Do you think I can write it off on my taxes?" Jules muses as he follows after me with the cart.

"Don't ask me, I don't know how taxes work," I say. My eyes catch over his shoulder, where a lone photographer has appeared. "Guess the paparazzi are here. Better choose fast."

Jules doesn't even turn around. "If I say I'll pay, are you going to cook something?"

"I can *bake* something," I offer instead, though what I should've said is *absolutely not*. "Or at least, I can try."

He looks at me for a long moment. "Can you make cheesecake?"

"I can try," I repeat with a shrug.

Jules considers this and then he nods, looking pleased for once. "I'll pay."

I grin and immediately start perusing the aisles for cream cheese, pulling up a recipe as I go. He follows after me, and I catch a hint of a smile on his face.

I'm halfway through the ingredient list when I pause, turning to face him. "I don't . . . have a kitchen right now. Since I'm staying at Barbie's."

Jules blinks. "You can't bake there?"

"I *can*," I say, biting my lip. "But I'll have to ask."

"Okay," he says, and then all he does is stare at me. I realize he expects me to ask *now* and I take my phone out of my pocket, wary of the photographer nearby.

I find Barbie's contact and then hold the phone to my ear, trying not to flush under Jules' intense stare.

"Summer? Is everything okay?" comes Barbie's voice.

"Hey," I say, fiddling with a lock of hair to keep my other hand busy. "Do you mind if I take over your kitchen tonight?"

"You're going to *cook*?" Barbie asks, aghast.

"God no," I say immediately. "I'm going to bake." Jules raises an eyebrow at me, and I add, "With . . . with Jules."

A long beat of silence stretches on the other end of the call. Then finally Barbie says, "Of course. What time?"

There's something faintly evil about her tone of voice. I narrow my eyes. "Maybe around six?"

"Perfect," Barbie says sweetly.

Before I can demand to know what she's doing, Zach yells, "See you there!" and the line disconnects.

I blink at my phone, and have to remind myself that someone is actively taking pictures of me so I don't call them back and start screaming.

"She said yes," I say to Jules, trying to hold in a grimace. "Uh . . . have you met Barbie before? Or Zach Murphy?"

"We've seen each other around," Jules says, tilting his head. "Why?"

I smile stiffly. "I'll be making cheesecake for four."

Jules' eyes widen only slightly before he manages his expression. "The more the merrier."

"Let's hope so," I mutter, and then continue down the aisle in search of sugar.

We spend a whole minute in front of the ice cream aisle, just smiling at each other for the sake of the camera, pretending to fight over two pints of Ben & Jerry's, but eventually I win, placing Chunky Monkey in the cart.

When we're about to approach the register, the photographer finally takes his leave, nodding at us before he disappears. I sigh, my posture finally relaxing, and Jules reaches in the grocery cart so he can wrap his scarf around his neck again.

"Really?" I ask. "Isn't it more embarrassing to be caught *with* a disguise on?"

"You're assuming anyone is going to catch me," Jules says, the words slightly muffled.

"I don't have a disguise," I point out, gesturing at myself widely. "If somebody recognizes me, the odds of them recognizing you are pretty high."

Jules reaches into the cart again and this time he pulls out the sunglasses, which he places on *my* face. I jolt as his fingers briefly touch my cheeks, his rings cold against my skin. "There. No one will recognize you either."

"For some reason, I don't think this is going to work," I say, but follow him dutifully to the register. The cashier is staring at us, a strange look on her face, and I know Jules' plan has already failed.

"Hey," I say, but Jules says, "*Shhh, darling.*"

I gape at him as he starts dumping our groceries onto the conveyer belt.

"I'd like to check this out, please," Jules says in the most outrageous British accent, and my mouth falls open further.

The cashier raises her eyebrows at him, and I resist the urge to slap my hand against my forehead.

Eventually, she starts checking his things out and placing them in flimsy plastic bags, but even as she does that, she continues to stare at him suspiciously.

"Hey," I say again, but Jules gives me a wide-eyed stare.

"Darling, please," he says. "Let's talk about it outside."

I sigh, shaking my head. "*Darling.* Your credit card has your name on it."

Jules falters at that before turning toward the cashier with puppy dog eyes. "Do you take Apple Pay?"

"Oh my God," I say, and hip check him out of the way, taking out my wallet. My legal name is Sumaira Ali, so I doubt she's going to clock me unless she already knows who we are. "I'll pay."

"Darling!" Jules protests, and I ignore him, swiping my card through the scanner.

"Make yourself useful and carry the bags to the car, *darling*," I say, drawing my signature on the screen.

I can't *see* Jules' pout under his scarf, but I can feel it. I give him a pointed look, and he grumbles something under his breath, grabbing the plastic bags.

The moment he disappears through the door, the cashier leans in, eyes wide. "You're Summer Ali, right? And that was Jules Moradi?"

I nearly groan, but I've taken enough media training classes to know better. "The one and only," I say instead, laughing sheepishly. "Do you mind keeping it on the down low that you saw us?"

"I—er, you're—wow. This is happening. All right, cool," the cashier says, looking incredulous. She's blinking rapidly at him but at least she isn't screaming. "Your secret's safe with me."

I offer her my most charming smile and put my credit card back in my wallet. She keeps staring at me, but eventually realizes I'm waiting for the receipt.

She turns back to grab it and hand it over to me, but before I can take it, she gives me a hesitant smile. "I really liked your debut album."

My smile feels a lot more genuine now. "Thank you. Really."

"Darling!" Jules calls from the doorway, popping his head back in through the automatic doors.

I roll my eyes. "I'm coming!"

I look back at the cashier, and she mimes zipping her lips shut before giving me the receipt. I give her a grateful nod and tuck the receipt in my purse before heading for the exit, all the while wondering *how* I got myself into this situation.

## CHAPTER NINE

## JULES MORADI SHARES PICTURES BAKING WITH SUMMER ALI, AND FANS THINK THEY MIGHT BE AT BARBIE LI'S APARTMENT!

I feel oddly exposed letting Jules into the apartment, and it's not even mine. I sheepishly gesture to the living room with a wave.

"Welcome to Barbie's Dream House," I say.

Jules glances around, eyes curious, and then his gaze lands on the kitchen, where Barbie and Zach are waiting, both grinning diabolically.

I resist the urge to make a wide-eyed gesture at them to *leave*.

"Hey! It's so nice to meet you," Zach says, bounding up and offering Jules his hand. He has a new haircut—his curls are gone and what little remains of the fuzz is dyed bright blue, contrasting with his black skin. "We've heard so much about you."

Jules takes it, and it seems like a switch goes off in his head, because he immediately offers my friends the widest grin I've seen on his face so far. "Good things, I hope?" He winks at me, and it takes everything in me not to gape at him.

"Jules, they—they know we're fake dating," I eventually say, a little thrown.

He gives me a puzzled smile. "Yeah, I figured as much."

"Uh—okay." I return the smile, feeling even more confused. Why else would he be pretending to like them? "I'm going to put the groceries away."

Jules nods, turning his attention back to Zach with a sparkle in his eye. My God, it's never been more clear that he's an *actor*. And this is the improv challenge of a lifetime. "So how long have you known Summer?"

I scurry into the kitchen, shooting daggers at Barbie. "Why did you rush home?"

She shrugs, a smirk on her face. "I wanted to meet the infamous Jules Moradi. Is that so strange?"

I smack her arm half-heartedly. "You've had multiple chances to meet him across your wide and expansive career."

"Yeah, but he wasn't pretending to date my best friend then," Barbie says, tilting her head. "How did the grocery shopping go?"

"It was fine," I say with a sigh as I start rummaging through the cabinets for supplies. "Don't say *I told you so*."

Barbie gives me a smug look that says as much anyway. "*Fine*, huh? But now you're baking something for him?"

"Not for him," I correct, bumping my head against the shelf when I shift abruptly to stare at her. "For everyone."

"I feel like you *just* uninvited us a minute ago," Barbie says, and somehow she looks even more like the cat that got the cream.

"What's your point?" I ask, eyes narrowed.

"That things don't always have to end in disaster for you,

Summer," Barbie says, nudging my hip with hers. "I know you've been a little off-balance after everything with your parents. But it's okay to have faith that everything will work out in the end."

"What does that even mean in this context?" I ask.

"That you should let yourself relax every now and then and enjoy the moment," Barbie says, pressing her chin to my shoulder. "I don't know much about Jules, and *trust* that I intend to change that tonight, but he doesn't seem all that bad if he's willingly hanging out with your friends without any warning beforehand. It might be nice to find a friend in him."

I glance at Jules, who's still animatedly talking to Zach—something about video games?—and nod slowly. "Yeah. Maybe."

"Don't say maybe, you're literally preheating my oven for him right now," Barbie says, rolling her eyes. "All right, I'm gonna go pester Jules."

I roll my eyes right back. "You do that."

Barbie presses a kiss to my cheek and skips over to the living room, half plopping herself in Zach's lap. He ignores her, his dark eyes bright with fascination as he listens to Jules. I stare for a moment, wondering if Zach might be forming a crush. He has a terrible habit of falling in love with straight boys, but I admittedly don't know Jules' romantic preferences.

Then I realize all of this is so far from my business that it doesn't even matter and I blow out a breath, pulling out my phone and opening up the cheesecake recipe I was looking at earlier.

The sound of laugher drifts from the living room, and slowly it relaxes my muscles. Eventually, I get into the swing of things, measuring and mixing as needed.

I lose myself in the motions, so when someone says, "Summer?" I startle so badly that the egg I was trying to crack into a bowl smashes in my hand instead, yolk covering my palm.

Holding myself eerily calm, I turn to Jules. "Yes?"

His eyes are wide. "Uh. Never mind."

"Are you sure?" I ask with a smile that feels deranged on my face. My heartbeat is still skyrocketing from the surprise, and it's making my anxiety feel sticky, like a strange second skin.

He nods quickly. "It's nothing."

"Give me a second," I say, and turn on the faucet, washing my hands. I take another moment to breathe in deeply through my nose. I should've been paying more attention to my surroundings.

But it's okay. One egg won't ruin anything.

By the time I turn back around, I actually feel calm. "What was it you needed?"

Jules scratches the back of his head, looking flustered. "I was just wondering when the cheesecake would be ready."

I wince slightly. "Well, it'll take four hours in the fridge alone," I say, which is something I should've realized before I agreed to do this. It only occurred to me in the last half an hour, and then I just didn't want to say anything, which was probably a mistake in and of itself. Jules definitely has better things to do than sit around hanging out with my friends while I attempt to bake a cake.

"I'm sure you have plans," I add, embarrassed. "I could freeze it and bring you some next time I see you if you want to leave?"

Jules blinks at me once, then twice. "Oh. I mean—I don't . . ."

I grimace. "I know, I'm sorry. I wasn't thinking."

"No!" Jules rushes to say, shaking his head. "No, I'm the one who suggested cheesecake. I forgot it needed time in the fridge. It's not your fault."

I try to smile. "It's okay. You can leave whenever you want."

Jules studies me for a moment. "Do you want me to leave?"

I stare at him. "Do you want to leave?"

Neither of us replies for a moment, then finally Jules nods. "I think freezing it is probably the best option. I'm sorry I suggested cheesecake in the first place."

"Don't be sorry," I say, waving him off. "Do you want to take a picture of me baking so you can upload it later?"

Something shifts in Jules' gaze, but I can't quite read it. "Yeah, that's a good idea," he says, taking out his phone.

I reach behind me, grabbing one of the bowls I was using, and offer him the brightest smile I can manage.

Jules takes the photo before showing it to me, making sure it's all right, and I nod in agreement. There's flour on my cheek, my dark hair has come loose from its high ponytail, and my pink apron would be better suited to a grandma, but it'll do. "Perfect."

Then I watch in confusion as Jules sets the picture as his background and tucks his phone back in his pocket.

"Why did you do that?" I ask, bewildered.

"Appearances," he says breezily. Before I can ask anything else, he nods at Barbie and Zach. "I think I'm going to head out, but let's all hang out again sometime."

*All* seems like a stretch since I was barely there, but I hum along anyway.

Before Jules can leave, Barbie hops off the couch, walking over. "Are you going to New York Fashion Week?" she asks Jules, and

I don't like the look in her eye.

He nods. "YSL invited me."

"Fantastic! Versace invited Summer. I'm assuming you both have a plus one? You should go together!" Barbie says, clapping her hands together delightedly.

I give her a curious look. What is she trying to do here? Force me and Jules to become friends through sheer will?

Jules considers the proposal, glancing at me. "I guess it wouldn't hurt to go together. You talk to your team; I'll talk to mine?"

"Okay," I say slowly, still suspicious of my best friend's intentions. "Do you know if YSL and Versace have their shows on the same day?"

"No, but I'll find out," Jules says before offering Barbie a smile. "That was a good idea, thanks."

Barbie flips her hair over her shoulder. "I'm full of them."

I squint at her and she grins at me.

"All right, until next time then," Jules says, turning his smile on Zach. "It was nice to meet all of you."

Then between one blink and the next, Jules is gone and I'm abandoning any and all pretense of baking to corner both Barbie and Zach. "Tell me *everything*."

Zach raises a brow, but he makes room for me to sit beside him on the couch. "I didn't realize you were this interested in Jules."

"*I'm* interested in Jules?" I ask incredulously. "I can't believe the both of you spent an entire hour talking to him!"

"He's pretty funny," Zach admits, leaning his head against Barbie's side as she comes to sit on the arm of the couch. "But I don't know how much of it is real."

Barbie nods. "Yeah, I'm not sure, but I want to give him the benefit of the doubt. I think you'll probably be able to figure out how much of it is real and how much of it is acting the more time you spend with him."

"Why did you rope me into spending *more* time with him?" I ask, stretching my leg to half-heartedly kick Barbie.

"You've been cooped up in this apartment all month long trying to write songs, and for *what*?" She lifts her chin. "Some time outside might help with inspiration."

I narrow my eyes at her. "When are we going to talk about the fact that *you* are writing songs about your bodyguard?"

"Never," Barbie says pleasantly at the same time Zach turns to her, mouth falling open.

"You like Spencer?" he demands.

"No," she says at the same time I say, "Yes."

"All right, well, if we're going to do this, then we should talk about the white boy from *Canada* that Zach has been seeing," Barbie says sharply.

"*Canada*?" I repeat, eyes wide. "I thought you were against long-distance relationships?"

"First of all, he lives in Seattle now," Zach snaps, which is as good as admitting to it. "Second of all, this isn't about me! Barbie, you're going to get Spencer fired if you do anything with him, you know that, right?"

"I'm not doing anything with him!"

"Yet," I add.

"Summer, don't make me kick you out of my home," Barbie threatens.

I smile at her, completely serene. "You would never. Over a boy? Come on."

"We'll see about that," she says, and launches herself at me.

I yelp and the three of us go down in a tangle of limbs onto the floor. There are some half-hearted kicks and punches, but eventually, I burst into laughter and they all follow.

Even if everything else is spiraling out of control, at least I'll always have this.

## CHAPTER TEN

## SUMMER ALI ON HER UPCOMING "TRUE TO ME" TOUR AND DEALING WITH WRITER'S BLOCK

The clock on the wall is ticking so loudly I swear I hear it echoing in the base of my skull. I try to keep my eyes focused on my journal, but the words are swimming on the page, a muddle of lyrics I can't make sense of.

My vocal teacher pulled me aside today after our biweekly lesson to ask if anything was wrong because I didn't seem as focused as usual. I shook my head, saying I didn't sleep that well last night—which wasn't *untrue* given my insomnia, but it's much more than that.

For weeks, there's been a tension brewing in my gut at the idea of going on tour without new songs to perform. It doesn't feel fair to my fans, the ones who have been supporting me since the very beginning.

I still think back on the first year of my career in disbelief and awe. The fact my debut album, *In My Shoes*, had three different songs make it into the Hot 100—one of which hit number one—

is unbelievable to me. Within months of releasing the album, I was invited to perform my lead single, "Scorpio Season," on the *Tonight Show* with Jimmy Fallon, *Late Night with Seth Meyers*, the *Late Show* with Stephen Colbert, *Good Morning America*, and the *Today* show, all of which I dreamed of performing on when I was a kid. I won awards for best new artist at the VMAs, AMAs, Billboard Music Awards, and so many more. My follower count shot up to the millions, and I got branded a "teen pop sensation" at sixteen years old.

For the last two years, I've been riding the coattails of that success. Lately, that seems like all I can do.

I'm stuck in this awful limbo where my label expects me to make them money, my fans are begging me for new music, and my brain just flat-out refuses to do anything about any of it.

Initially, I tried to push back with the label and suggest my next tour happen after the release of my second album, but the board of executives had looked at me and my parents and asked, "When will that be?" and I didn't have an answer.

So my parents readily agreed and gave me a look that said *shut up* when I feebly tried to argue again. Over and over, it's been drilled into me that musicians make most of their money from concerts these days, with the drop in physical album sales and the uptick in streaming, but it still doesn't feel right to get up onstage and sing the same exact songs that my fans heard me sing over a year ago. They want something new, and I want to give it to them, but I barely know who I am anymore.

I sigh and scribble out the last few lines I wrote in my journal, then turn to the next page.

I don't know how to do this. I just don't. It's ironic that my tour is called the "True to Me" tour when I've never felt more lost. My parents spent so long telling me who to be, and I *let* them. But now I'm adrift without them, struggling to put together the pieces of the new Summer Ali in a way that actually feels real and honest.

"Summy Apu, are you done yet?" Safi asks, tugging on my sleeve. "You said we could hang out together."

"We are hanging out together," I say, swatting her hand away. "It's called parallel play."

"What's parallel play?" she asks, giving Jana a curious look, but my other sister only shrugs, her eyes trained on the basketball game on the TV.

"It's when you do your things and I do my thing, but we're in the same space at the same time," I say, and then write down the new words floating through my head.

*Same space, same time*
*But the distance grows*

And then I cross those out too, frustrated with my internal cadence. None of this sounds right.

"I'm bored," Safi complains, flopping onto me, jostling my journal off my lap. "Let's do something."

I sigh, massaging the bridge of my nose. There's no distracting her when she's like this. "What do you want to do, Safi?"

"I want to do your makeup! Jana Apu has been showing me how to," she says, and I already know I'm going to look ridiculous by the end of the day, but nod all the same.

Jana finally looks away from the TV, eyes wide. "Makeup?"

And that's how I end up sitting on the floor of Barbie's guest room as the two of them pad different cosmetics onto my face.

"Hey, that's too much blush," Jana scolds, taking the brush from my other sister. "She's gonna look like a clown."

Safi shrugs. "So what?"

I roll my eyes but don't bother complaining. I've let Jana practice on me so many times that this is almost expected. It's not like I'm going outside, so I might as well let them have their fun.

My phone starts ringing, and I reach up, stilling Safi's hand so she doesn't poke my eye out while doing my mascara. "One second."

I glance at the screen and falter when I see *DO NOT ANSWER (BABA)* with a bunch of red exclamation marks next to it.

Jana peers over to look at the screen and blanches before scrambling to find her own phone.

The sound of my heartbeat in my ears drowns out the ringtone right up until the phone goes quiet. A moment later the screen lights up with one new voicemail. Oh God.

Safi finally seems to catch on that something is wrong, frowning at me. Jana keeps digging through the piles of cosmetics while I painstakingly click on the voicemail.

"What's wrong with you? Send your sisters home *now*. I know they're with you," Baba shouts out over the speaker, and I flinch, dropping my phone into my lap. Jana groans and Safi's eyes widen as she immediately starts packing things away in my makeup bag. "It's not enough that you screen your calls, but you're encouraging Jana to do the same? Do you have no shame? We raised you better than this—"

I reach down and press my thumb insistently against the volume button until the sound cuts off and the room fills only with silence.

My chest feels like it's caving in on itself, the way it always does when I fold and listen to one of their voicemails or read through their text messages. I know better, but I also can't help it.

"Did I leave it in the bathroom?" Jana mutters to herself, jumping to her feet and walking out of the room without an answer.

"Are we in trouble?" Safi asks me, and I break out of my stupor.

"What? No, of course not," I say, pulling her into my arms. "You didn't do anything wrong."

"Baba sounded really angry," she says, biting her bottom lip. "Are you gonna reply to him?"

I stare at her, unsure what to say. There's no way to explain to my eight-year-old sister that the cardinal rule involves no contact with them.

"Yes," I say, even though I already regret it. "Don't worry, I'll tell them you weren't with me, so they'll be less angry."

I open up my texts and tap out a quick message, my fingers shaking the entire time. **They're not with me. Please leave me alone.**

But then I falter, staring at it, wondering if I really want to send it. Whether I want to break the cardinal rule. It's not something I can take back. If I do—

Safi reaches over and presses send before I can snatch the phone away from her. There's a *whoosh* as the message disappears into the ether, and my heart drops.

Immediately my phone starts ringing again.

"You need to go," I whisper to Safi. "Both of you. Come on, get your stuff ready."

Safi opens her mouth like she's going to protest and I shake my head. "Come on, go grab your things." Louder, I say, "Jana, I'm calling you both a car. You need to go home right now."

My phone stops ringing for two seconds before it starts blaring again with a second call. Nausea curls in my stomach and I ignore it, pulling Safi to her feet.

She pouts at me before reluctantly going over to pack her bag. I can't meet her gaze or I'm going to have a mental breakdown.

Ignoring the call at the top of the screen, I book a car that will arrive in ten minutes to take my sisters home. The door opens and I look up, hoping Jana is ready to go, only to see Barbie standing there, hauling Jana into the room by the elbow.

"Why is this one digging through the bathroom cabinets like she's mining for gold?" she asks, and my phone goes briefly silent only to start ringing *again*.

She looks down at my phone and then back up to my face before sighing. "You broke the cardinal rule."

"I didn't mean to," I say in a small voice, though that's not exactly true.

My phone stops ringing again and this time rapid succession buzzes follow instead.

I look down at the screen before I can stop myself.

**Father Figure:** Pick up the phone, Sumaira.

**Mother Figure:** PICK UP NOW

**Mother Figure:** OR WE'RE COMING OVER THERE

**Mother Figure:** YOU THINK WE DON'T KNOW YOU'RE WITH BARBARA?

> **Father Figure:** Don't you dare ignore us right now.

Barbie rips the phone out of my hand. "Stop it! Summer, you can't let them—"

"They said they're going to come over here if I don't pick up," I say, my mouth dry. "I need to—"

"No, you do not," Barbie says sharply, and then turns around to face my sisters. "Pack up your things and say goodbye to your sister. Summer, you called a car?"

"Yes, but—"

"No," Barbie says. "Jana, what were you looking for?"

"I can't find my phone," my sister says uncertainly.

"I'll find it. Get your stuff ready to leave," Barbie says, and then herds them out of the room after they both hug me quickly and mutter goodbye.

Safi squeezes my hand tightly right up until she's out the door, and I feel the pathetic urge to cry.

"Sit down before you fall over, Summer, Jesus Christ. This is why you're not allowed to talk to them!"

When I don't move, Barbie sighs and gives me a gentle nudge toward the bed. I stumble a little and manage to soften my landing with the mattress.

Barbie turns her attention toward the rest of the room, scanning the floor, before she finally reaches down and picks Jana's phone out from underneath an eyeshadow palette.

"Stay here, I'll take them downstairs," she says, pointing a finger at me. "And then I'm going to come back and we're going to talk about how you need to follow your own rules!"

"I need to find a new place to live," I say, burying my face in my hands. "They—they know where your apartment is. They could show up here, they could drag me back—"

"I have a doorman, they absolutely could *not*," Barbie says. "Don't spiral, I'll be right back."

She leaves—still with my phone—and I force myself to take deep breaths. No matter what Barbie says, I know I have to find my own place. I can't live with the fear of them showing up.

It's not fair that one voicemail of my father yelling at me can make my hands shake. It's not fair that I left, and still, I'm haunted by them. It's not fair that no matter how far I go, they're always going to have this effect on me.

It's just not *fair*.

But none of this has ever been fair.

## CHAPTER ELEVEN

## PLUS ONES AT NYFW? SUMMER ALI AND JULES MORADI ACCOMPANY EACH OTHER AT YSL AND VERSACE SHOWS...

A limousine arrives outside Barbie's apartment at seven in the morning the Monday of New York Fashion Week, and my phone buzzes with a text from the driver. I try not to flinch. I'm still antsy around my phone, even though I've muted notifications from my parents to keep some semblance of sanity. I haven't spoken to Jana or Safi in over a week, and it's driving me up the wall, but I don't want to make things worse for them. I'll let them reach out first.

These fashion shows will be a good way to keep my mind off the whole situation. I give myself one more look in the mirror, trying not to wince at the dark circles under my eyes, before going outside. Jules is already in the car when I arrive, wearing sweatpants and a hoodie, and he looks as tired as I feel.

I'm a little surprised to see him, but I dutifully say, "Good morning," when I climb inside, sitting across from him.

"Good morning," he says, his voice is gruff with exhaustion.

I'm too sleepy to ask why Jules isn't in a car of his own. Instead, I ask, "Can we please stop for coffee?"

Jules hums. "You don't have a coffee machine at Barbie's?"

I blink one eye open to stare at him. "It's seven in the morning. I can barely function right now. I'm not going to try to figure out how to work that death trap."

Jules lets out a surprised huff, an almost laugh. "Better get used to it."

I groan and shut my eye. At some point the car stops, but I only blink my eyes open again when Jules passes me a cup from Dunkin' Donuts. I almost kiss him out of gratitude, before the thought startles me awake. Jesus Christ, it's too early.

"Coffee is my only friend," I mutter to myself darkly, and I see Jules give me a slightly amused look. I ignore him in favor of drinking as much of the sugary concoction as I can manage.

Half an hour later, when I actually feel alive, it registers again that Jules is in the same car as me. "I thought we were going to meet up later?"

Jules looks up from his phone briefly, meeting my gaze, before returning his attention back to the screen. I stretch my neck and find that he's intensely playing a level of some game that looks like a *Candy Crush* rip-off.

"I don't know if I should be offended," I say, but scoot over closer to watch his fingers as they match little jewels together. When Jules still doesn't say anything, I continue dramatically, "Here I am, the prettiest girl in all the lands, and I'm being ignored in favor of some random game on an iPhone. This is what the world has come to."

Jules raises an eyebrow at me. "Are you quite finished?"

"Are you?" I challenge.

He sighs in the same dramatic vein and throws his phone across the seat. It lands half-heartedly near the window. "All right, princess. You have my full attention."

"I'm not a princess," I say, but it comes off more haughty than I'd like, and Jules knows it if the look on his face is any indication.

"No?" He tilts his head. "What happened to being the prettiest girl in all the lands?"

I scowl at him, but it doesn't really have any heat behind it. "I was joking."

"I don't think you were," he says a little too knowingly. Clearly the coffee woke him up too.

I roll my eyes, ignoring him. *Darling, princess*, he's just full of pet names. "What are you doing in the same car as me, Jules?"

"Ariana thought it would be easier for us to get ready together," he says, finally relenting, leaning his head back against the seat. "She had both our styling teams sent to the same place. That way they can make sure we don't clash."

"Why didn't she tell me that?" I ask, frowning a little.

"Did you check your email this morning?"

"Who checks their email this early?"

"Anyone who has Ariana as a manager," he says, and taps my phone with two fingers, his rings clacking against the screen. "Check and see."

I regard him suspiciously but check my inbox. As promised, there's an email from Ariana with a timestamp of 5:32 a.m. I try not to gape at it. "What the hell was she doing awake that early?"

"I think she's a vampire," Jules says seriously. "There's no other explanation."

"Good Lord," I say, shaking my head. "All right. Note to self to start checking my emails first thing in the morning."

Jules gives me a salute in solidarity before reaching for his phone again, returning to his game. I pretend not to notice when I see him spend real money on getting more lives to keep playing. This dude is so . . . I don't even have words for it.

Ten minutes later, we arrive at our destination, a hotel based downtown, and the two of us are ushered into separate rooms as our teams flock us. I close my eyes and do my best to block it out, not wanting to get overstimulated. I only open them when Holly from makeup needs to do my eyeliner and curl my lashes, but keep my eyes firmly closed otherwise.

"All done," Holly says, and I finally stare at myself in the mirror. In a black chiffon gown and daring red lipstick, I look so much unlike myself I have to wonder if I've stepped into an alternate universe.

"This is . . . intense," I say, a little stunned.

"I know," Holly says, their lips pursed together. "I prefer you in more natural makeup. But Ariana said to match you with Jules, so who are we to argue?"

"I mean, it looks good," I rush to clarify. "It just doesn't really look like me."

"Your mom and dad didn't really let us do darker looks on you," Holly says, and I immediately turn to look at them. "They thought it would ruin your brand."

"My brand," I repeat.

"Summer, of light and love," Holly says, clearly repeating something they heard from someone else. "All things good and pure."

Something painful twists in my chest. "Yeah. Right."

I turn back to look at myself, wondering if this new look would be more familiar to me in a world where I was in control of my own career and made my own decisions.

"If you're really uncomfortable, we can give Ariana a call," Holly suggests, watching me in the mirror, a note of concern in their gaze.

"No," I say, shaking my head. "Let's leave it."

"Your choice," Holly says.

"Yeah," I say, a little thrown by the words. "My choice."

When I see Jules in the elevator, I know Ariana made the right choice. There's a little handkerchief in the jacket of his three-piece black suit, the same color as my lipstick, and his silver shirt matches the high heels they forced me into. His hair is slicked back out of his face, and he looks like he came out of a '50s noir film.

His eyes land on me and widen slightly. "You look good," he says, and it helps me feel a little more comfortable in my own skin.

"Not too bad yourself," I say with an unsteady smile. "Shall we?"

He offers me his arm, and I take it, holding it a little tighter than necessary as I mentally prepare myself for the onslaught of photographers waiting outside the hotel.

The moment we step outside, cameras start flashing in our faces. Aside from our bodyguards, there are also security guards on either side of us, clearing the way for us to get to the car, but Jules pulls up short when someone yells, "Summer! I love you! Will you sign my album?"

He gives me a curious look, waiting for my response. I stare at him, a little flummoxed. Usually my parents ushered me in and out of places, citing safety reasons for never letting me stop for fans outside of sanctioned events.

But Jules doesn't look worried, and security isn't rushing me.

I nod slightly and he gives me a lopsided smile, his left cheek dimpled, leading me toward the barricade on the left side of us. The girl with the aforementioned album is gaping at me incredulously, and my nerves disappear in the face of her awe.

"Hi," I say, taking the Sharpie from her hand. "Who should I make it out to?"

"Raisa," she says, stuttering over her own name. "R-A-I-S-A."

I dutifully write it down and sign underneath it, leaving a big heart next to my signature. Beside me, Jules is signing a film poster for a different girl, who looks like she might pass out from being in proximity of him.

"I love you so much," Raisa says, and I squeeze her hand as I return the Sharpie.

"I love you too," I say, and try not to well up at how genuinely touched she looks.

Jules grabs my free arm, lightly tugging on it, and I turn, following him, but not without a glance back at Raisa, who's screaming incoherently to the girl beside her. Warmth curls in my chest.

Inside the car, I give Jules a curious look. "Do you stop for fans a lot?"

"When I'm not in a rush, I try to," he says. "They're the reason we're this successful, you know?"

"Yeah," I say, and the sun in my chest threatens to burst. "I think I'm going to start doing it more."

Jules gives me a look, but he doesn't ask what I mean, which I appreciate. I don't even know why I said that.

The rest of the car ride is silent, but comfortable. I check the small clutch in my hand to make sure my phone is still in there alongside a tube of lipstick. It's my first time at New York Fashion

Week, and I'm more nervous than I care to admit. Barbie told me beforehand not to stress and that these things usually go smoothly, that most of my time will be spent sitting around watching the models.

Still, the moment we arrive, I feel out of place. I've never been the best at walking in heels, so I keep my grip on Jules' arm firm, relying on him to maintain my balance more than a few times. He doesn't seem bothered, keeping a bright practiced smile on his face as we walk past countless paparazzi. Inside the building, we stop on the red carpet, letting the photographers take as many pictures of us as they want.

With each flash, my anxiety ratchets up, but I do my best to keep a pleasant look on my face through it all. Unlike Jules, who's a YSL ambassador, I don't have to sit in the front row, but tomorrow at Versace, it's going to be the opposite since they're actively courting me.

Jules helps me find my seat before leaving for his own, and the moment his arm slips away from me, it all comes rushing back to me how much I truly don't belong here.

I adjust my dress and ignore the urge to take out my phone to attempt to look busy, because the last thing I need is to be seen or photographed tuning out. And I *swear* everyone is more focused on me than they ever have been before. When the woman beside me introduces herself, I do the same, but I barely remember the conversation afterward. Everything around me is a little too much, and I just want the show to *start* so the attention can be on the models instead of the people in the audience.

Maybe my parents were right in keeping me to such a strict event schedule and limiting my peer interactions to a minimum. I don't fit in here, with all these people who are meant to be stars. *You got lucky*, Ma would say, and it truly feels like it right now.

I don't have stage fright. Or at least, not in the typical sense. When I'm onstage in front of a crowd of my fans, it's one of the only times I feel like myself. But in situations like these, surrounded by other public figures, with so many cameras flashing and the weight of a hundred curious eyes, I lose all of that confidence, and I forget how to act like a normal human being, tripping over my tongue more often than not.

I don't know if it's imposter syndrome or something else altogether, but either way, it makes me want to scream.

I fidget a little more, before forcing myself to stay still, ignoring how many people are whispering and giggling on either side of me. Instead, I busy myself with the latch of my clutch, quietly doing and undoing it to keep my hands occupied. The repetition helps calm my brain a little.

When the show starts and the lights on the audience dim, I breathe a little easier. Okay. This is fine. Now this is about them and their clothes, not me and my nerves.

I watch with intense focus as model after model comes out, walking down the catwalk and around the rows of audience members. Some of the people around me take out their phones, taking photographs, but my hands are too numb to do much of anything. Instead, I nod along to the upbeat music and try to commit to memory which outfits I like best.

Before I know it, the show is over and Jules is at my side again. I don't realize until his hand wraps around mine, making me nearly jump out of my skin.

"Summer?" he asks, and there's a careful note to his voice.

I look up at him, blinking a few times to bring him into focus. "Oh. Jules. Hi."

He crouches slightly until he's at my eye level. "Are you all right?"

"Never better," I say cheerily, but there's something wrong with my tone. I don't expect him to notice it, but he clearly does given the way his eyes darken.

"Come on," he says, tugging my hand lightly. "We've got interviews to do."

"*You've* got interviews to do," I correct, but let him draw me to my feet.

"I'm not leaving you alone," Jules says, quiet but serious. "There are too many people around to talk now, but later, okay? Until then, stay by my side."

"As you wish," I say, but his touch on my skin helps to ground me more than I thought it would.

I feel almost normal by the time the first interviewer approaches Jules, and he lets go of my hand, but gestures toward the space beside the interviewer's camera for me to wait. I nod, wrapping my arms around myself and standing to the side.

The interviewer casts me an intrigued look, but then Jules draws his attention away from me with an easy smile.

Three interviews go by like that, and I'm a little surprised to find how charming Jules can be when there's a camera pointed at him. Each of the interviewers look like they've fallen in love with him over the course of a five-minute interval.

"Hey," someone says, and I don't realize they're talking to me at first. "Summer, right?"

I turn and nearly trip when I realize who's speaking to me. Nora Terris, Jules' ex-girlfriend from two years ago, is beside me, in her six-foot glory. She's only two inches shorter than Jules, likely taller than him when she wears heels like she's doing right now. She's beyond beautiful, and I'm nearly at a loss for words.

"Nora," I manage to say, and then want to staple my lips shut. "I—hello! It's nice to meet you."

Nora laughs a little, taking the awkward hand I just offered her. "It's nice to meet you too. So, you're Jules' girlfriend?"

"I . . . No labels yet," I say, suddenly nervous. From what the media says, Jules has left all of his exes terribly heartbroken before moving on to the next without a care in the world. His and Nora's breakup was the talk of the town for weeks, given they were costars on Jules' most notable film, a thriller called *Aftershocks*.

"But you're dating him," Nora says, raising a perfect eyebrow at me.

I swallow, a little too loudly for my own liking. "Uh. Yes."

Nora considers me for a long moment, looking me up and down in a way that makes me want to crawl into a hole.

But then she breaks into a wide smile that makes absolutely no sense. "Take care of him, will you? He's never been the type to look out for himself."

The words don't compute at first. "Take . . . care of him?"

Nora nods, giving Jules a fond look. He meets her eye and winks before returning his attention to his interviewer. "He's a sweetheart. You're lucky to be with him."

"Lucky to be with him," I repeat, feeling more bewildered by the second, since none of these words are making sense. Am I missing something? Is this a real conversation?

"The luckiest," Nora says, squeezing my hand. "The two of you should come have lunch with me and my boyfriend sometime. Tell Jules it's an open invite."

Then she disappears without a trace, leaving me entirely too befuddled.

Jules comes to my side a moment later, finally finished with his interviews. "Were you speaking to Nora?"

"Yes," I say, drawing the word out slowly. "She said we have an open invitation to lunch with her and her boyfriend."

"Did she?" Jules' face softens. "Let's take her up on it sometime."

"I am so confused," I mutter before patting his arm. "Can we go then? Are you finished?"

"All done," Jules agrees, and when he wraps an arm around my waist, I lean into his side and let his tall frame shield me from everyone looking our way.

Outside, as we're waiting for our car, Jules takes his suit jacket off and drapes it over my shoulders. I realize belatedly that I've been shaking, though it was more from overstimulation than the cold. Still, I give him a thankful smile and wrap the coat tighter around me.

The moment we're in the car, Jules turns to me, a look of deep concern on his face. "Are you all right?" he asks again.

"I—yes," I say, shaking my head to clear my thoughts of Nora and their weird dynamic.

"I looked into you before we started this whole thing," Jules says, which immediately draws my gaze up to meet his. "And I read your personal essay about how anxiety affects your songwriting process."

My lips part in disbelief. "I—*why?*"

"Because I wanted to know what kind of person you are," he says, still watching me. "My sister has anxiety too. I'm guessing yours is more high functioning than hers, though, if you've managed to survive in this industry this long."

I don't have anything to say to that, too busy being astonished. I've never bothered looking him up outside of what Ariana has told me, knowing enough from the media and figuring I'd learn the rest firsthand, but even if I had, I'd never *admit* that to him.

"Were you having an anxiety attack in there?" he asks, which only throws me off even more.

"What? I—no," I say immediately, defensive, but then I realize he's asking because he's *worried*. I bite my bottom lip, looking away from him. "It wasn't an attack. But I . . . I sometimes get really anxious in big crowds. Especially when I'm surrounded by people like that. It's . . . it's nothing I can't handle."

Jules frowns at me and reaches over to pull his jacket tighter across my shoulders. "Are you going to be okay for tomorrow's show?"

"I'll live," I say, voice quiet.

He touches my hand. "Is there anything I can do to help?"

*Why?* I want to ask, but I think I know the answer. Because Jules is a good person. It's there in the cracks of him, past the cool and detached facade he puts on for my benefit.

*If I break you*
*Will I finally know what's inside?*

The lyrics surprise me enough that I decide to tell him the truth, even though it makes my cheeks flush with heat. "Touching helps. It grounds me. Gives me something else to focus on. Not that you have to—"

"Touching you how?" Jules asks, turning my hand over and squeezing it in his. "Like this? Or more?"

"This is more than enough," I say, and I mean it, but he doesn't look satisfied.

"What about hugs?" he asks.

I'm not even surprised at this point. Of course he'd catch on.

"Hugs work best, yes," I hedge. "But you don't need to give me hugs if you don't—"

Suddenly I'm wrapped in Jules' arms, and the rest of the world seems to still. I freeze up, but slowly, inch by inch, my body unwinds in his hold.

He keeps hugging me, longer than I thought he would. When he finally lets go, I realize I'm more relaxed than I've been all morning.

"Whenever you need a hug," he says, his brown eyes warm, "just tell me. I'll always give you one."

"You don't have to—"

"Summer," he says. "I'm serious. Anytime. Anyplace. Promise me you'll ask if you need it."

I swallow back the rest of my protests. Finally, I nod. "Okay. But only if you promise you'll tell me if I'm being too much."

He shrugs. "That day will never come, but I promise."

I turn away from him, folding my arms across my chest. My heart is racing, but it has nothing to do with my anxiety. "You're strange."

Jules gives me a long, considering look before nodding to himself and turning to face the front. "So are you."

# PART TWO: SPRING

## SUMMER ALI'S SPRING-ISH PLAYLIST
### March to May—*new beginnings and new endings*

1. "Delicate" —Taylor Swift
2. "the way things go" —beabadoobee
3. "Can't Go Back, Baby" —Troye Sivan
4. "Ribs" —Lorde
5. "All This Time" —Louis Tomlinson
6. "Stained Glass" —Madison Beer
7. "Forgive Me" —Chloe x Halle
8. "FRAGILE THINGS" —Dove Cameron
9. "Don't Smile" —Sabrina Carpenter

## CHAPTER TWELVE

## SUMMER ALI SPOTTED AT REAL ESTATE OFFICE: IS THE SINGER TRYING TO MOVE CLOSER TO ACTOR JULES MORADI?

Looking for an apartment is both easier and harder than I thought it would be. Jana insists on helping me, sending me listings every few hours. I set a hard budget when I click on one of the links and see a penthouse apartment with a rent price so high that I nearly gag.

The problem isn't how much it costs—more so that with each passing day, I grow more aware of the fact that I have no idea how to budget appropriately. My parents have always been in control of my money, and for the first time in my life, it's *my* responsibility. I don't want to spend it recklessly or splurge on things I don't need.

A simple two-bedroom apartment will do. One for me, and one for Jana and Safi to sleep in whenever they want to stay over. Half the apartments Jana sends are in Manhattan, but I'm too attached to Queens to agree. It may be a little too close to my parents for comfort, but it's also been my home for the last five years, and I don't know if I'm ready to leave it behind. Even now, living in

Barbie's apartment in SoHo, I'm a little taken aback by how noisy things are and how often I see rats outside.

I also don't want to be afraid of getting recognized every time I step out of my apartment. I have no idea how Barbie copes with it, but probably by having a bodyguard accompany her everywhere. It helps that she's half in love with Spencer, though Barbie has taken to turning alarmingly red every time I bring it up.

So for the past week, I've been in and out of different apartments throughout Queens, trying to find some place I like. After looking in Forest Hills, Sunnyside, and Jackson Heights, I decide I like Long Island City best, close to Manhattan but still firmly Queens.

More importantly, it's right by Jana's middle school.

I pick her up after she's finished with classes so she can come with me to visit a few listings, two of which she suggested after I gave her my new parameters.

"What did you tell Ma and Baba this time?" I ask once she climbs into the car, tossing her backpack on the floor.

"Speech and Debate," Jana says with a shrug.

I give her a dry look. "You hate public speaking."

"Yeah, but they don't know that," Jana says, rolling her eyes. "Besides, it's not as if I could tell them I'm on the basketball team. They'd lose their shit."

"Language," I reprimand, but I don't really mean it. By the time I was Jana's age, I was sneaking off to audition for *Stars of America*. I think she can cuss every now and then.

Jana rolls her eyes again, and it's a wonder they don't disappear in her head. "Whatever, Apu. Which apartment are we going to see first?"

I show her on my phone, and she nods approvingly.

But when we get there, it turns out that three of the windows won't close properly, letting in a chilly breeze that makes me regret not bringing a heavier jacket.

Jana makes a face at the apartment and says, "Next!" and I agree wholeheartedly.

We visit two more apartments, the first with mold in one of the closets and the second with water stains on the kitchen ceiling that make me fear for my life.

"Why is this so hard?" I grumble, climbing in the car again.

"If you would just get a penthouse—"

"Jana."

My sister huffs, slumping in her seat. "Fine. Whatever. Where does Jules live?"

I give her a sidelong look. "Why does it matter?"

"I'm just curious," Jana says, a little too innocently.

"He lives on the Upper East Side."

Jana gives me a pointed look and I ignore it, sending the driver the link to the next apartment building we're visiting.

"So how are things going with him?" she asks.

"I'm sure you can find out the answer to that online," I say, with a raised eyebrow, knowing all too well how much time Jana spends doomscrolling on the internet.

"Why would I check E! News when you're my *sister*?" she asks, scowling at me. "Answer the question, Apu."

"There's nothing to say."

Jana harrumphs. "Have you told him yet?"

I give her an exasperated look. "Told him what?"

"That you're pansexual," my sister says, and my muscles lock up as I nervously eye the divider between us and the driver.

I told Jana my sexuality a year ago, when I finally mustered up the courage to tell someone the truth. She'd been confused as to why it mattered what gender I like, and I had to painstakingly explain that Ma and Baba would never approve. *That* she understood well enough.

"Why would I tell him that?" I ask, lowering my voice pointedly.

"So you know he loves you for *you*," Jana whispers, like it's obvious. "If he doesn't know all of you, what's the point?"

"Have you been reading romance novels again?" I ask with narrowed eyes. "I thought we agreed you aren't old enough for those."

"You're avoiding the question," Jana says, squinting right back at me. "Have you told him?"

"We just started dating," I snap. "I don't need to tell him everything about myself."

"No, but this is important!" she insists. "Especially since Ma and Baba—"

"Jana, I don't want to talk about this."

"Aren't you supposed to be the grown-up?"

"I'm barely eighteen! Newsflash: I'm still a teenager too!"

Jana groans, shaking her head. "You're being ridiculous."

"*I'm* being ridiculous? I've been seeing Jules for two months, and you're saying words like *love*. Be serious, Jana."

My sister looks unconvinced, and my skin starts to crawl uncomfortably. "Why are you so against telling him?"

"I'm not—that's not what this is," I say sharply. But she's landed on something delicate, something I can't think too long about or my hands start to shake. I don't like telling people about my pansexuality. The only people who know are Barbie, Zach, my sisters, and my PR team. Already, my team knowing makes me want to dunk my head in the toilet. Anyone more than that feels dangerous.

At the end of the day, what Jules and I have is temporary. I don't know if he deserves to know something so permanent about me.

"I'm dropping you home," I say finally, leaning over to tell my driver the address.

"Hey!" Jana protests, smacking my arm, but I ignore her. I can't deal with this on top of everything else, and Jana always likes to needle at something when she senses it makes people uncomfortable.

"You're so immature," Jana mutters when I finally sit back in my seat.

"Good," I say, equally irked. "Maybe you should try it sometime."

Jana turns away from me, giving me the cold shoulder. I silently fume, and don't say anything either.

When we pull up in front of the house, something sticky and disquieting spreads through me. It's been over three months since I've been back here, and it looks the exact same, unchanged, while I feel entirely new and different and *wrong*.

Jana picks up her backpack, grumbling under her breath as she gets out of the car. "You're so annoying. I hope you know that."

"Yeah, yeah," I say, rolling my eyes and flicking the back of her head as she goes.

I fully intend to sit there and wait until she gets inside, but then the front door opens and Baba steps outside, his eyes narrowed as he looks at the car on the street.

My heart catches in my throat instinctually and I immediately lower the divider to say, "Drive. *Drive*."

My driver gives me an alarmed look but shifts the car's gears.

"Faster," I insist, watching as Baba starts to stalk toward the car, his hands curled into fists at his side. "*Please*."

The car accelerates, and I jerk forward, nearly crashing into the seat in front of me. I glance backward in time to see my dad standing where the car was only seconds earlier, glaring after us.

I groan, thunking my head against the seat and wishing I were anywhere but here, now.

*I keep running and running*
*But you're nipping at my heels*

## CHAPTER THIRTEEN

# FOOTAGE SURFACES OF JULES MORADI CLEARING OUT AN ENTIRE FRENCH BOUTIQUE TO SHOP WITH SUMMER ALI

The next time I'm with Jules, I can't stop thinking about what my sister said. She's all but forgotten our conversation, texting me new apartment listings like we never had an argument in the first place. I want to ask what happened after I left—if Baba yelled at her—but I already know the answer, so I don't bother.

Instead, I think about her saying, *Have you told him yet?* over and over, even though there's no reason for it. Jules and I aren't in a real relationship. I barely know anything about *him*. Why do I owe him truths about myself?

But with all those thoughts floating around in my head, I realize how strange it is that I barely know this boy beside me, yet see him every other week for outings. We've already been at it for well over two months.

"How's your audition going?" I ask, and Jules falters. I pull him off the street as the road sign in front of us changes from *Walk* to *Don't Walk*.

"It's okay," he says, a little hesitant. "It's a several-part audition."

Today is more low-key than our previous pap walks, with no specific destination in mind. Ariana said it's important for us to be seen doing normal things together, even if it's just strolling out and about. Across the street, there's a pap taking photos of us from afar.

Both of our bodyguards hang back a few feet as they follow us down Fifth Avenue. They're dressed in civilian outfits, which I think is their attempt to be discreet and blend in. It doesn't work that well though, considering how big and buff they are, and the way they radiate an aura of danger.

I'm not sure if it's because of them or because Jules is so clearly recognizable, but there are a few people staring at us, their phones out, whispering among themselves. I dutifully ignore it, focusing on Jules' hand in mine and the furrow in his brows as he waits for the walk sign.

In the last few weeks, dozens of photos of us have circulated the internet. Every time we're in public, fan photos join in alongside the pap pics, giving some credibility to our outings.

Both Jules and I have had an increase in followers and engagement. I barely go on social media these days if I can help it, but even I notice that my posts are getting more and more likes, and more importantly, incessant comments—and questions—about Jules. And I have to admit, I'm starting to grow more curious about my fake boyfriend too.

"What are the different audition parts?" I ask.

Jules runs his free hand through his hair, a few loose strands falling across his forehead. "It's complicated."

"I'm a good listener," I say, just to be contrary.

Jules' nose wrinkles, and he swerves right, taking me with him. I stumble a little but follow him inside a French boutique, absolutely bewildered. We were supposed to go our separate ways after our walk—not go shopping.

"What—?" I start to ask, but then Jules is greeting the woman behind the desk with a bright smile, saying, "Bonjour," with a perfect French accent.

I gape at him, and have half a mind to just lie on the ground and never get up. I've heard Jules speak French before—I'm pretty sure he only learned it for a role he had a few years back—but hearing it in real life is an entirely different thing.

"Bonjour!" the woman says in delight, but then she falters, eyes raking over the two of us. It takes a moment, but her mouth falls open as she blinks, startled. "You two are . . . Jules Moradi and Summer Ali?"

"Oui," Jules says, offering her an affable smile. "C'est un plaisir de vous rencontrer. J'aurais une petite faveur à vous demander?"

The woman nods furiously along to whatever Jules is saying, but I'm at a complete loss, watching the exchange incredulously.

"Serait-il possible que vos clients quittent les lieux, s'il vous plaît? J'aimerais magasiner seul avec mon amie," Jules says, gesturing toward me.

I stare back blankly in response because I have absolutely no idea what any of the words coming out of Jules' mouth are.

The woman turns to give me a look and her eyes widen further. "Est-ce alors votre petite amie? Il me fera plaisir de libérer les lieux pour vous. Donnez-moi cinq minutes!" she says, eyes darting between us quickly before rushing off towards the other side of the store.

"Ce n'est pas ma petite amie!" Jules calls after her. "Not yet anyway." He glances at me. "She'll be back soon."

My mouth purses into a tight pout. "What did you ask her to do?"

He shrugs in reply, turning that stupid, charming smile on me. "I requested for her to have the other customers leave."

My eyebrows rise so high I fear they're going to disappear off my forehead. "*What*? Why?"

Jules shrugs again. "Distractions, of course. Oh, look, they're leaving!" He points toward a cluster of people making their way through the exit, most of them looking confused or annoyed.

I can't help but feel a little bad, except then the woman comes back, grinning. "Tout le monde est parti. Vous pouvez maintenant magasiner, et si vous avez des questions, n'hésitez pas de les poser. Il me fera plaisir de vous répondre!"

"Merci," Jules says to her before pressing a hand against the small of my back. "Come on then, we've got the shop to ourselves."

"I don't—what's wrong with you?" I demand in a hushed whisper before turning back to the woman working the desk, repeating, "Merci!" because it's one of the three French words I actually know.

Jules ignores me, walking over to the counter, taking out his wallet as he goes. When he offers the woman his black card, my eyes nearly bulge out of my head.

"Buy whatever you want, ma chérie," he says to me, and I resist the urge to walk over and knock the living daylights out of him.

Jules grabs my hand, guiding me deeper into the shop as sales assistants start to flock to us, their eyes wide with excitement.

"Are you serious?" I ask. "Tell me you aren't serious."

I've never met anyone this frivolous with their money. Granted, I'm not close with a lot of celebrities aside from Barbie and Zach, but even then—who shuts down an entire store? This isn't a *movie*.

"Surely you don't go shopping with other people around?" Jules asks, raising an eyebrow at me. "I mean, I guess if you're quickly running errands, sure, but something like this?"

My cheeks heat. "I—I don't go shopping that often," I say, and don't bother explaining that my parents had a significant amount of say in what I wore over the last few years. "But even if I did, I wouldn't do *this*. Are you genuinely telling me you do this often?"

"As often as I need to," Jules says, playfully wiggling his brows at me. I feel like I'm looking at a complete stranger. "Don't be so uptight."

I gape at him. "I am not being—" I cut myself off when I notice the sales assistants still watching us. I doubt they'd risk our future business by reporting this to a gossip rag, but there's no way to know for sure. I can't afford to slip up in front of them.

"Treat yourself," Jules insists, looking over a pair of suede boots that probably cost as much as half my wardrobe. "It's on me."

"I'm not doing that," I mutter, crossing my arms. "Whatever. Can you just hurry and buy what you want so we can go?"

Jules immediately turns toward me. "Summer. I'm not letting you leave this store without buying something."

"Then I guess we're not leaving," I say, shrugging.

He tilts his head, considering me. There's a strange light in his eyes, quickly transforming into something mischievous. "All right. Challenge accepted."

"Wait. Wait a second. That wasn't a challenge," I say, but Jules is launching into motion, moving toward the sales assistants and speaking in rapid French. They all nod along like they understand what he's saying, while I stand there like a gobsmacked fool.

There's a sudden flurry of motion as the sales assistants go off in ten different directions, all of them reaching for different clothes.

"What—" I start to say, but then one of the sales assistants comes up to me, holding a shirt against me, frowning. "No, not your color," she says with a shake of her head before disappearing again. Another sales assistant comes up to me with a measuring tape, running it from my hips to my ankles before I can protest and nodding to herself seriously.

"Jules!" I shout, but he's busy looking at a rack of scarves, holding a silk blue one between his fingers. "Jules, what did you say to them?"

"Learn French if you want to know so badly," Jules says idly before holding up the scarf, glancing between me and the blue fabric. "Do you like it?"

My eyes lock in on the price tag. "That's almost three hundred dollars, are you out of your—"

"No, you're right," Jules says, as if I'm not even speaking. "Red is more your color."

"You're not planning to buy these for me," I say in disbelief.

Jules gives me an amused look. "No, I brought you here so we could look at them," he says, and the words are so purposefully pointed that I consider taking the scarf from his hand just to strangle him with it.

"You can't—you don't need to buy me anything," I say, trying to be as firm as I can be. "I have enough clothes. Don't spend your money on me."

"My love language is gift giving," Jules says innocently. "Now be a darling and give these poor ladies your attention."

"I'm going to kill you," I warn him, but reluctantly turn to the sales assistants despite myself, all of them looking up at me with hopeful smiles. "Uh . . . Hello."

The next half an hour is a whirlwind as all of them attempt to dress and style me, enthusiastically pushing me into the changing room with an armful of clothes. The entire time, Jules sits in an expensive-looking armchair and drinks champagne offered by the owner, which is *illegal*, not that anyone in the store seems to care.

Then the real nightmare starts as the sales assistants begin to ring clothes up at the counter. I pull the cashmere sweater off, mussing up my hair in the process, and stalk over to the register.

Jules doesn't move from his chair, watching me with hooded eyes and a sliver of a smile. "They already have my card, darling."

"I don't care, darling," I say, sugary sweet with the promise of violence, and turn to the owner, hoping to God she doesn't only speak French. "Have you charged him yet?"

She raises an eyebrow, glancing between us. "Not yet."

"Good," I say, and take one of my credit cards out of my wallet, praying that my spending limit is high enough for this. "Charge this instead, please."

Jules immediately gets to his feet. "Wait, Summer, I don't—"

"Now," I insist, giving the woman my most serious, intimidating stare. I don't think it actually works, since there's an amused smile on her face through it all, but she dutifully slides my card through the machine.

"Fuck," Jules says as he approaches my side. "Summer, you didn't have to do that."

"I'm not going to let you pay for an entirely new wardrobe for me," I say sharply.

"You wouldn't even be buying a new wardrobe if it wasn't for me," he argues, shaking his head. "You don't have to—"

I shove the scarf on the table into his mouth. Jules' eyes widen in disbelief.

"Looks like I have to pay now," I say cheerfully, and nod at the woman behind the counter. "Receipt, please!"

Jules spits the scarf out. "You're impossible."

"Look who's talking, darling," I say, tucking the receipt in my purse for safekeeping. Thank God the purchase cleared. I would've died of humiliation otherwise. "Shall we?"

He stares at me for a long moment, clearly weighing something in his head that I'm not privy to. I try to focus on that rather than the fact I just spent a ridiculous amount of money on clothes that I don't need and have nowhere to put since I'm *couch surfing*.

"This too, please," Jules says, taking something from the side of the counter, tucked away where I hadn't noticed it. "On my card."

I squint at it, only catching a glint of gold before the woman grabs it, nodding.

I try not to wince when I see the price come up on the screen, ringing in at somewhere around five hundred dollars for the one piece. I didn't look at the final number on my receipt, nor do I want to until I'm tucked away in a safe corner of Barbie's apartment.

The woman hands it back to Jules a moment later, and I realize it's a gold necklace with a small *J* hanging from the bottom. A ruby hangs beside it, shaped like a teardrop, gleaming red.

"You're not serious," I say, simultaneously awed by how beautiful it is and aghast at the thought of wearing it. "This isn't *High School Musical*."

Jules raises an eyebrow at me. "I owe you a necklace, remember? From when we first met?" My hand goes to my throat on instinct, remembering the snap of the chain between us, and his eyes twinkle. "And isn't it a grand romantic gesture? One that hundreds of thousands of people might find sweet?"

I glare at him, catching on to his intention. The paparazzi are probably still outside, waiting for us to leave. "Fine."

Jules smiles at me and unhooks the necklace from its casing. "Turn around."

Grumbling under my breath, I present him my back, gathering my hair in one hand.

Jules' fingers brush against the skin of my neck, warm and gentle, and I try not to shiver at the touch. He carefully places the necklace around my throat, fastening the chain securely, before moving back.

I let my hair fall back into place, my neck still tingling from his touch. "Happy now?"

"Delighted," Jules says, and the only reason I don't flip him off is because there are at least five sales assistants swooning behind him.

Later, when I get back to Barbie's apartment, the internet is having a breakdown over the photos of me wearing the *J* necklace, and I'm too busy considering bankruptcy as I stare at the receipt from the store.

It's by *far* the most outlandish purchase I've ever made in my life, and beyond irresponsible. My parents would kill me if they knew what I did. Even if I can afford it, I have no reason to be spending this much money in one go.

I groan, burying my face in my hands for a solid ten minutes, before I finally get up and start sorting through the clothes. I barely remember any of it, but as I start pulling them out of the bags, I'm surprised to find how much they suit me.

I've never really had my own style before, wearing whatever was handed to me. But I like the thick, comfy sweaters, and the silken dresses that feel expensive, and the long coats, beautiful and sophisticated. I pick up a red corset, wondering when I would ever wear this, before it occurs to me that I could wear it whenever I *want*. And that's the point.

These clothes are for me, to wear when I want them, wherever I want them. It's my decision, it's my choice.

I frown at the clothes, a little irritated that Jules actually had a good idea, even if he went about it in the most deranged way possible.

And then my eyes narrow as I realize he never answered my question about his audition. So *that's* what all this was: a distraction.

I'll have to get to the bottom of it next time I see him.

## CHAPTER FOURTEEN

## SUMMER ALI FANS GO WILD AFTER SHE APPEARS TO WEAR "J" NECKLACE FOR JULES MORADI

Songwriting is going absolutely terribly. Every time I stare at my lyric journal, my brain goes entirely blank. It's never been this bad before and it makes me want to rip out my hair.

I've finally managed to write one coherent song, and it's a song that can never see the light of day, about an unnamed girl I had a crush on ages ago.

When I decided to audition for *Stars of America*, I never anticipated how hard it might actually be to *be* a celebrity.

At the time, all I wanted was to chase my dreams. I wanted my name on billboard signs. I wanted my face plastered all over Times Square. I wanted everyone to know my name.

I wanted to do something, I wanted to be something, I wanted to change lives. I wanted to change the whole *world*. And I had every intention of doing it.

But now I wonder if maybe my ambitions are too big for my

actual capabilities, if I've flown too close to the sun and now my wings are melting.

Between my parents and not knowing if I want to come out, it feels like there are invisible strings pulling me in every which way, and no matter what I do, I'm never going to be able to sit and be happy with myself.

I sigh, shutting my lyric journal.

Behind me, the front door opens and Barbie comes inside holding a stack of packages. I raise my eyebrows when I see Spencer coming in after her, carrying groceries.

"This is for you," she says, handing me a large box.

I take it but don't bother inspecting it, too invested in the way Spencer is looking at Barbie like a lost puppy. It's probably my tour merch, since the label mentioned they wanted me to be seen wearing some of it ahead of my first concert date.

"Thank you for your help," Barbie says, turning to Spencer with a warm smile and stretching on her tiptoes to wrap her arms around his neck in a hug.

Spencer nods, and the tips of his ears turn pink as he steadies her with a hand on her back. "Of course. You can call me anytime." He pauses, the flush spreading across his face as she pulls away from him. "For help, I mean. So I can help you. Like in my job description."

Barbie also begins to blush, twirling a strand of dark brown hair around one of her fingers. "Right. Yes. I will call you. For work."

I bite my lip to keep from giggling at them. This is so unserious. She's really going to deny her feelings for him when she's standing around like a lovesick girl because he carried her *groceries* for her?

Spencer does some kind of bow thing, then looks extremely embarrassed, and ducks out the door.

Barbie closes it behind him and then immediately sinks to the floor, groaning.

I finally let out my laughter, walking over to sit beside her. "Babs, come on."

"I do not wanna hear it," she says, shoving her hand in my face. "I do *not*."

I roll my eyes. "He's literally obsessed with you. You may as well start dating already."

"He's my bodyguard," she reminds me, like I don't know that.

"I've always been a fan of star-crossed lovers," I muse. "The world keeping you two apart but your love defies it all."

"Summer, I'm begging you to shut up," she says, groaning. "I can't think about this or I'm going to start screaming and never stop."

I snort, and tuck my face against her shoulder. She leans her head against mine and exhales deeply. I pat her knee, letting her lean against me for as long as she needs.

As much as I've been poking fun at her about the situation, I don't know what I'd do if I were in her shoes. The only equivalent I can think of, in terms of someone I want to be with but can't, would be if I were to date someone who isn't a boy.

I've never really given dating much thought before. There's never been any time, and even if there were, my parents would never have approved of my having a relationship, knowing it might distract from my career.

But I think a part of me has also been terrified of falling in love with anyone other than a boy. If I were in a steady relationship with someone, I don't think I could hide it. It wouldn't be fair to the person I was dating, and it would be a pain in the ass for my team to deal with.

Suddenly, I sympathize with Barbie a lot more. Why does love have to be so complicated? "Hey," I say quietly. "You know if you really need to talk about it I'm here, right?"

Barbie nods, squeezing my hand. "I know. I love you."

"I love you too," I say, and I'm glad that this love is easy, if nothing else.

In between vocal lessons, tour rehearsals, and endlessly staring at my empty journal, I schedule an appointment with Ariana for a conversation I'm dreading more than I can begin to put into words.

On a Tuesday at the beginning of March, I step into my manager's office and remind myself to breathe.

"Summer! It's so good to see you," Ariana says, looking up from her computer. "Would you like anything? Coffee, tea, water?"

I shake my head and sit down across from her, anxiously fidgeting with my sleeve. "I'm good, thanks."

Ariana offers me a reassuring smile as she takes a sip from her own mug. "All right. So what's up?"

I grimace. So we're getting straight to the point then.

I take a deep breath and try not to hyperventilate. "I—I wanted to tell you something. About me."

Ariana cocks her head to the side. "Is this about your writer's block again? I've already spoken to your label. I was going to email you later this week when I had everything in writing, but they offered a fall deadline if that works for you, maybe October or November?"

"No, that's not . . ." Oh God. November is so far away yet so much closer than it has any right to be. How am I going to—

I force myself to focus on the issue at hand, setting that deadline aside to worry about later. "November is fine," I say, the words strained. "But I wanted to talk to you about my personal life."

A light of worry enters Ariana's eyes and she reaches for the phone on her desk. "Are you seeing someone? Oh God, all right, hold on, I can phone in Jules and his team, and we can—"

"No! No," I hurry to say. "No, nothing like that."

Ariana's hand pauses midair. "Then what is it? Is it your parents?"

"No," I say, and resist the urge to start banging my head against the wall. I need to spit it out. I just need to spit it out. *Just spit it out.* "I'm queer. Pansexual, if that matters."

And then I slump into my chair, bracing for the potential blow.

Ariana blinks. "Oh."

I clench my teeth, waiting for more to come, but she only smiles at me.

"Summer, it's completely fine, don't look so worried," she says gently. "Thank you for telling me. Do you want to come out? If you do, I'll work with your PR team to make sure it goes as smoothly as possible and help you on your way. It shouldn't have any effect on your arrangement with Jules, so there isn't any issue with timing—"

"No," I say, and the word seems to stick inside my throat. Come *out?* That's not—I can't—the entire room feels like it's closing around me. "I don't want to—not right now. But I just . . . wanted to keep you in the loop."

"I see," Ariana says, studying me a little too closely. "Then thank you again for telling me, Summer."

"Yeah," I croak, and then get to my feet. "That was all. Thank you."

Then I flee the room, wishing the earth would open up and swallow me whole.

\*\*\*

Unsurprisingly, I end up at Zach's apartment, on the edge of an anxiety attack. He takes one look at me outside his door and pulls me in, wrapping me in a blanket before bringing us two mugs of warm cocoa.

I bury my face in my arms and try not to cry, unable to even explain *why* I feel so unstable. Ariana was supportive, even encouraging, yet there's nausea swimming in my stomach and wet warmth pressing at my eyelids.

*Do you want to come out?*

No, I don't. No, I *really* don't.

"What the hell happened?" Zach asks, tugging me toward him and stretching his arm around my shoulders. He knows as well as Barbie does how much physical touch tends to calm me. "Was your vocal teacher hard on you today? You had a lesson this morning, right?"

I shake my head and press the heels of my palms into my eye sockets. "I came out to my manager."

A beat of silence, and then Zach says in a deadly calm voice, "She didn't take it well?"

I look up immediately, swiping at my face. "No, she was fine about it. But—she asked me if I wanted to come out, and I don't . . ." I stare at him at a loss.

"You don't . . . ?" Zach asks, squeezing my shoulder.

"I don't know what I'm doing," I say, small and pathetic. "I don't . . . I don't want to come out, Zach. I don't know if I'll ever want to."

Zach's face grows weary with understanding. "You don't have to, Summer. You know that, right? You don't owe anyone that information, much less the world."

"But it's not—it's not about the world," I say, then wince. "Well, it's a little bit about the world, but it's mostly . . ."

"About your parents," he finishes.

I don't answer, but he already knows it's true. We're both aware of exactly how homophobic my parents are.

"I'm scared," I finally whisper. "How did you do this?"

"I took it one day at a time," he says, equally quiet. "That's all we can do."

I make a low noise of dismay and press my face into a couch pillow. Zach sighs and kisses the side of my head. "Do you want a distraction?"

I nod without moving the pillow, trying and failing to ignore how my insides feel like they're caving in.

*There's a rockslide in my chest*
*Falling into the sinkhole of my heart*

"I think my parents might be getting back together," he says, and I peek one eye out from the pillow to stare at him in disbelief. "I *know*. Right after I wrote a song called 'Divorced.' It feels kind of pointed, doesn't it?"

"I thought they hated each other," I say, finally setting the pillow down in my lap, though I keep fidgeting with the fringe. "They wouldn't even come to your birthday party last year because they both thought the other might show up."

"Right, so you can imagine my shock when I decided to surprise my mom and visit her but walked in on them . . ." He trails off meaningfully.

My lips part. "No. *No.* You saw them—?"

He grimaces. "Tragically, yes. I've considered bleaching my eyes at least half a dozen times since."

"Jesus Christ. So you think they're back together?"

"That, or they're having some kind of hate-sex situation," he says with a gag. It's a little over the top, clearly intended to make me smile, and it does for half a beat.

"Ew," I offer.

"Ew," he agrees, and lets go of me to flop backward on the rest of the couch, throwing his legs over my lap. "So I've decided the only thing I can do at this point is scream into the void."

I lean my head back to stare at the ceiling. "I think that's all any of us can do."

## CHAPTER FIFTEEN

## JULES MORADI IN TALKS TO BE CAST IN LEAD ROLE OF MINA RAHMAN'S DIRECTORIAL DEBUT, "RIGHT AS RAIN"

This time, Ariana decides to send Jules and me to the aquarium. She sends the email at 5:43 a.m. and then follows up at 5:48 a.m. to say: *Also just checking in, Summer. Let me know if you need anything! Here to talk.*

I reply with a brief *Thank you!*

I don't want to talk. I don't want to be perceived. I don't want *any of this.*

Instead of spiraling, I try to focus on the aquarium. It's the first time I've been to one in years, the last time being on a school trip in elementary school. I do my best to muster up energy and enthusiasm, but I can't really manage it after this last week. All I've done for days is lie in bed and helplessly wonder why my life is the way it is. Coming out to Ariana has left me raw and aching in a way I didn't anticipate. Usually I'd ride out my bad mental health days with my sisters, but even that isn't as easy as it once was.

It would help if my useless brain could at least write a song with all this free time, but it struggles to do even that. I'm just so tired of feeling this drained all the time.

When the car pulls up outside of Barbie's apartment in the late afternoon, I get in with a quiet hello and then spend the entire drive to the aquarium staring out the window.

Jules seems confused by my silence, but he doesn't ask. Even if he did, I don't know that I'd have anything much to say.

At the aquarium, I let him take my hand and lead me toward the spineless exhibit. Jules gestures to an octopus with a bright grin, and I nod but don't say much else.

Jules purses his lips but keeps us moving without commenting on it, instead pointing out the different aquatic creatures loudly. There are no paps today, since Ariana doesn't want people to catch on that we only spend time together when we're being photographed. Instead, we have to rely on the people around us to recognize us and snap a few blurry photos, and hope that they'll go viral enough for the media to pick up on it.

I don't really understand it, but Barbie is right—it's not really my job to worry about it. I just have to show up. I can do that if nothing else.

And at least we're *here* today, of all places. I've always loved animals, and even in my pit of despair, they're enough to make the day a little more bearable. I even manage a small smile when we see two otters holding hands in one of the exhibits.

"There you are," Jules says, startling me.

"Hm?" I ask, looking up at him. He's wearing earmuffs, but I can see the tip of one of his ears anyway, red from the cold.

"You've been down all day," he says, squeezing my hand. "You're usually so cheerful."

A bitter sort of smile passes over my lips. "I guess you're right."

Jules falters, stopping us in the middle of the hall. The people behind us have to swerve to stop from bumping into us, giving us annoyed looks as they walk around us. Jules doesn't seem to notice, tugging me to the side.

"Hey," he says, his brown eyes intent on my face. "Do you want to talk about it?"

"Not really," I say, digging my toe into the ground absently.

A frown touches the corner of Jules' mouth. "Do you want a hug?"

I shrug instead of answering, but then I'm enveloped in Jules' warm heat, his arms slipping around my shoulders, holding me tight against him. I let my own arms rest lightly against his waist and listen to his steady heartbeat for a few moments.

I'm the one who pulls away eventually, tugging the sleeves of my sweater over my knuckles. "Can we keep walking?"

Jules nods, but wraps one arm around my shoulder as we go, draping his warmth against my side.

"What's your favorite sea creature?" he asks as he leads us toward the dolphins across the hall.

"I don't know," I say. "Maybe sharks."

"Sharks?" he repeats, giving me a surprised look. "Why?"

"They're cute," I say, and Jules only looks further bemused. "What's yours?"

"I like turtles," he says, gesturing to some on either side of us. "I used to have one as a pet."

"I've never had a pet," I admit, following the path of one turtle with my eyes as it dives toward the ground. "I always wanted one, but I wasn't allowed."

"Why not?"

"Ma and Baba said I spent too much time traveling and I wasn't responsible enough to take one on the road with me," I say, dragging my eyes away from the turtle to look at the floor, carefully matching my steps to Jules'. "And they refused to help me take care of it, so . . ."

Jules nudges me. "So?"

"So that's it, I guess." There's something acidic climbing up my throat, and I swallow it back down. "They said it wasn't allowed, so I never got one. End of story."

"Lots of celebrities travel with their pets," Jules says slowly.

"I know."

"Did you tell them that?"

"I did."

"And they didn't care?"

I give Jules a bleak smile and let go of his hand to go look at the dolphins, the tip of my nose brushing against the glass. A little kid beside me does the same, eyes wide in wonder, and my spirits lift just the teeniest bit.

When I finally turn around, Jules has his phone out, but he quickly puts it away when he sees my attention on him. He presents his hand, fingers outstretched. "Come with me?"

"Where to next?" I ask. "I think I saw they have penguins—"

"There's a spring fair on the boardwalk," he says abruptly. "Do you want to go?"

I furrow my brows. "Do you think there are enough pictures of us?"

"We'll still be in public," Jules points out, his hand still hovering in the air between us.

I nod slowly and put my hand in his. He gives me a beautiful smile, one so earnest that it surprises me. Is this the real Jules? Is this what he's like with no cameras around? He interlaces our fingers, pulling me along, and I'm helpless but to follow him.

Outside, Jules seems to know exactly where to go, walking around tourists with an ease that can only come from years of living in New York. I match him step for step, taking in the determination in his gaze.

Eventually, he stops in front of a booth with water guns and mini-targets, and digs in his wallet for a five-dollar bill.

"What are you doing?" I whisper.

"You'll see," Jules says and picks up the water gun, looking the most focused I've ever seen him.

And then he proceeds to miss the target five times in a row.

I press my lips together to keep from laughing as Jules glowers and hands over another five-dollar bill.

"What are you doing?" I ask again, and it comes out significantly fonder.

Jules keeps shooting, and on his eighth try, *finally* hits the target. He turns to me, his expression bright and happy, and I finally let myself smile back at him, unable to resist his joy.

"I want the shark, please," he says to the owner of the booth, and something warm settles in my chest at the realization of what we're doing here. Jules holds the shark out to me, bowing extravagantly. "For you, my lady."

"You are so silly," I say, but take the shark, clutching it to my chest. "Thank you, my lord."

Jules grabs my hand again, pulling me along the boardwalk. "Want to hear a joke?"

"Do I?" I ask, but there's still a small smile on my face.

He clears his throat, and then says, "How do you make an octopus laugh?"

I play along. "How?"

His grin widens. "You give it ten-tickles!"

"Oh my God," I say, shaking my head. "That was the worst joke I've ever heard in my entire life."

"Tentacles!" Jules says insistently.

"You're so silly," I repeat, matching his tone. I can't help but feel cheated that he's kept this version of himself from me for so long. A part of me wonders if he didn't see me as a real person until today, if I was *Summer Ali* rather than Summer. In his defense, I think he may have been *Jules Moradi* rather than Jules to me up until this very moment too.

Jules shrugs a shoulder, his eyes crinkling in the corners from the force of his smile. "I think you need a little silly in your life, Summer Ali," he says, almost as if he heard my internal monologue.

*Who am I without my name?*
*Who are you without yours?*

The air between us feels charged with something I can't define. Jules must realize it too, because he looks away from me, swinging our hands back and forth between us with more momentum than necessary.

"Who *are* you, Jules Moradi?" I ask, shaking my head. "I feel like I can't quite put my thumb on you."

"Anything you want to know about me can be easily found through a Google search," he says.

I snort at the irony. "I said the same thing to my sister the other day."

Jules' nose wrinkles. "It's a bad habit, isn't it?"

"Probably," I agree.

Usually, I feel tired when I talk about this with other people. So much of my life is for public consumption that I hardly know which parts of my life are my own. It's not as if I regret becoming a famous musician—because I *don't*. I never will. This is my dream, and I get paid to do it as a job. I doubt many people can say that.

But I wish someone had told me about all the baggage that comes with it. I would've still done everything the same way, but at least I would've been better prepared for it.

"It's not even true," Jules says, pulling me back to the conversation. "You can hardly Google me and find out my mother likes to plant cucumbers in our backyard."

I look up at him. "Is she into gardening?"

"She's into saving money," Jules says, with a fond shake of his head. "Which is ridiculous, because I keep telling her to ask me if she needs anything, but she says it's the principle of the matter, and that she refuses to buy cucumbers from the grocery store when she can grow them for free in our backyard."

The words hit a sore spot inside of me. My parents have always been all too delighted to spend my money, and if it weren't for Safi and Jana, I would've cut them off entirely. Even then, I've moved most of my money into a new bank account as advised by my lawyer. Thinking about it—and Ma and Baba's anger in the aftermath—makes me slightly nauseous.

But it's nice to know Jules has people in his corner that don't only view him as a commodity, who see him for who he is rather than what he can be to them.

"Tell me about your family," I say softly.

Jules runs a hand through his hair, his expression contemplative. "Well, my parents are both doctors. Fulfilling stereotypes and all that," he says with an amused huff. "But they've never pushed me or my sister to follow in their footsteps. Obviously, if you couldn't tell by the fact I've been on *World of Tween* since I was five years old."

"A little bit of a giveaway," I agree, smiling slightly, though I had no idea they started him on the show so young. He must've gone from a side character to one of the mains with time. "How'd that happen?"

"My aunt actually," Jules says, grimacing a little. "She married my uncle, who worked at a casting agency at the time, and arranged for me to audition after I kept nagging her. Or so I'm told. I don't really remember it. But it makes me a little bit of a nepo baby, I suppose."

I shrug. "You're a person of color. Who cares. Get a leg up however you can."

Jules gives me a long look at that, searching for something in my face. "Iranians are *technically* considered white."

"Technically my ass," I say, rolling my eyes. "You know you're not white."

He opens his mouth like he's going to protest and I cut him off.

"And before you claim you're white passing, you're really not," I say, giving him a pointed look up and down. "Do you think your nose looks like a white person's nose? Be serious, Jules. And have you seen your eyebrows? They're thicker than mine! The palest shade of brown is still brown, even when you're wearing an *alarmingly* light shade of foundation. You know you're supposed to match your neck, right?"

"Alex always said it didn't really count," Jules says, almost under his breath, as he touches his face absently.

"Alex?" I repeat. "Alex who? Is this some white dude?"

A flash of momentary dread passes over Jules' expression before he quickly recovers. "It doesn't matter."

"I think it matters if some white guy is telling you you're just as privileged as he is when that's not the truth," I say, a frown pressing at my mouth. "You know that's not true, right?"

"Summer, I don't—"

"Have you ever played a role where you're a person of color?" I ask with narrowed eyes. "Have you tried?"

"It doesn't feel right to take other roles when I know I can mostly pass for white," he mutters. "Alex said—"

"*Fuck* this Alex person," I say in disbelief. "Why don't you let the casting director decide who's best for the role instead of counting yourself out early? I understand not wanting to audition for characters who are supposed to have a darker skin tone, because yes, I agree, you're privileged when it comes to colorism within our community, but that's *within our community*. It does *not* mean you're only allowed to audition for white roles! Have you—what's the ethnicity of the new character you're auditioning for?"

"There's no specific ethnicity," he says with a sigh, scrubbing a hand over his face. "Summer, I really don't want to—"

I round on him. "You're allowed to play your own ethnicity. *Please* tell me you know that."

Jules gives me a stiff smile that tells me he's done with this conversation. "Yeah. Sure. Anyway, as I was saying, my parents are definitely supportive of my career, but they're also really busy, so I don't see them as often as I'd like. Mom's a pediatrician and Dad's a surgeon, so you can imagine. My older sister, Laila, visits me pretty frequently though. I'm sure you'll meet her at some point."

I purse my lips, wanting to push more but sensing the boundary Jules is drawing. "Buy new foundation," I say finally, and then allow the subject change. "Are you and your sister close?"

"Pretty close," Jules agrees, some of the tension in his shoulders fading and we start walking again. "What about you and yours?"

The left corner of my mouth turns up without my permission. "Yeah. Sanjana and Safina are both menaces, but I'd die for them. At least yours is older. Mine are thirteen and eight."

"Oof," Jules says, giving me a rueful smile. "So you're the oldest?"

"Guilty as charged."

"Summer, Sanjana, Safina," he lists off, a small dent forming between his brows.

I glance around, taking note of the girls a few stalls behind us, whispering rapidly as they hold out their phones. I wince a little and then lean closer, so only Jules can hear me. "Sumaira."

He looks down at me. "Sumaira," he repeats.

I nod, pulling back. "*Stars of America* said it would be better if I had a Western name, and I *do* like the name Summer, so it worked out fine."

Jules leans closer this time, his lips brushing against my ear. "Juyan."

I blink, a little startled. "Juyan?"

He nods and his eyes dart behind us, to the same girls I noticed before, and then he presses a kiss to my forehead before pulling away. I pretend not to hear the sound of a camera shutter behind me.

"Nice to meet you, Juyan," I whisper.

Jules keeps leading us down the boardwalk, his hand warm and solid in mine. "Nice to meet you too, Sumaira."

## CHAPTER SIXTEEN

## FANS SPOT SUMMER ALI AND JULES MORADI COZIED UP ON A DATE AT THE FAIR; COULD THINGS BE GETTING SERIOUS?

A week later, I'm supposed to be packing for tour, but instead I'm being forced to sit still as Safi paints my nails, her tongue poking out in concentration.

"Not a bad color," I muse, considering the red nail polish. I'm starting to grow more and more fond of it. "But pink would've been better."

Outside, the sun is starting to set, clueing me in to the fact it's getting late and that the girls need to get home soon, but I already get such little time with them nowadays that I'm reluctant to send them off. I've been scared to have them over for the past few weeks, but they both threatened to throw a temper tantrum if I didn't see them before tour, and I was helpless but to agree. I might nag them frequently, but at the end of the day, they'll always have me wrapped around their fingers.

"I'm painting *my* nails pink. And red is a nice color on everyone,"

Safi says, and then slaps my wrist when I try to take a closer look. "Don't move!"

I pout at her to no avail as she goes over my nails with a second layer of clear nail polish. I grimace, hoping I don't actually smudge it.

"God," Safi says, blowing out a breath. "Jana Apu, can you hold Summy Apu's hand still for me? This is preposterous!"

"Big word," I say, and give her a sheepish smile when she glares at me.

Jana looks over from where she's painting her own nails. "Sure, give me a second." She calmly sets the bottle to the side before skipping over to us. She takes my hand in hers, and I try not to flush as I remember the last person who held my hand was Jules.

As if Jana can hear my thoughts, she zeroes in on the necklace at the hollow of my throat and squints. "Is that a *J*?"

I don't say anything, keeping my gaze focused on my youngest sister as she starts applying a third coat of nail polish.

"It is," Jana says, accusatory.

"It's nice," Safi says without looking up. "I like it."

My phone starts ringing, and I reach for it with my free hand, ignoring both Safi and Jana's shouts of protest. On the screen is a picture of Jules with the fluffy shark he won me.

"Oh my God!" Safi shouts. "Can we talk to him? Apu, oh my God, can we talk to him?"

Jana nods, her gaze almost menacing as she looks at my phone. "I want to speak to him."

"Neither of you is speaking to him," I say sharply. "Promise me you'll be quiet or I won't pick up."

"But Apu!"

"*Promise.*"

"Fine," they both mutter, neither looking pleased about it.

I pick up the call with my free hand, taking care not to smudge my nails, since Safi *will* yell at me if I ruin all her hard work. I set the phone on speaker, giving both my sisters a warning look as I balance it on my thigh. "Hello?"

"I got the part!" Jules says, his voice loud with excitement. "Summer, I got it!"

My eyes widen, my hand jerking in Safi's grip. She hisses at me, but I barely notice. "Oh my God! Jules, that's amazing! Congratulations!"

"I'm already speaking to them about the soundtrack, they said—"

I grin ear to ear, shaking my head, though I know he can't see it. "Oh my God, *forget* the soundtrack for a minute. This is so incredible! Isn't this your dream role?"

"Yeah," Jules says, and his voice is so warm it makes me want to burst from joy. "I can't believe . . . I mean, I hoped, but I didn't think . . . Wow."

I smile at my phone helplessly. "Congratulations, Jules. Really. I'm so happy for you."

"Thank you," he says, earnest. "I couldn't have done it without you."

"I mean, I hardly—" I cut myself off, realizing what he means. The PR stunt. I glance at Jana and Safi, both of them rapt with attention as they stare at the phone. "I suppose I helped. Do you know if we still have to . . . ?"

A beat of silence, and then Jules clears his throat. "Ariana says we should, since I haven't finished securing a song for you. I swear I'm actively working on it. You don't mind, do you?"

"I don't mind," I say, still cognizant of my sisters sitting beside me. "Do you know how much longer?"

"Your guess is as good as mine," Jules says with a laugh. "Ariana would know better."

"All right, I'll speak to her then," I say, and kick Safi lightly when she starts to open her mouth. She glowers at me but doesn't say anything. "Congrats again, Jules. Really."

"Thank you, Summer," he says, and I can almost see him smiling in my head. "And I wasn't referring to our situation earlier. I meant that I took your advice for my last audition. I acted . . . I acted like myself. And I think it made a difference."

"Oh," I say softly. "I'm glad. I'm proud of you."

"Yeah, well," he says, sounding sheepish, even across the phone. "It's good to try new things, I guess."

"Is it too early to say I told you so?" I ask, grinning to myself.

"Give it a week or so, I think," he says with a laugh. "But anyway, I wanted to wish you good luck with your tour. We'll coordinate throughout?"

"Yeah," I say, and without meaning to, my hand drifts up to touch my necklace. "Sounds like a plan."

"I love you!" Safi shouts, and I groan, shoving a hand over her mouth.

"Oh?" Jules says, the glee obvious in his voice. "Who was that?"

"An eight-year-old that's about to be very, very sorry," I say, narrowing my eyes at Safi. She looks unrepentant, licking my palm, but I'm used to her war tactics.

"If you hurt my sister, I'm going to kill you," Jana says matter-of-factly, and I slap my other hand over her mouth.

"Two very different ends of the spectrum," Jules says cheerfully. "Nice to meet you, Sanjana and Safina."

Both of them startle at that, and I drop my hands only so I can grab my phone. "All right, I'm gonna go before either of these two menaces says something else. I'll speak to you later."

"Bye, darling!" Jules says, and I hang up, rolling my eyes.

The moment I set the phone down, both of them launch themselves off my bed, running for the living room, screaming for help from Barbie.

I sit down on the edge of the stage the moment I finish rehearsing the last song in my set. It's my favorite song off my debut album, and one I could perform a thousand times over, but I always go a little too hard and exhaust myself by the end. Barbie and Zach come up to the stage a second later, Zach tossing me a water bottle I barely manage to catch.

"Thank you," I call to my band, who grin at me. The drummer comes forward to ruffle my hair before joining the others as they head backstage.

"You were great," Barbie says, jumping up to sit on the stage with a boost from Zach. "Are you nervous?"

"More nervous about being away from all of you for the next few weeks," I say, and it's not even with the intention of being cheesy. I've never been alone on tour before. Sure, I'll have my band and my tour manager, but it isn't the same as having my parents with me at every stop.

They used to accompany me every time I left the state, leaving Jana and Safi in the care of our Dadu. As irrational as it was, I used to feel jealous of my sisters, enjoying peace and quiet with our grandmother while I suffered at the hands of our parents.

Now our positions are flipped, and it doesn't feel half as great as I thought it would.

"It won't be that long," Zach says, squeezing my knee. "I'll see you at the Seattle date."

"Of course you will," Barbie says, rolling her eyes.

"Mind you, Spencer is quite literally *right over there*," Zach says, gesturing toward the exit where Barbie's bodyguard is standing alongside ours, scanning the room for threats.

"Don't be petty," Barbie says, making a face at him. "You're the one that brought up Seattle."

"Both of you behave," I say, whipping them lightly with my sweaty towel. "No ripping out each other's throats while I'm gone."

"No promises," Barbie says, baring her teeth at Zach, who flips her off. "I'll be at whatever date you need me to be at. Just give me a call and I'm there."

"You are *so* annoying," Zach says, and I sigh, pulling them in for a hug. Both of them immediately retract their claws in favor of holding me.

"I don't know how I'm going to leave my sisters," I whisper to them in the quiet space between us.

"We'll be here if they need anything," Barbie says, knocking her head against mine lightly. "Don't be afraid to ask us for help."

It's a little easier said than done, but I nod all the same. "You guys will call *me* if you need anything too, right?"

"Oh, trust me, you'll be hearing all about my family drama at Easter," Zach says, pulling away to grin at me.

"And at the rate my love life is going, I'm sure I'll be having a mental breakdown in the group chat soon enough," Barbie says with a sigh, resting her chin on her fist as she stares at the back of the venue.

I rub her back consolingly. "At least it'll make for good songs?"

Barbie glances at me. "How's your writer's block going anyway?"

"And on that note, I will see you guys in three months," I say, hopping to my feet and running away before they can protest. Barbie curses after me and Zach laughs so loud it echoes through the concert hall.

## CHAPTER SEVENTEEN

## SUMMER ALI AND JULES MORADI REPORTEDLY HAVE LONG-DISTANCE DATING PLAN IN PLACE AMID THEIR RETURN TO TOURING AND FILMING

My favorite part of being a singer is undeniably performing at concerts. No matter which way I slice it, that will always be true.

Even now, when I carry an immense guilt knowing that I have nothing new to show my fans, I still look forward to performing for them more than anything else.

I love being able to see them in person. I love hearing them sing back the same words I spent so long writing. I love seeing a physical embodiment of the community that music can build. I love knowing that so many of my fans were able to form meaningful relationships with each other because of my existence. I love knowing that my music has saved some of their lives the same way it's saved mine.

This is everything I dreamed of when I imagined becoming a singer all those years ago, and it makes all the hard parts worth it beyond measure.

For a brief few hours, I'm able to ignore how bad my writer's block is. I can stand on a stage, sing my heart out, and have a fun and silly little time with my fans.

The problem is the hours when I'm *not* onstage, when we're traveling between cities and I stare out of airplane windows and wonder what the hell I'm gonna do if I can't come up with a second album soon.

At least a quarter of my set is cover songs because I barely have enough original ones to last a whole concert. It's embarrassing. As much as I love finding a new song to perform every night, to make each concert unique and individual to the people there, I can't help but wish I had new *songs* to perform instead.

I don't go on social media much aside from posting tour-date-specific photos every night, but nowadays, I find myself lying in large beds in empty hotel rooms and scrolling through multiple platforms despite myself. There's a surprising amount of people talking about me and Jules, and when I click into one of the posts, it leads me down a rabbit hole of countless pictures of Jules on set with his *Right as Rain* cast members.

When I realize I've been inadvertently staring at Jules' face for the last half an hour, I close the app and switch to a different platform, my cheeks flushing even though there's no one around to see me.

When I check my mentions, there are so many fans asking me about new music amidst all the photos and videos from tour. I search my name and find hundreds of posts from people looking forward to "SA2" and speculating what the songs might sound like.

It all fills me with a heavy sense of dread.

During my concerts, I tend to stop halfway through for fifteen minutes to read signs and banners, and engage with the fans in the venue. When a fan holds up a sign in Dallas asking when they can expect my next album, I paste on a fake smile and pinky promise it's coming soon.

I want to keep that promise, but I don't know *how*. Every time I sit in front of my journal, my head is completely empty.

I don't understand why my brain is refusing to work with me. This shouldn't be that hard.

I never really write songs about my personal experiences—not that there's much going on in my love life to write about anyway. I've never been in love before and I've only had fleeting crushes otherwise. Most of my songs are based around books and movies that I've watched, putting myself in a character's shoes and imagining what kind of song they'd write if they were given the opportunity.

Most people don't know that—the media certainly doesn't, and I never plan to tell them. There's so much of my life that's public now, and the very few songs I really write about my life are tucked away, secret and hidden in the back of my lyric journal.

My phone buzzes and I glance at it to see a text from Jules. I click into it to find a picture of a pink YSL purse.

> **Jules Moradi:** saw this and thought of u

> **Jules Moradi:** should I ask YSL to send it over

> **Me:** there's no way that doesn't cost like $2k... be so serious rn

> **Me:** where did u even see this???? aren't u supposed to be filming

**Jules Moradi:** I /am/ capable of multi-tasking

**Jules Moradi:** aren't YOU supposed to be asleep rn?? didn't u have a show earlier

**Me:** I'm in the same timezone as you lmao I'm in portland

**Me:** actually LA is pretty soon if you wanna come? I can set aside tickets for you

**Me:** for the stunt I mean

**Jules Moradi:** ohhh yeah that's a good idea

**Jules Moradi:** will you come visit set then??

**Jules Moradi:** I'm sure everyone will be excited to meet u

**Jules Moradi:** and u can get a feel for the movie's vibes for when u write ur song

**Me:** sounds like a plan

**Me:** let me know the details when you can

**Jules Moradi:** you got it

I set my phone down and look back at my empty journal. After a moment, I pick up a pen.

*Tumbleweeds roll through the back of my head*
*And the world is calling me a fraud*

I frown at the words, considering them for thirty seconds, and then I sigh. This is impossible. I cross the lines out and finally force myself to roll over and go to sleep.

And maybe it would all be fine if writer's block were the only problem I had to deal with during tour, but my life has never been that easy.

"What's up, Seattle!" I shout into the mic halfway through my set.

The crowd screams, and in the back of the pit, Zach is cupping his hands around his mouth and yelling my name right along with them. I shoot him a secret smile before turning back to the thousands of adoring fans. "It's so good to be back here! It's been, what, a year? A year too long. If I could tour all the time, I would. Did you guys miss me?"

Another round of affirmative cheering greets me.

"I missed you too," I say with a grin. "Are you guys having a good time? What's been your favorite song so far?"

They start yelling different song names, and I nod as if I can hear each of them individually. "All right, I hear some 'Cheers,' some 'Wash It Away,' and a *lot* of 'Scorpio Season' out there. Any Scorpios in the crowd?" Hands shoot up throughout the pit and I laugh. "Anyone share a birthday with me? November 11?" A piercing scream comes from my left, in one of the upper sections, and I swirl to face them with raised eyebrows. "All right, seems like someone up there for sure."

"It's my birthday today!" someone shouts near my feet, and I focus on the barricade. The girl in question looks like she's about to pass out when we lock eyes.

"Did you say it's your birthday?" I ask, crouching so I'm closer to eye level. She starts nodding vigorously. "Can I see some ID?"

She gapes at me before she starts digging in her purse like it's the last thing she'll ever do. I giggle, and the fans around her scream loudly. She finally manages to get it out and hands it to a security guard, who passes it along to me.

I hold my hand above my eyes to block out the stage lights, squinting down at the driver's license. "Lynn? Oh, yes, I see right here, May fourth. Hey, may the fourth be with you! A little Star Wars moment, love it," I say, my smile stretching wide. "Do you like Star Wars, Lynn?"

Lynn makes a face and I burst into laughter.

"All right, I'll take that as a no," I say, handing the license back over to the security guard. "Well, happy birthday! Come on, everyone, let's sing happy birthday to Lynn."

The entire crowd gathers together to sing her happy birthday, and I blow her a kiss before walking to the other side of the stage. "Anyone over here a Star Wars fan? Yeah? Oh, you look like you'd love Darth Vader," I say, pointing at a random girl near the catwalk.

"His name is Anakin," she shouts back.

"You're so right, that's my bad, his name *is* Anakin," I say with a grin before scanning the crowd for any interesting signs.

I falter when I see someone holding up a lesbian pride flag. The person beside them has another one in bisexual colors.

There's a lump forming in my throat and my gaze jumps to Zach in the back. He tilts his head in question, and I immediately return my expression to neutral. If he can tell something's wrong, someone else might be able to as well.

I point a few feet away from him. "Sorry, does that sign say, '*today's my 2nd anniversary with my bf and he broke up with me because I wanted to come here instead*'? Good riddance!"

I keep going like that for ten more minutes, but my eyes keep returning to the pride flags without meaning to. Now that I've noticed those two, I'm hyperaware of the fact there are more littered throughout the crowd.

During the last song, someone throws a pansexual pride flag onstage as if they *know*, and I stare at it for a beat too long considering whether I'm brave enough to pick it up and parade it around.

But I'm not, even if I wish I were.

I finish the concert with a bow, my arms wrapped around my guitarist and bassist on either side of me. As I leave, my fingers itch with the urge to grab the flag off the stage, but I clench my hands into fists to contain it.

Backstage, I change into my normal clothes and come outside to find Zach holding his arms out for a hug.

I lean into his embrace.

"I saw the flag," he whispers into my hair. "You all right?"

I pull back, smiling thinly. "As right as rain."

We both know that isn't the truth, but Zach doesn't call me out on it. He only reaches down and squeezes my hand, and it doesn't fix anything, but it does make everything marginally better.

## CHAPTER EIGHTEEN

## CONFIRMED: ANGELINA RODRIGUEZ AND JULES MORADI TO STAR IN MINA RAHMAN'S DIRECTORIAL DEBUT "RIGHT AS RAIN"

When I arrive on the set of Jules' film with two deli sandwiches in my tote bag, I'm not sure what to expect, but it isn't a line of trailers parked on the side of the road outside of a high school and both paparazzi and reporters camped out right in front. I guess it makes sense, but it takes me a little aback.

An assistant greets me the second I step foot out of the car. Damon stays behind me, pushing through the crowd as they throw questions at me. I ignore them, following the assistant as she leads me inside the school.

I glance around, taking in all the rows of lockers. This is where I would be in an alternate universe where I never became famous. I finished homeschooling a few months ago, but if I were a student here, my graduation would probably be right around now.

It feels strange to think that. I feel out of place, like I'm crossing a line and entering uncharted territory where I don't belong.

Sometimes I wish for a normal life, where things are less hectic and less intense, but coming right from multiple weeks of tour, I can't find it in myself to want *this* over performing in front of thousands, over bright lights and adoring fans.

The assistant pushes open the doors to an auditorium and gestures for me to sit in one of the last rows, out of view of the cameras as they film something on the stage.

Jules is making a speech, but I can't hear it. I'm too far away. He looks impassioned, completely overtaken by this character, and I realize I don't even know what this movie is *about*.

It's obvious that Jules is in his element though, near breathtaking as he fills up the stage with his presence. I lift my phone, taking a photo of him, knowing I can't post it until after the movie trailer is released—and we may not even be fake dating by then—but doing it all the same.

There's passion in his movements as he gives the speech, his eyes blazing with determination and confidence. There are rows and rows of people sitting in the front, extras who look up at Jules with awe, and I wonder if it's because that's what their characters are supposed to do or if they're as mesmerized by Jules' acting as I am.

My lips curl into a small smile. I'm glad Jules looks so at home here, in front of a camera. It's obvious this is his dream, the way singing is mine. He's practically glowing as he runs through the scene over and over, giving it his all each and every time.

I flash Jules a thumbs-up when I see his gaze dart toward the back during one of the breaks in between cuts. Jules grins, returning the thumbs-up, before tuning back in to the scene.

"Cut!" the director calls again, and the entire auditorium seems to exhale in relief at her voice. "That was a good run. Let's break for lunch."

Members of the cast start flocking down the auditorium aisles, disappearing from view. A few cast members give me knowing looks, and one of the girls even winks at me as she pushes through the double doors.

Jules finally reaches me, a quiet smile on his face, so different from the impassioned person I saw on the stage mere moments ago. "Hey. You made it all right?"

I nod, getting to my feet. "There's an awful lot of paparazzi out there."

"Yeah, I know," he says with a wince. "There's a back entrance, but since the point is for us to be seen . . ."

"I get it," I say, waving off his concerns. "So do you have your own trailer?"

Jules lights up. "Yes, come on, I'll show you."

I follow him out the doors and can't help but feel out of place again. Jules puts a hand on the small of my back, leading me without any real pressure, and it settles the kernel of anxiety in the back of my brain.

"Don't want you to get lost," Jules murmurs in my ear, but then one of his cast members comes up beside him, asking him a question, and he's whisked away momentarily.

Suddenly, the girl who winked at me is standing by my side. She's so familiar, but I can't place her. "You would think Jules would know better than to whisper sweet nothings to you on set, but that's Jules for you, isn't it? Quickie in his trailer, then?"

I nearly choke on my saliva. "*Excuse* me?" Then I abruptly start shaking my head, eyes wide. "He wasn't—this isn't—" I splutter, and the girl chuckles, bumping her hip into mine and pushing me closer to Jules.

"I'm only kidding," she says before holding her hand out. "Angelina. I'm Jules' costar."

It clicks in my head then. Angelina Rodriguez, Oscar-nominated actress. The star of the movie alongside Jules. The girl I once had a crush on.

She looks at odds with the image of her in my head, her hair and makeup done completely differently from what I'm used to. She's also older, reminding me how *weird* the passage of time is.

"Summer," I say, blinking a few times to get my bearings, but shake her hand all the same.

"I know," Angelina says, grinning. "And I really was joking, but if given the opportunity, I hope you'd sing 'Partition' at the top of your lungs."

"I would *never*—" I start to say, but the protest dies in my throat when Angelina starts laughing heartily.

"Keep your dirty jokes to yourself," Jules says, coming up beside me and batting Angelina's hand away.

"It wasn't even that dirty," Angelina complains, crossing her arms over her chest.

Jules gives her a pointed look.

She huffs, throwing her hands up. "Fine! Let's all be puritans, I guess!"

"Go away," Jules says, drawing the words out on a whine as he gives her a light push. "Leave me and my girlfriend alone."

She sticks her tongue out at him petulantly and then disappears into one of the classrooms.

"Wait," I say, a little too late, biting my lip. "Should I have let her think we're having sex in your trailer? I wasn't thinking about appearances, I—"

"Don't worry," he says, giving me a faint smile. "Angelina's not the type to talk to the press either way. I know she's a little . . . extra, but she's got a good heart underneath all that."

I nod, but my thoughts are ricocheting back and forth in my head. Ma and Baba insisted I always retain my "pure" image, keep up the good-girl act, be sweet and lovely, and never stray from that.

But who was that for? What did that gain me? A few extra sales from people who were never my target audience anyway?

I've only ever kissed two boys and one single girl in my entire lifetime, and all three of them are secrets I've guarded like my life depends on it. Ma and Baba would have had a conniption if they knew. Given the way they're losing their minds over Jules, I don't think adding fuel to the fire would do me any favors.

Not that Jules and I have kissed yet. The idea of doing so makes me nervous for reasons I can't quite put into words. My skin starts to itch, and I scratch at my wrist until Jules' fingers gently wrap around my hand.

"Do you need a hug?" he asks quietly.

"Please," I say, and he pulls me into his arms, resting his chin on the top of my head.

We stand there for a while, swaying lightly, and I will myself to calm down, to focus on Jules' arms around me, his skin pressing against mine.

"Come on," he says after a while, leaning back and brushing my hair out of my face. "Let's eat lunch."

I smile faintly, holding up my tote bag. "I brought sandwiches."

Jules laughs. "Perfect, I have dessert waiting for us."

After we finish eating our sandwiches, tuna for me, turkey for Jules, he pulls out two Popsicles from his mini-fridge and hands me the pink one.

"What if I wanted the green one?" I ask, hopping down the steps of his trailer, trying to ignore the paps that immediately jump at the chance to photograph us. Worse are the reporters, asking us nonsensical questions.

Damon is already at my side, keeping them a safe distance from me, while Jules' bodyguard, Rivus, does the same on the other side.

"You didn't," Jules says before adding, "You snooze, you lose," and showing me his green tongue.

I snort and shake my head at him. "They're going to get pictures of that."

"Let them," he says with a careless shrug. Once we're back inside the school building, it's quieter, though there are plenty of cast members drifting through the halls.

"Jules! Come join us!" says one of the actors down the hall, gesturing toward a classroom.

Jules looks to me for permission, and I nod. I expect it when he takes my hand in his and leads us into the room.

There are a few other members of the cast in the room, with Angelina sitting on the teacher's desk eating a burrito bowl. The person who called us over nods at me with a smile. "Darien. They/them pronouns."

"Summer," I say, returning the smile. "She/her pronouns."

Jules takes a seat at one of the desks in the front row, and I take the seat beside him readily. He doesn't let go of my hand, stretching his arm out to the side so he can hold it comfortably. His touch steadies me, which is probably the point.

"Leo, Darien, Renee, and Angelina," Jules says, pointing them out to me. "Everyone, this is my girlfriend, Summer."

It's the second time he's called me his girlfriend, though we never discussed it. I suppose it's not a real relationship, so we don't *need* to discuss it, but it's still strange to hear the word come out of his mouth. It's only been five months of this PR stunt, but it's not like these people know that. In fact, these are probably the people we need to fool the most.

"Nice to see Jules settle down finally," Darien says, sitting atop one of the desks, swinging their legs back and forth. "Never thought the day would come."

"Fuck off," Jules says, but he's grinning, a dimple pressing into his cheek.

"I'm serious, dude," Darien insists, their eyes bright with amusement. "Summer, what did you do to lock him down?"

"Wrote him a song," I say dryly, though it couldn't be further from the truth.

"Must've been some song," Angelina says through a mouthful of food. She doesn't seem to care that people are looking at her, and I can't help but find that admirable.

"It was beautiful," Jules agrees.

I look at him out of the corner of my eye, but he tells the lie seamlessly, as if it's the genuine truth. I suppose he wouldn't be a good actor if he did anything else.

"I'm surprised it was enough," Leo says, his head tilted to the side. "Alex mentioned you had commitment issues."

Jules' hand tightens in mine, but that's the only indication that the words have an effect on him. "Did he?" he asks placidly.

There's that name again. *Alex.*

I tap my thumb against the back of Jules' hand insistently until he turns to glance at me subtly. I give him a pointed look. *Who is Alex?*

He shakes his head slightly, but enough for me to understand that if I want an answer, I'm not going to get it now.

"Alex had a lot to say," Leo says, still watching Jules, an almost predatory look on his face.

Jules' entire hand goes stiff, the veins in his forearms prominent as he holds himself still. I keep my face impassive, even though I want to glare at Leo.

"So what's the movie about?" I ask brightly, turning to look at everyone else. "Jules didn't want to spoil the surprise, but maybe the rest of you will? I hear it's going to be the biggest movie of the year."

Renee laughs. "Well, we can hope, right? With Mina directing, it should at least be a decent success."

"Mina?" I ask.

"Mina Rahman," Darien clarifies. "This is her film debut. She's dating Emmitt Ramos?"

The last name *Rahman* makes me feel a sharp spark of delight. I wonder if she's Bangladeshi, too? I'll have to ask Jules later.

"Emmitt Ramos . . . The one from the superhero movies?" I ask, racking my brain for the name.

"The very same," Renee says, clasping her hands to her chest, hearts shooting out of her eyes. "I hope I get to work with him someday."

Angelina snorts. "Are you trying to get fired, bro? You better not let Mina hear you."

Renee waves her off. "As if anyone could steal Emmitt from her. They've been together for over half a decade."

"*Anyway*," Darien says, rolling their eyes. "Mina's directing, and everyone's been waiting for her film debut for years."

"Ah," I say, nodding in understanding. The words ring a bell, reminding me of when Ariana first proposed this PR stunt. "So what's the movie about?"

Everyone trades looks, and I sigh when it becomes obvious none of them is willing to cross Jules and tell me. "Well, what *kind* of movie is it?"

"Coming-of-age," Angelina says, finally tossing her empty burrito bowl into the trash. "And that's all we can tell you."

"I'll get it out of him," I say, a pleasant threat, squeezing Jules' hand hard enough to hurt. "Don't worry."

Angelina laughs. "Good luck with *that*."

## CHAPTER NINETEEN

# FROM "WORLD OF TWEENS" TO THE WORLD OF HOLLYWOOD STARS: JULES MORADI AND ALEX ROBINSON'S FRIENDSHIP OVER THE YEARS

Jules eventually goes back to filming, and I sneak out the back door this time, thankfully avoiding all the vultures outside. Usually when they're called by publicists, they have some modicum of respect for us, but the ones outside the movie set are decidedly not respectful.

Back at my hotel, I take a shower and then call Barbie and Zach in a three-way FaceTime. Zach picks up first, then Barbie.

"Do you guys know who Alex is? It's come up a few times with Jules," I say, wiping a towel through my hair.

Barbie lets out an evil laugh. "I told you. You owe me ten dollars."

Zach groans. "Summer, *why*."

"What did I do?" I ask, looking back and forth between them.

"It's what you didn't do," Zach mutters. "Why haven't you looked up your fake boyfriend on Wikipedia yet?"

I squint at him. "Because Wikipedia is hardly a reliable source of information. Ariana already told me everything I need to know about him. There was a one-sheet!"

"Ten dollars," Barbie says gleefully. "I accept Venmo."

"Ugh," Zach says, shaking his head. "Fine."

Barbie grins, perfect teeth on display. I still remember when she had braces two years ago, and it makes me ache for a version of us that had less on our plates.

"Stop making bets about me," I whine, "and tell me who Alex is."

"I love you," Barbie says, shaking her head fondly. "Alex was Jules' costar on *World of Tweens*. He was the main character? Or, well, he was the main character after the original actors aged out of the show."

"I've seen like two episodes," I admit, scratching the back of my neck. "Back when I was a kid. I don't remember much."

Zach thunks his head against the table in front of him dramatically. *"Summer."*

"Sorry!" I say. "I just—I didn't see the point, this is all temporary, and—"

"My God," Zach says, edging on pity. "You're hopeless."

I give him a full-blown pout. "Zachary, tell me who Alex is."

"He's an asshole, from what I know," Barbie says, still cheerful. "All he does is talk shit about Jules."

"*What?*" I ask, and immediately pick up my phone to Google the two of them.

"Oh, now she'll look him up," Zach grumbles, and shoves a cookie in his mouth.

Dozens of articles come up about the two of them, but none of them mentions Alex dragging Jules through the dirt.

"I don't see anything," I say, perplexed.

"He doesn't say it outright. I've heard it's a lot of 'a source close to Jules says' and 'an insider reports' and that he badmouths him to everyone within the industry," Barbie explains, the distaste obvious in her tone.

"How do you know?" I ask, looking back up at her.

She tilts her head toward Zach's side of the screen. "Zach heard it all from his ex."

Zach finishes eating his cookie, wiping his mouth with the back of his hand before nodding. "Yeah. Derek says they used to be best friends but apparently Jules won some award that Alex was also nominated for, and since then it's been"—Zach clicks his tongue, running a finger along his throat—"*bad*."

"But why?" I ask, eyes wide. "What happened?"

"Well, Jules won," Zach says slowly. "And Alex lost."

"Because of *that*? Barbie has won awards I've lost! And vice versa!"

"Well, yes, but we're not backstabbing pieces of shit," Barbie says easily.

"That can't be it," I say, shaking my head. "There's gotta be more to it."

Zach shrugs. "That's all Derek told me. That and that Alex tried to blacklist Jules from his new movie. The one you just visited."

My eye starts to twitch. "He tried to do *what*?"

"All right, I don't like the look on your face, so I'm gonna go ahead and hang up," Zach says, eyes wide. "Don't kill anyone."

"I'm not gonna—" Zach's face disappears from my screen.

Barbie sighs. "Have you asked Jules about Alex?"

"I tried, but he avoided the subject," I say, frowning. "Do you think that's why he was so insistent on fake dating? Because Alex tried to blacklist him?"

"Could be," Barbie agrees. "Do you want me to ask around?"

I shake my head. "No, no . . . I'll figure it out. Thank you, though."

"Of course, Summer," Barbie says, giving me a soft smile, one of the ones she rarely gives out in public. "For what it's worth, I think Jules was in the right."

"Yeah," I say, and I'm quietly seething with the urge to fight Alex on Jules' behalf. "Me too."

My last concert of the tour approaches sooner than I expect. After three nights in the Kia Forum, I expect it to feel old, but an hour before the show I'm thrumming with excitement.

I don't want it to end. I hate the thought of going back to New York, where I don't even have my own place. At least out here, the fans make every stage feel like home.

I forget Jules is supposed to attend until one of the venue's security staff leads him into the waiting room, and he greets me with a warm smile and open arms.

I stop mid–vocal warmup to fit myself against him, letting him hold me for only a few beats before I pull back, too amped with adrenaline to stand still. "You made it!"

"As if I would miss it," he says, reaching for one of my iron-pressed curls, bouncing it lightly. "You look gorgeous."

My cheeks flush almost immediately. "Thanks. How's filming?"

"Good, good," he says, taking in the waiting room with curious eyes.

For a brief moment, I want to ask about Alex again, but it's neither the time nor the place. Instead I ask, "Have you been to any of my shows before?"

He shakes his head. "It'll be my first. What should I expect?"

"Singing, probably," I say, and he cracks a smile.

"Are you going to sing the song you wrote for me?" he asks, batting his lashes. More and more often, I get to see this playful Jules, and it makes me happier than it should.

"Wouldn't you just love that?" I ask, shoving him away from me.

"I would," he agrees.

"Should've come to one of the earlier shows then," I say with a cheerful smile. "By the way, have I mentioned I'm learning French?"

He levels a look at me, and my grin only widens.

"Better get to your seat," I say, giving him a light shove toward the door. "Make sure fans have time to photograph you in the crowd before the opening act."

He sighs loudly. "If I must."

"Enjoy!" I call as he leaves. "Don't forget to leave a review on Yelp!"

"I won't," he says, holding up his phone pointedly, and I laugh as the door closes behind him.

Onstage, it's easy to lose myself. I stride up and down the catwalk, singing my heart out as I stare out into a crowd of bright lights.

I introduce the band midway through the show, letting them each have their moment as I catch my breath and chug a bottle of water. As I do, I finally catch sight of Jules in the crowd. He's in the one hundreds, in one of the aisle seats, and ridiculously enough, he's holding up a sign that says *SUMMER'S #1 FAN*.

I grin, shaking my head. "Are you serious?" I mouth.

"Deadly," he mouths back, and shakes his hips in a little dance that makes me splutter with laughter.

I turn away from him, and launch into the next song, "Flying

Kites," but my eyes start drifting over to him more and more often.

The fans near the front of the stage seem to notice, their phones swingingly wildly back and forth between Jules in the crowd and me on the stage.

But one fan in particular doesn't seem to care, too busy arguing with a security guard. I keep singing but walk a little closer, trying to figure out what's going on, but then I see the rainbow flag in her arms and I realize the issue.

Even as my brain stutters in surprise, my lips know to keep moving, singing the words of a song I could recite in my sleep.

It's obviously not the first time a fan has brought a rainbow flag to one of my concerts, but it's the first time I've actively seen security keep it away from me. Does this venue ban flags? *Why?*

I glance at Jules again, and he's watching me with bright eyes, still holding that stupid sign. I remember the weight of one of his hugs, and it gives me enough strength to walk forward, tapping the security guard on the shoulder.

He turns to me, and I gesture to the flag, making grabby hands. He looks bewildered, but dutifully takes it from the fan, who's watching with wide-eyed awe. I grab the flag firmly, pulling it up onto the stage and waving it behind me. It's only a few seconds, ten at most, before I hand it back to the security guard, but it feels like a lifetime.

My heart is pounding unevenly in my chest, and I force myself to return to center stage, still singing along. The world in front of me is blurry at the edges, but it's second nature to perform, so I keep going and going and going.

Even if it feels a little bit like the end of the world.

* * *

Backstage, I go into my dressing room and shut the door. I can barely breathe, and I wonder if there are even lungs inside my body anymore. Why is it so hard to get air inside my chest?

I slide down the wall, hitting the ground. My tailbone aches and I let out a pathetic sob. What's wrong with me? I didn't even do anything that crazy. Lots of celebrities hold pride flags and wear pride pins. It's not a big deal.

But it feels like one. It feels terrifying and scary and *real*, and I want to go back in time and stop myself from ever doing it.

The door opens behind my back, and I nearly fall over in surprise. Jules steps inside, takes one look at me crouched on the ground, and immediately drops down beside me.

"What's wrong?" he asks urgently, reaching up to wipe the tears streaming down my face. "What happened?"

I shake my head, unable to offer him anything except for ragged breathing.

Jules wraps me in his arms, but instead of a hug, my back is pressed to his chest, and I'm almost sitting in his lap. He smooths a hand down my hair, murmuring quiet words I barely hear over the rush in my ears.

Eventually, I make them out. "It's okay, Summer. I've got you. It's okay, it's okay. Breathe, darling, breathe."

I shake my head, burying my face in my hands. He doesn't try to pull me out, still gently carding his fingers through my hair. "Just breathe, darling. That's all I'm asking."

I force a mouthful of air into my seemingly nonexistent lungs, and it seems to kickstart my body. Suddenly, I can't get enough air, almost gasping for breath.

"It's okay, it's okay," Jules says, squeezing me tighter against him.

"Can you feel where I'm touching you? Focus, Summer."

I try to do what he says, forcing myself to pay attention to his arms around my waist, his legs underneath mine, his chest against my back.

Slowly, slowly I start to come back to myself, though it doesn't stop the hiccupping sobs escaping my mouth. I twist in Jules' arms until my face is buried in his chest, hidden from view. He makes quiet shushing noises, cradling the back of my head.

"It's okay, it's okay," he murmurs. "I'm here, Summer."

It takes ages for me to feel okay enough to acknowledge his presence. In that time, my tour manager knocks on my door at least twice, asking what's going on, but Jules quietly yet firmly tells her I'm busy.

Finally, I pull away from him, unable to look him directly in the eye as I wipe my face with the back of my hand. Eyeliner smears across my skin and makes me want to whimper. I must look *awful*, makeup running in rivulets down my face.

Jules helps me up and onto the couch, grabbing makeup wipes without missing a beat. He hands me one and uses the other to gently wipe my face while I scrub my hand, pointedly refusing to meet his eyes.

"Hey," Jules says, lightly tapping my jaw, urging me to look in his direction. "It's okay, Summer."

"I'm sorry," I say, focusing on the defined edge of his left cheekbone instead of his eyes. "I shouldn't have—thank you for putting up with . . ." I can't finish the sentence.

Jules tilts my chin up again, so I have no choice but to meet his gaze. "I wasn't putting up with anything. You are not a burden to me. I am always, always happy to help you when you need it."

Any words I have left die in my throat. His brown eyes are gentle and earnest.

"Do you understand?" he asks.

I nod slowly, unable to do anything else.

"Good," he says, and then finishes taking off the rest of my makeup, his brows furrowed with concentration.

I watch him in silence, wondering why Jules is bothering with this. I've dealt with anxiety attacks on my own before, but this is the first time I've had someone take care of me in the aftermath, and it's so *strange*.

And there's something different about Jules. I didn't notice it before, too caught up in my emotions, but there's a new light in his eyes as he looks at me. Something has changed, and I have no idea what it is.

"Thank you," I whisper finally.

Jules leans in, pressing his lips against my forehead. "Always."

# PART THREE: SUMMER

## SUMMER ALI'S SUMMER-ISH PLAYLIST
### June to September—*me, myself, and I*

1. "Matilda" —Harry Styles
2. "I know it won't work" —Gracie Abrams
3. "Run and Hide" —Sabrina Carpenter
4. "You're On Your Own, Kid" —Taylor Swift
5. "Blue & Grey" —BTS
6. "Slow Down" —Laufey
7. "Good enough" —Xdinary Heroes
8. "Jigsaw" —Conan Gray
9. "teenage dream" —Olivia Rodrigo

## CHAPTER TWENTY

## JULES MORADI SPOTTED AT "TRUE TO ME" TOUR HOLDING UP "#1 SUMMER FAN" SIGN AMIDST RUMORS OF THE TWO OFFICIALLY BECOMING A COUPLE

With the end of the tour comes a return to New York, and I finally narrow down my apartment choices and put in an application for a two-bedroom in Long Island City with a high-rise view of the East River.

When I find out I'm approved, I call Barbie first, who insists I take as much time as I need to move out. Then I call Jana, and by proxy Safi, and tell them I'm officially moving into one of the apartments Jana picked out—and they spend the entire time screaming in excitement, demanding to come over as soon as possible. I promise them they can help me unpack when I move in.

Finally, I call Ariana to tell her my new address for mailing purposes.

A text comes in at the top of my screen midway through the call.

> **Father Figure:** Is it true what Jana and Safi are saying? You're moving into your own apartment?

> **Mother Figure:** YOU'RE TAKING THINGS TOO FAR SUMAIRA

> **Mother Figure:** CALL US BACK

I ignore the texts but make a note to myself to remind Safi and Jana to keep their voices down when they're at home.

When I'm finished speaking to Ariana, I go over to the windowsill, where my poor strawberry plant has been struggling to grow for months.

I gently touch one of its leaves, a faint hope blooming to life in my heart. "You're going to have a real home soon," I say. "A place to grow."

Jules shows up bright and early on Tuesday morning, and I try not to think too hard about the fact that the last time I saw him, I had a mental breakdown in his arms.

For his part, he doesn't mention it, greeting me with a tight hug that leaves me a little breathless before pulling away to crouch in front of Jana and Safi.

"Hello," he says brightly, and his brown eyes are sparkling in the sunlight. "I'm Jules."

"We know," Jana says, staring him down, but her glare loses its effect when Safi pounces on him, jumping into his arms.

Jules laughs in surprise, easily lifting her up. I try not to pay attention to the way the muscles in his arms flex as he carries her.

"I'll leave you to the welcome party," I say with a mini-salute, heading for the moving van with my belongings in it, mostly to get myself to stop staring at Jules. Amidst the tangle of attraction is a seed of guilt over our last interaction.

He never asked for an explanation for my anxiety attack, but I feel compelled to tell him the whole story, even though I *know* I don't owe him a coming out. Still, the combination of Jana's urging and the fact that with time, I've genuinely come to trust Jules and feel safe with him makes a compelling case for telling him the truth.

Across the street, a flock of paparazzi takes pictures of me carrying cardboard boxes into my new apartment building. Jules joins in after a while, as my sisters race ahead of us into the lobby. I glance at the photographers a little warily, but remind myself I already brought this up with Ariana, and my sisters will be safe. The last thing I want is for their faces to be plastered across social media. There are pictures of them around if someone goes digging, but for the most part, the general public doesn't know who they are, and I'd like to keep it that way.

When I finally take the last box out of the moving van, Jules comes hurrying out of the building to help me carry it. I hand it over in favor of grabbing my strawberry plant. Behind me, the cameras go *click, click, click* and I can already see the headlines.

Inside the building, I let out a sigh of relief. "Well, that's done then."

"Not too bad," Jules says, glancing out the doors as the paparazzi get back in their cars and vans. "We'll look sweaty, though."

"Proof that we're real human beings, I guess," I say with a roll of my eyes, then falter, staring at the bead of sweat running down his cheekbone. It's the first time I've gotten a good look at his face all day and it's slightly different from usual. "Your foundation, it's . . ."

"Yeah," he says, a little sheepish. "Looks a little bit more like me, don't you think?"

I grin, unable to help myself. "The real prince of Persia."

"Jake Gyllenhaal was in that movie," he points out.

"And when white people stop fake tanning to play roles they have no business playing, then we'll know some peace," I say cheerfully. "Do you want to come up or are you busy?"

"Your sisters have forbidden me from leaving," Jules says with a fond shake of his head that makes my stomach twist and turn. "My flight back isn't until Thursday anyway, so I've got time on my hands."

I nod and lean down to press the button for the elevator with my nose.

Jules laughs under his breath, but doesn't comment.

Part of me was expecting him to leave as soon as we finished. For the most part, we haven't really spent time by ourselves without cameras around—and I suppose my sisters will be there, so we're not *really* alone—but it's still weird to think about hanging out with Jules when we're not obligated to spend time together.

Upstairs, Safi and Jana are sitting at my new dining table with a box of pizza in front of them that I ordered an hour ago when they started to get fussy.

As soon as we step inside, Safi starts gesturing to the seat beside her. "Jules, come sit!"

"So that's how it is," I say, raising an eyebrow. Safi doesn't acknowledge me, still grinning at Jules.

I set down the strawberry plant on the closest windowsill and walk over to the table, just as Safi says, "This is your official seat now, Jules! I called dibs on you last night," and glares at me and Jana meaningfully.

"That's not fair," I say, though I let Jules take the seat, sitting next to Jana instead as I grab a plate. "I wasn't with you last night. What if I wanted to call dibs?"

Safi's glare doesn't waver. "Well, maybe if you'd been there, you would've been able to."

Ouch. I wasn't expecting that.

"I'm sorry, Safi," I say quietly, sinking lower in my seat.

Safi sighs, turning to share an exasperated look with Jules. He looks a little confused, but as always, doesn't push where there are obvious boundaries drawn. Safi looks back at me, her lips pressed into a stubborn pout. "Fine. I forgive you. But I already called dibs, so you're going to have to deal with it."

I pout back at her while my hand creeps across the table, toward her plate. "Can't we do a recount or something?"

Then, while she's still considering it, I snatch the pizza off her plate, taking a quick bite before she can protest.

"Hey!" Safi says, blinking in disbelief. Jana giggles from my other side, and Safi retaliates by stealing the pizza off Jana's plate.

"Hey!" Jana says this time, and it starts off a round of yelling, both girls abruptly shouting in each other's faces.

I look over at Jules, who watches with wide eyes, holding his pizza close to his chest as he slowly chews. I burst into laughter despite myself. Quietly, in the safety of my own head, I think I could get used to this.

\* \* \*

Hours later, after unpacking most of my belongings, I stuff my sisters in a car and warn them to behave before shipping them off back home. Both of them frown at me, asking if they can come back soon, and I say *of course*, all the while wondering if I can actually keep that promise.

Ma and Baba are undoubtedly wondering where they are—and likely suspecting they're with me—and it's only a matter of time before it all comes crashing down on my head.

But I try not to think about that as I finish organizing my bookshelf by color, turning to Jules as I consider which shade of blue is darker.

"Left," he says from the kitchen, rinsing all my kitchenware even though I told him not to bother.

"I thought so," I agree, slotting the book into place before standing up and dusting off my knees. "If you're going to do all that, at least let me dry."

Jules tilts his head, considering, before he nods. "All right. Deal."

I grab the dish rag from where it's hanging in front of the stove and come to stand beside him.

When Jules hands me the plate, I say, "They really liked you."

"Who?" he asks, then tacks on "Your sisters?" as an afterthought.

I finish drying the plate, putting it away in the cupboard before grabbing a handful of utensils from Jules. "Yeah, my sisters. They don't usually take to strangers that well."

Jules' eyebrows knit together as he works to clean a tough spot on one of the plates. "They were lovely. I'm glad I met them."

I smile faintly, drying in between the prongs of a fork. "They are lovely." And then in the quiet of my new apartment, I allow myself a little vulnerability, a little honesty for this boy who's washing my dishes for no reason except that he can. "My parents are a little . . . much. They used to be my managers, but I fired them a few months back, when I started working with Ariana. We haven't really spoken since then."

Jules gives me a sideways glance before handing me a pot. "I'm glad you have Safina and Sanjana then."

"Yeah, me too," I say, taking it from him and drying it absently. "You never asked me about . . . about what happened after the concert."

Jules doesn't reply for a moment, squirting some more dish soap onto his sponge. When he does, his voice is soft. "I don't want you to feel obligated to tell me anything, Summer."

"You're not obligated to stand here and do my dishes, Jules," I say, a little exasperated. "But you're doing that, aren't you?"

"It's not the same," he says.

"It's not," I agree, "but it means something to me."

Jules stops washing the dishes to look at me, a frown tucked into the corner of his mouth. "It means something to me, too. But that doesn't mean you owe me all your secrets now. I'd never ask that of you."

I swallow nervously, turning my gaze down to the pot in front of me, drying it intently. "Maybe I want to tell you."

He follows my lead, turning back to the sink. "Then I'm all ears. But please don't feel like you have to."

There's silence for a while, the two of us working together seamlessly as a unit. Jules washes, I dry. Jules washes, I dry. Jules washes, I dry.

I finally break the quiet. "I'm pansexual. Most people don't know, and I'm not—I'm not ready to come out yet. At the concert the other day, I picked up the flag on instinct, and afterward, I realized the repercussions and I . . . I panicked, I guess."

Jules reaches over, turning off the sink. "Summer," he starts to say, but I shake my head.

"No, wait, just—let me finish. I know, I *know* the real fans won't care. I know there will still be people who love my music, no matter what gender I like. But it's not about . . . it's not about the world. I mean, it is a little bit, but it's mostly about . . ." I blow out a breath, setting down the dish towel. "It's mostly about my parents. I know if I ever came out, they'd never . . ."

Jules doesn't interrupt me, though he does take my hand in his.

I force myself to laugh a little awkwardly. "Yeah, well. Let's just say they're not the most open-minded people in the world."

"Can I speak now?" Jules asks quietly.

"Yes," I say, matching his volume.

"Thank you for telling me," he says, his thumb brushing over my knuckles. "I want to say that this doesn't change the way I feel about you, but I'd be lying. It does."

When I inhale sharply, he shakes his head.

"Now I think you're even stronger than I ever realized. I think you're so much braver than anyone could ever give you credit for. I know we haven't really talked about our relationship beyond this PR stunt, but I need you to know that I consider you one of my friends, and you telling me this doesn't change anything for me. I—I can't imagine how hard it must be to keep this part of yourself hidden, especially from your family, and I'm so sorry I can't make it any easier. But I'm here, okay? Anytime it all feels like too much, I'm here. If you want a hug, I'm here. If you need someone to talk to, I'm here. If you want someone to sit with you in silence, I'm here."

My eyes are wetter than I want them to be. "Really?"

"Really," he says.

I smile, and it feels all kinds of wrong, and all kinds of right. "Okay. I'll add your friendship application to the pile."

Jules laughs. "Oh, there's a pile, is there?"

"It's pretty high," I say, reaching up to my wipe my eyes. Jules' gaze softens and he brushes a tendril of hair out of my face. "And you're all the way at the bottom, dude."

He shakes his head, amused. "Is there any way to bump my application higher?"

"You can watch an episode of *World of Tweens* with me," I suggest, gesturing toward the newly set up television in the living room.

Jules blinks at me, then gapes. "You're not serious."

"Deadly serious, Moradi," I say, and let go of his hand so I can walk toward the TV. He lets out a groan of protest but follows me anyway. I take those few moments of refuge to rub my eyes a little more furiously, making sure no tears remain.

I didn't think Jules would take it badly, but something in my soul settles knowing how well he did take it. Every time I come out to someone, a small part of me is afraid they're going to react the way my parents undoubtedly would if I ever told them—in horror and disgust.

But Jules' quiet acceptance and support is like a balm against my wounds, and I hold it close to my chest gratefully.

I sit on the couch and Jules sits down beside me, but then curls up, so his head is leaning against my thigh.

"I can't believe you're going to make me do this," Jules says, grabbing a couch pillow and holding it in front of his face. "It's evil, Summer. I hope you know that."

"I'm a little evil," I accept, pulling the pillow away from him. "It won't be that bad."

"Yes, it will," he says, shaking his head. "Are you sure I can't offer you anything else?"

I pretend to consider it, tapping a finger against my chin. "I mean, I guess I *can* take your firstborn."

"Evil," he says again, sighing dramatically. "I'm never coming over again."

"Why is it that I don't believe you?" I ask, and for the first time, allow myself to touch him back, my hand drifting down so I can run my fingers through his hair.

Jules' eyelashes flutter as he sinks into the touch. "Don't ask me. My head's empty, no thoughts."

I snort and reach over him to turn on the TV.

## CHAPTER TWENTY-ONE

### SUMMER ALI AND JULES MORADI SEEN CARRYING MOVING BOXES! COULD OUR NEW FAVORITE COUPLE BE PLANNING TO LIVE TOGETHER SOON?

After Jules wraps up filming for *Right as Rain*, he comes back to New York and starts making it a habit to come over to my place. The first time he shows up with takeout and board games, I'm taken aback, but slowly, it becomes a ritual. Jules always takes photos for Instagram, which helps draw the lines a little better, a stark reminder that this is business, even if we are friends now. I start doing the same, trying to uphold those same boundaries. Half my camera roll is Jules doing something stupid nowadays, and Safi makes a point to comment on it the next time she plays games on my phone. I snatch the device away from her, warning her not to go through my camera roll, but she just looks pleased, grinning like the Cheshire cat.

It's almost freaky, how easy it is to get used to Jules as a constant presence in my life. But it also becomes a little harder to hide that I've been struggling with writer's block, and I know he's picked up on it after a few visits.

He doesn't bring it up at first, though I can tell he's waiting to.

When he shows up one night and drags me out of my apartment toward a karaoke bar near his place, I know I'm in for it. "Why?" I ask, shaking my head as he pulls me inside the bar.

"Barbie said—" Jules starts to say.

"Barbie is a traitor and a liar, and we mustn't ever speak of her again," I say seriously.

Jules rolls his eyes. "You would die for Barbie."

"That doesn't mean she's authorized to give away state secrets!" I protest, batting uselessly at Jules' hands as he continues pulling me through the bar. I've never been inside one before, and while I have no plans to drink alcohol here, I'm worried they're going to card us anyway. This is the last thing either of us needs to get caught up in, but Jules doesn't look worried.

He finally stops walking and turns to me, holding my hand against his chest, and my cheeks immediately flush. More and more often, my body reacts before my mind can. I try to remind myself it's because of close proximity to an attractive boy, and nothing else, but it's hard when Jules is staring at me with twinkling brown eyes, like he knows exactly how flustered he makes me.

"Please sing with me?" Jules asks. I take one look at our hands and then Jules' pleading face before sighing. Resistance is clearly pointless.

"All right," I say. "But any Taylor Swift and I'm out. I'm not mentally stable enough for that, and I *will* break down in tears if I hear a single song from *Reputation*."

"Deal," Jules says easily, and drags me over to the stage before I can change my mind. I follow along, wondering when I started letting Jules Moradi determine my evening plans.

The girl that's running the karaoke machine—Emily, according to her name tag—looks close to fainting as she recognizes us. It occurs to me that Jules, who is far from a professional singer, is about to attempt karaoke with me in public.

"Are you sure *you* want to do this?" I ask him, a little stunned.

"Of course," Jules says with a sly look on his face. "I'm trying to become your muse."

And then he pulls me up onto the stage before I can see what he chose.

The music starts, and in the split second it takes me to recognize what song this is, I realize Jules might know me far better than I thought.

Jules grins, and when he opens his mouth, he starts belting out the lyrics to "You're the One That I Want" from *Grease*.

"Oh my God," I whisper to myself, but then Emily is shoving a microphone in my hand, and I have no choice but to sing the next line.

I hear a gasp in the crowd, and suddenly there are blinding lights as people turn on their phones to record the two of us.

I give Jules an exasperated stare, but he only winks, still singing Danny Zuko's lines without missing a beat. His voice is nice, and he can hold a tune, which is more than I can say for most actors. I try not to outshine him too much, but he must realize what I'm attempting to do, because he pulls his mic away from his mouth and says, "Don't hold back, Summer. Come on!"

I roll my eyes, but allow a little more of my true voice to sink into the words. The crowd is cheering, swaying together, and Jules looks so, so enthusiastic that it's hard not to share in his joy.

The song comes to an end, and I'm smiling so widely my cheeks hurt.

"Encore! Encore! Encore!" the crowd chants.

Jules gives me a questioning look, and I shake my head. "Come on," I say, grabbing his hand and pulling him off the stage. The crowd groans, but I ignore them, leading us toward a more secluded corner. "What was all that about?"

"You've been holed up in your apartment for days," Jules says, gesturing for me to sit on the only empty bar stool. I oblige, but regret it a moment later when he steps in between my legs so I can hear him over the sound of the bar. We're so close that I can count his individual eyelashes. "I thought you could use some time outside. I was going to suggest a day cruise actually, but figured this would be a good warmup."

"A day cruise?" I ask, raising my brows.

"Next week," he says, resting his hands on my thighs. I nearly jolt, but manage to restrain the reaction at the last minute. "What do you say? It's supposed to be nice weather. You could invite Barbie and Zach."

"You're not going to invite anyone?"

Jules nods. "I was thinking of asking my friend Raj. Have I mentioned him before?"

I rack my memory for the name and come up blank. "I don't think so. Tell me about him."

"He's my best friend," Jules says, smiling slightly, but something shifts in his gaze, a little uncertain as he looks at me. I don't know what he sees on my face, but he continues, "Last year, I went through a bit of a rough patch. He staged an intervention and helped me get things back on track. I . . . I'll tell you about it sometime, when we're not out and about."

"Okay," I say, studying him. This is one of the first pieces he's offered up about himself, and I can't help but be curious. I've always wondered about his year of solitude, but I've been hesitant to outright ask. "Well, I'm excited to meet Raj, then."

"So you're agreeing to come?" he asks with a smile.

"As if I was going to say no," I say, lightly shoving his shoulder. "Though there were better ways to convince me than dragging me out to a bar we're not legally allowed to be at."

"We're not drinking anything," he says, matching my amused tone. The low lights of the bar drown Jules in a red haze that accentuates the cut of his jaw and the sharp lines of his cheekbones.

I tilt my head. "Are people going to believe that when pictures of us inevitably leak?"

Jules hums, glancing around. There are countless people watching us, though they hastily look away before they can meet Jules' eyes. "We could give them something else to talk about."

I wrinkle my nose. "Like what?"

He shrugs at me, his eyes hooded. "You tell me."

I don't understand what he means, not until his gaze flickers to my lips and back up, and then suddenly my heart is beating so loud that I'm surprised the entire bar can't hear it.

I figured it would be a matter of time until we had to kiss for the cameras, but I wasn't expecting it tonight, when Ariana hadn't even instructed us to be seen outside.

"You want to kiss me," I say, and it's not really a question, though it is in all the ways that matter.

Jules smiles, and there's an edge of a dare in it. Everyone else in the bar seems to fade away to nothing, until the two of us are the only ones in the entire space.

"Okay," I say, and the word comes out hoarse.

Jules shakes his head, reaching up to brush my hair out of my face before resting his hand against the side of my neck. "No. Only if you ask me."

"Ask you?" I repeat. I wonder if he can feel my racing pulse underneath his fingers.

He nods. "You have to ask me. I don't want you to agree just because I'm suggesting it."

My entire faces scrunches up. "I don't like that logic."

Jules shrugs, tapping his thumb against my jaw. "If you can't ask me for it, then I shouldn't be kissing you."

I huff. "It's not like I'm drunk. I can consent, Jules."

"Then ask me," he says again, undeterred.

I consider how serious he's being, and if it puts me at a disadvantage to ask him to kiss me. Our entire relationship is built on false pretenses, and *asking* him to kiss me feels more real than it should. But he brought it up, didn't he?

And a small part of me wants to, even if admitting that is terrifying. But I'm no longer the girl I used to be—the one who was afraid of desiring things, much less taking them for herself.

Finally, I relent, tilting my face toward him. "Will you kiss me, Jules?"

He smiles, slow and beautiful. "Yes."

Then he leans in, pressing his lips to mine, soft but unyielding. I close my eyes and sink into it, something sharp igniting in my stomach and exploding through my chest.

I stretch forward, one of my hands going to the side of his face while one of my legs curls, pulling him closer toward me.

He laughs against my mouth, and I find myself giggling too, helpless to it.

I kiss him and I kiss him and I kiss him, until nothing matters, until everything does, before I finally pull back.

Jules looks down at me, his eyes bright and effervescent, and lyrics write themselves in the back of my head. *Am I prisoner to the stars or am I prisoner to him?*

I let my hands drop down to his waist, toying with his belt loops. For the first time in months, I wish I had my journal so I could write the words down.

The thought jars me back to reality. My heart feels double its normal size and it's unnerving. I don't know what I'm supposed to do. How much of this is even *real*? How much of this is to play into our fake dating arrangement? Does this mean anything to him?

"This is going to be all over the internet tomorrow," I say weakly.

"Kind of the point, isn't it?" he asks, still smiling.

"Yeah," I agree, but the word sounds far away. "I guess so."

## CHAPTER TWENTY-TWO

## JULES MORADI AND SUMMER ALI SPOTTED MAKING OUT IN UES BAR? THINGS ARE GETTING STEAMY WITH HOLLYWOOD'S FAVORITE NEW COUPLE!

"Maybe we should turn around and go home," I say, fidgeting with the straps of my bikini top. "I feel like I didn't think this through properly."

Barbie leans over me to glance out the van's window. The cruise ship is already waiting for us, but it's *empty*. Or at least, empty aside from the silhouette of Jules and who I assume is Raj. I thought there would be more people around, but I never actually asked, which is admittedly on me.

"We're going to be the only ones there," I say, not without an air of despair.

"No, look," Zach says, pointing over my shoulder. "There are paps here already. Jules must have run this by Ariana first."

I follow his finger until I see the smaller boat with a load of people on it, holding their cameras, and I make a face.

Barbie elbows me. "What? First it's too private for you and now it's too public?"

"No, I—" But I don't know how to put the thoughts in my head into words.

"But you kissed Jules and now you're overthinking everything," Barbie supplies, and I turn a glare on her. She's right, though, even if I don't want to admit it. "It's fine, Summer. He knows it's a PR stunt."

*What if I'm the one who's forgetting?* I want to ask.

Zach takes one look at my face and swears under his breath. "Summer..."

"I know," I groan, burying my face in my hands. "It's ridiculous. I know it's ridiculous. I'm just—" I look up, giving them both pleading eyes. "If it seems like I'm going to do something I'm going to regret, please intervene."

"Define something you're going to regret," Barbie says, placing a hand on my shoulder and squeezing.

I swallow nervously, looking back and forth between them. If there are two people in the world who would never judge me, it's them, but it's still hard to say the words out loud. "This is all pretend. I know that. For fuck's sake, he's one of the best actors of our generation, I *know*, but I... I'm afraid I'm going to get too caught up in it. I—I don't want to fall for him. Please don't let me."

Zach reaches over, taking my hand in his. "We won't." He cuts a look at Barbie. "Right?"

Barbie's expression is affronted. "Why are you looking at me?"

"Because I can *tell* when you're scheming," Zach says, narrowing his eyes. "Barbie, Summer is asking us for help. You know how hard that is for her. We have to do our best."

"Of course I'm going to help her!" Barbie says, throwing her hands up. "If you'll recall, I literally let her stay in my apartment for *months*."

"I'm sitting right here," I say dryly, but their familiar bickering settles something in my chest.

"Sorry, sweetie," Zach says, squeezing my hand before letting go. "We're going to take care of you. Don't worry."

"You're so annoying," Barbie mutters to him before turning to me. "We won't let you slip up when you're with us. But you spend an *awful* lot of time with him alone, Summer, and there's only so much we can do."

"See, you're doing it again," Zach complains. "She's asking us for help and you're just stressing her out with other shit. It's not our place to—"

"I'm her best friend, I think I'm allowed to—"

"Good Lord," I say, and get out of the van. I'd rather deal with paps than listen to the two of them go on and on. At the end of the day, they always settle things, but a girl can only put up with so much.

"Summer!" Jules shouts, waving at me. "Come on up!"

"Coming!" I call back. Damon gets out of the van behind me, helping me take my bags out of the trunk. Both Barbie's and Zach's bodyguards follow suit, grabbing the ice chest and picnic baskets full of food.

Spencer keeps stealing looks backward at the vans when he thinks no one is looking at him, and it makes me smile.

"She'll be fine," I say to him.

Spencer turns to me with wide eyes. "Oh—I know, I just . . ."

"You worry about her," I finish. "It's sweet."

He makes an awkward noise of agreement, refusing to meet

my gaze. "It's my job. I'm her bodyguard."

"Your job is to protect her, not care about her, but you do both anyway," I say with a fond shake of my head. "I'm glad she has you."

Spencer mumbles something that I can't quite make out and rushes ahead of me, onto the boat. I snort to myself.

The paps on the other boat finally take note of me, turning their cameras in my direction, and I pull my wrap tighter around my body. I can't help but feel oddly exposed. My parents always forbade me from wearing anything they deemed inappropriate, and wearing a bathing suit is inarguably the most skin I've ever shown in my entire career.

Zach and Barbie exit the van a moment later, neither of them looking entirely pleased, but they've stopped arguing at least. I offer Barbie a wide-brimmed hat, matching mine, and Zach a tube of sunscreen, since he's always going on about how having melanin doesn't protect us from UV rays.

Once the three of us have gathered our things, we follow our bodyguards up onto the boat.

"Here goes nothing," I mutter, adjusting the strap of my bikini again before stepping onto the sundeck and pasting on my most cheerful smile. "Hello!"

"Summer!" Jules says with a wide smile. It's different from the smile I usually see on him, a little more open, a little more vulnerable. Raj stands next to him with an arm around his shoulder, and I wonder if that's why. "And you brought Barbie and Zach!"

"I did," I agree, meeting him across the deck. "And you brought Raj?"

"At your service," Raj says with a dramatic bow. "I've heard so much about you."

"Oh?" I glance at Jules, who smacks Raj on the arm. "Do I want to know?"

"Let's just say I've been looking forward to meeting you," Raj says, smirking slightly, and Jules steps on his foot.

"Anyway!" he says loudly, gesturing toward the front of the sundeck. "We're all set up over here. Everybody good to go?"

"As long as there's alcohol involved," Zach says, making for one of the chairs.

"My kinda man," Raj says approvingly, before glancing back at me. "We'll catch up later, when Juyan isn't looking."

"I'll kill you," Jules says to him flatly, and Raj laughs, ignoring him in favor of following after Zach.

Barbie doesn't say anything, observing the situation with a knowing look in her eye that hardly bodes well for anyone.

"Don't," I warn her, before grabbing her hand, pulling her toward the others.

We all settle in on the front deck. Barbie immediately lies down to tan and Spencer gives her a look of despair before directing his gaze skyward. I snort and sit down beside Zach, who's lathering sunscreen onto his legs.

"So, Raj," I say after checking that Jules is distracted grabbing drinks from the coolers. "What was Jules like as a kid?"

"I'm *so* glad you asked," Raj says, immediately sitting down in the chair in front of me. "I have an entire album dedicated to his baby photos."

My eyes light up. *"Really?"*

"Really," he says, and starts scrolling through his phone.

I lean forward but then immediately shift back when I realize the position reveals even more of my skin.

It's so *strange* wearing something like this. I hate that I feel this uncomfortable wearing something that other people put on without a second thought. I hate that my body is conditioned to act a certain way, to feel a certain way. I never really thought about how much I would have to unlearn after leaving my parents behind. It's yet another reminder that they're always going to follow me wherever I go.

*Foreign to myself in ways I don't understand*
*Can I crawl out of my body and into yours?*

By the time Jules comes back, Raj has shown me pictures of Jules from age four to ten, and I've crooned no fewer than a dozen times.

"What are you doing?" Jules demands, grabbing at Raj's phone. Raj seems used to it because he quickly shifts out of the way, shoving one of his hands into Jules' face to push him back. "Raj, I swear to God!"

"This is payback for when you did the exact same thing with Priya," he says, unbothered. To me, he adds, "She's my girlfriend, and Jules loves to embarrass me in front of her."

"Embarrass—bragging about you is not embarrassing you!" Jules protests.

"By that logic, neither is what I'm doing!" Raj says, readjusting his grip so he's squeezing Jules' cheeks. "And Summer's not your real girlfriend, so it's not even *half* as bad as what you did to me."

"That's not—" Jules splutters. "You're *literally* showing three world-famous musicians baby pictures of me!"

"Oh, I'm not looking," Barbie says, flipping to the next page of her magazine. "So only two world-famous musicians."

"You're literally a child star!" Raj throws back. "*Half* of the pictures of you on the internet are baby pictures."

"That is not true," Jules says with a pout. "And two world-famous musicians is still two too many!"

"I was trying to uncork this bottle, so I wasn't really paying attention either," Zach admits, but then proudly brandishes the champagne. "Shall we?"

Raj lets go of Jules' face and eagerly picks up a handful of glasses. "Please, let's, or he's going to keep going."

Jules flips Raj off, though it doesn't stop him from sitting beside him. When he reaches for the buttons of his shirt, undoing them so his bare chest is revealed, my jaw nearly unhinges itself.

Zach reaches over and subtly touches my chin, and I immediately close my mouth, looking anywhere but at Jules.

"Wait, pass me a drink," Barbie says, lifting her sunglasses to look over at us. I fidget with my bikini, even more aware of my body now that Jules' skin is on display. She frowns at me for a second before looking at Zach. "Hey, can you—"

"Absolutely not. No drinking by yourself! Come over here so we can play a game," Zach says, waving her over with the bottle. "And Spencer, don't even *think* about giving her a drink when I'm not looking."

Spencer gapes, and behind him, Damon cracks a smile. "I wasn't going to—"

"Oh, save it for someone who believes you," Zach says, rolling his eyes.

Barbie marches over, pointedly stepping on Zach's foot as she grabs a champagne flute. "You are the bane of my existence," she hisses to him before plopping down in my lap, hiding half my body from view, and I honestly want to burst with affection. She must've realized how uncomfortable I was feeling. "Summer, keep the evil man away from me."

I lean my chin against her shoulder. "I will do no such thing. What drinking game are we playing?"

"Anything but King's Cup," Jules says, making a face. "Raj makes the most disgusting cup known to mankind, and I refuse to ever drink it again."

"Then don't lose," Raj says brightly.

"Ride the Bus?" Zach suggests, pulling out a pack of cards from his bag.

"That sounds good to me," Jules says, shoving Raj half-heartedly when he pretends to protest. They bicker like brothers, and it puts a smile on my face. I know Jules doesn't have that many friends, so it's nice to see that he does have someone like Raj in his corner.

Not for the first time, I find myself feeling incredibly grateful for my own friends, who have always been so deeply supportive of me and my career. I'm all too aware of how toxic relationships can be among the Hollywood elite, even if my parents kept me sheltered from the worst of it. Honestly, it's probably one of the only good things they did for me. I can't imagine what I would've done if I ended up befriending someone like Alex only to have them turn around and stab me in the back. Probably given up on making friends entirely.

But I found people like Barbie and Zach, who might argue incessantly but would also lay down their lives for each other in a heartbeat. Their friendship is one of the things I value most in my life, and one of the only things that's kept me going ever since cutting my parents off. In all the ways that matter, they're my real family.

"I love you," I whisper to Barbie halfway through the game.

She looks at me with a quirked eyebrow. "Are you drunk already?"

"No, I just . . . I appreciate you," I say, squeezing her arm. Then I turn to Zach. "I love you, bro."

He gives me a confused look, but readily says, "I love you too, bro."

I smile at him and keep holding on to Barbie as the game continues. Jules watches me across our little circle, his head tilted to the side, but he doesn't ask. Instead, when our eyes meet, he winks.

I roll my eyes and focus on the cards in front of me. The longer the game continues, the more I wish I'd worn something else. Then I *hate* that I feel that way, hate that I'm still allowing my parents power over my body. And the vicious cycle continues to repeat over and over in my head until I feel nauseous.

It doesn't help that the straps of my cross-tied bikini are digging into my skin uncomfortably. I'm beginning to wonder if I ordered a size too small. I should've tried it on in the store before ordering it, but I didn't want to spend any more time thinking about it than I had to.

"I'm gonna use the bathroom," I say suddenly, and get to my feet. I'm a little wobbly but I can walk.

Barbie gives me a look of concern. "Do you want me to come with?"

"No, I'm good," I say, and force myself to walk away from the game and toward the bathroom. The staff directs me with a smile, and I give them one back.

Away from the noise of my friends, I'm all too aware of the sound of camera shutters going off. I glance to the side, where half the paps are following my trajectory to the bathroom while the others focus on the front deck.

I wrap my arms around my chest self-consciously and duck into the bathroom as soon as I can. After relieving myself, I look in the mirror and consider the straps of my bikini. My vision blurs a little but I blink through it. Maybe if I loosen them, it'll help?

With a concentrated set to my brow, I set to work, adjusting them until they stop digging into me so insistently. There are faint marks from how tight they were and I try to massage them away.

Satisfied, I exit the bathroom and start to make my way back to the front deck.

And then the world decides to take a shit on my existence, and I stumble, tripping over nothing.

"*Shit*," I say, and hit the deck with a loud thud.

"Summer!" Barbie calls, but I'm too busy focusing on the fact my fucking bikini has come loose. *Fuck. Fuck, fuck, fuck.*

I immediately pull the straps back up, but it's too late. The camera shutters are going off at rapid speed, and I know if I look up, I'll find all the paparazzi focused on me.

Oh my God.

This can't be happening.

Barbie appears in front of me, eyes wide as she stares at my bikini. I've managed to haphazardly cover up my chest, but the straps are still undone.

"Did they see—?"

I nod, unable to speak, my entire throat closed up.

"Fuck," she whispers, and reaches for the straps of my bikini, pushing my hands aside so she can fix it. "Fuck, was it bad?"

I nod again and my eyes start to well up without my permission.

I'm so fucking *stupid*. How could I let this happen?

I don't realize Jules is beside us until his hands come around my shoulders, draping his shirt over me. "Wear this," he says urgently.

Barbie takes over for him, buttoning up the shirt quickly. "It'll be okay, Summer. They won't run the photos. We won't let them."

"It'll be okay," Jules repeats, but the words are as shaky as I feel.

Zach appears over Barbie's shoulder, holding a towel up, blocking us from view of the paparazzi. "Come on, we can go inside. They won't be able to get photos of us in there."

I whimper and bury myself in Barbie's arms. She wraps me in a tight hug and leads me indoors, but even being out of sight doesn't do anything for my nerves.

"It'll be okay, they won't run the photos," they all say, and I don't believe a single word. An awful sense of foreboding builds inside of me, and I'm certain that in refusing to listen to my parents, I've signed my own death certificate.

## CHAPTER TWENTY-THREE

### SUMMER ALI'S "NIP SLIP" IN TINY BIKINI AT "WILD" CRUISE PARTY

### SUMMER ALI SUFFERS WARDROBE MALFUNCTION AND FLASHES FRIENDS WHILE WEARING RACY BATHING SUIT

### SUMMER ALI RISKS NIP SLIP IN BOOB-BARING SWIMSUIT AFTER JULES MORADI KISS EXPOSED

---

For days, I simmer with anxiety, waiting for the ball to drop. My team does everything they can to hold off the pictures for as long as they can, but one morning I wake up, and there they are.

I call Ariana, hang up, call my PR team, hang up, and then go scream pathetically in the shower until the tears stop running down my face.

My phone is ringing nonstop, but I ignore every call that isn't from my PR team, especially when I realize half of them are Ma and Baba, incessantly blowing up my phone.

I curl up in bed with wet hair and consider never getting back up. I'm so *stupid*. Why did I think I could handle any of this by myself? I should've never agreed to a PR stunt, should've never agreed to be photographed in public, should've never gone on a cruise, should've never worn a bikini. What was I thinking?

My parents never would've let me do any of this. If my career were still in their hands, this entire situation would've never existed.

Maybe they were right. Maybe I got too in over my head in a bid for independence, and now I'm paying the awful price.

There are pictures of my naked chest circulating the internet. *Multiple* pictures. From *multiple* angles. Despite the fact my bikini slipped for less than five seconds, there are so. many. fucking. pictures.

I scream hysterically into my pillow, resisting the urge to smother myself.

I'm so stupid, I'm so fucking *stupid*. Why did I think I could do this? Every time Ma said *you're a child* is flashing through my head, and for the first time, I have to acknowledge that she's right.

I imagine the look of disappointment on Baba's face right now, the way I know he would barely be able to stand to look at me, and I feel bile climb up the back of my throat.

I shouldn't have gone. I shouldn't have gone.

They would've never let me go.

I scream and scream and scream, until my throat is hoarse and my temples throb with a furious headache.

Eventually, I have to set my phone on do not disturb to keep from giving in to the temptation to pick up when one of my parents calls and blubber hysterically, taking them back as my managers with open arms.

If I had the energy, I'd get up and throw things, just to hear them crack, just to see them break, but I'm completely wrung out and miserable. There's nothing to do but hope and pray that this shitstorm blows over.

My doorbell rings.

Slowly, I pull my blankets down. I didn't order food, though my stomach has been grumbling in protest for hours, so I don't know who else could be at my door.

Again, the doorbell rings.

I sit up in bed, blinking rapidly. My parents don't know where I live, so it can't be them. Barbie is in LA, working on a collaboration with Third Eye. Zach is in Seattle, spending time with the Canadian guy he's seeing. Jules is in Pennsylvania, visiting his family.

The doorbell rings once again.

I painstakingly climb out of bed, scrubbing a hand over my face. My legs feel unsteady, but I somehow manage to get to the door without falling over.

I unlock it, tugging it open a crack, and whoever's on the other side pushes forward, nearly knocking me into the wall. Suddenly, I have my arms full of Safi and Jana, both of them hugging me like they haven't seen me in years.

"What . . . ?" I say, my voice coming out as a croak, and when I look up, Jules is standing behind them, hands in his pockets.

He offers me a small smile that doesn't reach his eyes. "Hey. I heard you weren't feeling well, so I brought your sisters over. I hope that's all right?"

I don't say anything for a moment, so perplexed by the situation that words escape me.

"Summy Apu," Safi says, squeezing her arm around my waist. "We missed you."

"I missed you too," I say, smoothing a hand down her braid. "I missed both of you."

"Jules said you're sad, so we bought ice cream and popcorn and he said we could have a movie marathon," Safi explains, looking up at me with wide brown eyes.

"I brought you cookies and cream," Jana says, holding up a grocery bag, and I know *she* knows, even if Safi doesn't. But she doesn't say anything about it, instead holding my gaze and offering me only love and warmth.

I glance at Jules again as he stands awkwardly in the doorway, as if he's not sure if he's overstepping. I think about how immeasurably kind it was of him to leave behind his family to track down mine, to bring me the two people in the world that might actually make me feel slightly better.

"Come in," I say, holding the door open wider. "All of you."

Our movie marathon goes as follows: *Tangled, The Princess and the Frog, Moana, Turning Red*.

After *Turning Red*, Safi starts yawning, and I reluctantly help them put their coats and shoes on, calling a car for them. If I could, I'd never let them leave, but that's hardly an option. I have to go back to reality at some point.

I close the door behind my sisters and Jules comes to stand beside me, a hesitant look on his face. "Do you want to talk about it?"

I turn toward him, staring at him for a few moments before I shake my head. "No. I'm all right. But thank you for checking up on me."

"You don't seem all right," Jules says softly. "Is there anything I can do to fix it?"

And I'm hit with the urge to cry, because the only thing that can fix this mess is turning back time and making it so I never agreed to go on that stupid cruise, but I don't want to say that. It's not Jules' fault I'm an idiot, but if I answer honestly, he'll take the blame onto himself anyway.

I take a deep breath, blinking a few times to keep any possible tears from forming. "No, I'm good. Really. Don't worry about me."

Jules gives me a hard look, eyebrows drawn together. "You don't have to lie to me, Summer. I know—I know that the world hasn't been kind to you today. But they're going to forget about it, I promise. Stuff like this blows over before you even realize it."

I shake my head. "No, it doesn't, Jules. This is going to follow me for the rest of my career."

"It won't," he insists. "They'll move on to something new tomorrow. They always do."

"You don't know that," I say, biting my lip and trying to keep my emotions in check. "*Right as Rain* . . . they might not even want me on the soundtrack after this. I've never had a scandal before, and I don't—"

"The movie won't care," he says. "I promise, Summer. This isn't going to change anything."

"Yes, it is," I say, a little more sharply than I intend.

"I won't let it," he says firmly. "I'll talk to them, but I'm telling you, they won't care about any of this. It's just the media making noise like they always do."

"You don't get it," I snap, and it all comes spewing out of me without permission. "You're a dude. It doesn't matter if a picture of your chest is plastered across highway billboards. This is going to affect my career. People are going to call me a whore, a slut. They're going to sexualize me left and right, even if I tell them not to. That picture is *never* going to leave the internet. When people think of me, they're not going to think about my music first—it'll be this. This is going to define me for weeks, months, maybe years! Who fucking knows!"

Jules opens his mouth, then closes it, like he doesn't know what to say.

I laugh, but it's hardly a pleasant sound. "You know, I used to hate that my image was 'good' and 'pure' or whatever. The idea that I could do no wrong. It felt like my parents were using that to exert control over me, to keep me from being who I wanted to be, from doing the things I wanted to do. But look at me now. It hasn't even been a year since I stopped letting them manage my career and now my fucking boobs are on the front page of TMZ!"

The sharp words hang in the air, echoing through the small space of my apartment for what feels like a lifetime.

"I'm sorry," Jules says finally. "I'm sorry. I shouldn't have—you're right. I don't understand. I'm sorry for speaking over you, Summer."

"It doesn't matter," I say, shaking my head. "None of this matters."

"It does matter. I'm sorry, Summer. I'm sorry this happened to you. It's bullshit, and I wish I could make it all disappear. I—I may not know what it's like to be on the other side of this, but . . . the media made a circus of my love life, so I get that it fucking sucks. I shouldn't have tried to make light of it."

I sniffle, leaning back against the wall. "How did you deal with it?"

"What? The media circus?" Jules sighs, running a hand through his hair. "I mean, it's different for me. It was kind of my fault to begin with."

I frown at him. "What do you mean?"

"I shouldn't get into it right now, this is about you and your feelings. I don't—"

"No, I want to know," I insist. "Tell me."

Jules makes a face, but it's directed at the floor rather than me. "If you really want to know . . . my old film agent told me I was typecast."

"Meaning?"

"Meaning that I would only ever book one type of role. The best friend. The comic relief. And I—I hated the idea that I was going to be boxed in for the rest of my career. I wanted to be the main character. I wanted to be the love interest. I wanted to be more than someone on the side, getting only a few lines of actual depth, if that." Jules folds his arms across his chest almost defensively. "But my film agent said that I should be glad for it, because it meant that I would get a consistent check, and that was better than nothing."

"That's so fucked up," I say, scowling. "Did you fire him?"

"Eventually," Jules says before wincing. "First, I thought I could solve it on my own. I wanted Hollywood to romanticize me so I . . . did my best to make myself look romantic? It was stupid, I wasn't really thinking, but I had to do something. So I started calling the paps on myself and going out with all kinds of girls, going to clubs, flirting with anyone in hearing distance. I thought it would make everyone take me seriously, and it wasn't like it was hard—I like meeting new people and forming connections. But then suddenly they were branding me as a childhood star on a bender, a playboy out on the town, and it made me so *mad*—it wasn't even like that. All of the people I was—" He cuts himself off, looking up at me. "Sorry. You don't want to hear this right now."

I shake my head. I want to say it's nice to have a distraction, but that isn't the right word for the unflinching honesty Jules is giving me right now. "No, I do. It's . . . talking to you makes everything feel a little less terrible."

Jules gives me a pained smile. "If you're sure."

"I'm sure," I say, and raise my chin, gesturing for him to continue.

"I don't know how much else there is to even say. I was trying to form genuine connections, you know? It wasn't some malicious thing where I met girls and then tossed them aside like they didn't matter. Especially not with my costars. I honestly was planning to keep business and pleasure separate, but Nora from *Aftershocks* and I were talking one night, and things got a little out of hand—and then the media was having a field day about *that*, even though neither of us ever intended to for it to be anything more than a hookup. And in my next project, my costar came on to me because she thought all the rumors were true, and I wasn't exactly opposed since I liked her well enough and then—I don't know. I guess shit spiraled. And then just kept spiraling."

He sighs, pinching the bridge of his nose. "There were such fucked up headlines about all of it. They started speculating on who I'd date next, on if I was taking roles specifically to land dates with famous women, on if I even cared about acting at all or if I was in it for a hot date. It was so—" He blows out a harsh breath. "Anyway, the point is, I know how vicious the media can be. And I'm not the best person to turn to for advice, since I dealt with it by shutting down. I stopped talking to people, stopped trying to make friends. Really, I mostly kept to myself and only spoke to Raj, because he wasn't a part of this world. He knew who *I* was, not the person the media was making me out to be."

The puzzle pieces start clicking together in my head. "That's why he had an intervention?"

Jules nods, and a muscle in his jaw shifts. "My reputation was in shambles. My life was falling apart. If he hadn't picked up the pieces, I . . . I think I would've been just like every other burned-out child actor."

"But you came back," I whisper. "You found a way."

He finally looks up at me, his brown eyes shining with aching sincerity. "This movie was my last chance, Summer. Without you, I don't know that I *could* have come back."

"You didn't tell me that," I say, eyes wide.

"I didn't want to put unnecessary pressure on you," he says with a shrug. "You didn't sign up to help me fix my life. You agreed to fake date me, and I wasn't going to make anything else your problem."

"If I'd known, I would've . . ." I shake my head. "I would've tried harder. To make people think I was in love with you. I didn't realize how much was at stake—"

"Summer," Jules says, finally crossing the distance between us and placing his hands on my shoulders. "Listen to me. You did more than enough." He sighs, looking down. "If you want to end things, I understand. You wouldn't have even been on that cruise if it weren't for me. I didn't—I didn't expect to become your friend. I didn't expect to enjoy hanging out with you. I should've kept things professional between us, and never invited you—"

"Shut up," I say, and reach up, wrapping my arms around his neck and hugging him tightly. "Just shut up, Jules."

Hesitantly, his arms slide down to my waist, slipping around me. "I wouldn't blame you if—"

"This shit sucks, okay? I'm fucking miserable and I want to cry and scream and be anyone but Summer Ali," I say, holding him tighter. "And from what it sounds like, there was a time when you wanted to be anyone but Jules Moradi."

He runs a hand down my back, gentle and comforting. "Yeah, but . . ."

"Shut up," I say again. "All I need right now is for you to be my friend and stick with me through this shitstorm. Can you do that?"

Jules nods slowly. "I can do that."

"Then that's all that matters," I say, and I mean it.

## CHAPTER TWENTY-FOUR

# SUMMER ALI JOINS "RIGHT AS RAIN" SOUNDTRACK WITH UNTITLED BALLAD

My phone starts ringing at ten in the morning, waking me up abruptly. I try not to groan as I slap my hand around my bedside table until my fingers close around my phone.

I glance at it only briefly to make sure it's not my parents, abiding by the cardinal rule, and my brain fully wakes up upon seeing it's Ariana.

"Good morning," I say, sitting up in bed and rubbing my eyes. "What's going on?"

"Have you seen the news?" Ariana asks.

I stand up, moving for my desk, where my laptop is. "What news?" I ask, already opening up Google Chrome, my pulse throbbing in my neck. Are there more pictures of me that leaked? Why won't this nightmare end?

"You're going to be on the soundtrack! It's official!" she shouts.

I falter, my brain still functioning at half capacity. "The soundtrack for *Right as Rain*?"

"What other soundtrack?" Ariana asks with a laugh. "Yes, Summer! For *Right as Rain*. Congratulations!"

"Oh my God," I say, my fingers faltering on my keyboard. "*Oh my God*. Are you serious?"

"I'm deadly serious," she says excitedly. "They confirmed it via press release this morning. I sent you an email with all the terms. I'm hoping we can finalize the contract soon."

"Holy shit," I say, holding a hand to my head. "I can't believe—this is really happening? You're not joking?"

"I'm not joking," she confirms. "Go out and celebrate! You deserve it!"

"I—oh my God, okay. Thank you! Thank you! Tell them I said thank you too, holy—*wow*."

Ariana chuckles. "I will. By the way, have you spoken to Jules yet? Did he mention taking you on vacation to meet his family?"

I blink. "Meet his *family*?"

"Yeah, I told him it might be a good idea for you to be seen visiting them. I know your parents are closer, so I would've suggested them, but given you're not on the best terms, I thought a little road trip to Pennsylvania might be a fun alternative," Ariana says, unaware of the crisis every new word is triggering in me. "Anyway, I'll leave you to it, but talk to him about it, all right? Congratulations again!"

And then she hangs up while I sit there, astounded. I check her email first, clicking into the press release, and my eyes widen as I read the headline. This is really happening.

I lean back in my chair, blowing out a deep breath. This has to be because of Jules. I mean, it was always going to be because of Jules, but between now and the last time I saw him, he obviously did or said something to make the *Right as Rain* team finalize their decision.

As happy as I feel about the news, the idea that *I* might be nominated for an Oscar because of this, I can't help but wonder if Jules went out and rushed them into making this statement because of me, because I was afraid I might lose this opportunity due to my scandal.

I glance down at my journal, lying open on the table. The page in front of me is empty aside from a few crossed-out scribbles.

I sigh, rubbing my eyes. Well, now that it's confirmed, I have to get to work. I can't sit around moping and hoping someone else will write the song for me.

I reach for my phone, shooting Jules a text.

> **Me:** do I finally get to know what the movie is about now that I officially have to write a song for it?

> **Jules Moradi:** you heard the news then???
> Congrats :D

> **Me:** I know you had something to do with this

> **Jules Moradi:** I plead the fifth :)

> **Jules Moradi:** I'm sure someone will send you the rough cut of the movie soon

**Jules Moradi:** I wouldn't want to spoil it too early

**Me:** you're a menace

**Jules Moradi:** yeah yeah

**Jules Moradi:** do you have vocal lessons at the studio later? wanna grab dinner after?

**Me:** yes I'll be done at 6

**Me:** also ariana suggested something about meeting your family?? did she mention it to you

**Jules Moradi:** yeah

**Jules Moradi:** let's talk about it at dinner

**Jules Moradi:** I'll be outside the studio at 6

I react to his last message with a thumbs-up and force myself to *inhale, exhale,* and get to work.

"Why are you trying to kill me?" I complain, wrapping my silk scarf tighter around my neck and pointedly ignoring the curious looks we're getting.

"No one is going to try to murder you, Summer," Jules says

calmly, and I can almost see him roll his eyes behind his sunglasses.

"Some of your fans are terrifying, Jules. Do you have any idea how scary teenage girls can be when they want to be?"

Jules turns to look at me pointedly. "I think being around *you* has clued me in, yes."

"I would flip you off if it wouldn't be caught on camera," I mutter.

For the most part, I try not to linger too long in midtown, especially near Times Square and Rockefeller Center, where a majority of early morning and late-night television shows are filmed. There tend to be legions of teenagers waiting in standby lines to see their favorite celebrities, and I don't exactly want to run into them. I adore my fans to pieces, but it's not *my* fans I'm worried about.

Ever since the pictures of me leaked, there have been hundreds of people slut shaming me and sending me death threats, and too many of them had some variation of *Jules Moradi* in their usernames or his face as their profile pictures.

Damon and Rivus follow behind us dutifully, so we should be fine in theory, but that doesn't make me feel any less anxious walking out and about near this many people.

"Getting dinner is not worth this much effort," I say under my breath, but I don't stop following Jules. When he reaches down and links our fingers together, I let him without protest.

In the back of my mind, I wonder if allowing him to hold my hand is only going to lead to more trouble, but it's such a nice, comforting weight that I can't bring myself to let go.

"Are you sure no one's going to kill me?" I ask a minute later. More and more people have started to follow us, at what they might think is considered a respectful distance, but really isn't. All it does is make me want to duck into the nearest store and hide in a back room until they go away.

Jules brings us to a stop, turning to look at me. "I promise it'll be okay. If anything, Rivus will fight off any lunatic with the nerve to throw themselves at you," he says, gesturing to his bodyguard, who nods gruffly.

"So you don't deny it could be a possibility," I say, narrowing my eyes at him.

Jules leans forward, taking my face in both of his hands. "Summer, I would never let anything happen to you."

"I know," I say with a sigh. "It's just . . . scary to be outside right now."

"If you let them intimidate you into staying home, you're never going to be able to go outside again," he says softly, and I hate that he's right.

"This better be the best fucking dinner I've ever had in my life," I mutter.

Jules smiles, and then unexpectedly leans in and pecks my nose. "If it's not, you can yell at me all you want."

My cheeks flush despite myself. "I'll hold you to that."

I don't expect Jules to lead us to a small hole-in-the-wall Persian restaurant and greet the owner by name, but he's always been good at surprising me.

Jules gives me a smug look after I take my first bite of the sabzi polo ba mahi I ordered as per his suggestion. "Well?"

"You're the most irritating person I've ever met," I say instead of answering that it's probably the best food I've had all month.

He chuckles. "High praise coming from you."

"Ugh, whatever," I say, waving him off. "Tell me about this thing with your family."

"It's honestly not anything worth talking about," Jules says, wiping his mouth with a napkin. My gaze lingers on his lips for a beat too long before I force myself to look down at my food instead. "Ariana suggested it awhile back. I never got around to asking my family about it, but then Laila said she wanted to meet you, so I thought why not? It might be good to get out of town for a while, right?"

I choke on my food slightly and have to gulp down half a glass of water before I can speak. "Your sister wants to meet me?"

Jules grimaces a little. "Well, she's never seen me date someone this long, so . . ."

"Oh," I say, clearing my throat. It's hardly my place to judge him when I haven't told my sisters either, preferring to leave them out of all the nonsense that comes with being a public figure. "But what about your parents? I don't want to intrude—"

"They're excited to meet you too," Jules says, but there's something off about his voice, and for the first time, I realize he's *nervous*. From the sound of it, he's never taken anybody home before. This is a private part of him that no one has really seen, and he's offering it to me despite how tense he is.

"You don't have to do this to cheer me up," I say. "I'll be okay, Jules."

"It's not—" He shakes his head. "I want you to meet them, really. It's only fair, isn't it? I've met Safina and Sanjana so many times already."

I frown at him. "Are you sure?"

"I'm sure," he says, giving a firm nod. "How about next weekend?"

"Yeah, that's fine," I say before tilting my head. "Are there paps in rural Pennsylvania?"

"I sincerely doubt it," Jules says with a snort. "So you don't have to worry about them harassing you."

*Then why am I coming?* Except I can't make myself say the words.

"Thank you for inviting me," I say instead.

He smiles at me, and despite the tremor in the corner of his mouth, his eyes are earnest and warm. "Don't thank me yet. My parents are going to smother you. Maman *loves* to cook and won't let you leave without seconds, possibly thirds."

There's a pang in my chest, a little painful, a little bitter. "I'll have a light breakfast before we leave then."

The day before we head out to Pennsylvania, I host Jana and Safi for a dinner that consists entirely of fast food. My parents would never let me have any, and I doubt that's changed for my sisters since I moved out.

As soon as I open the door, Jana greets me with crossed arms. "Why am I hearing rumors that you and Jules are going off on a vacation together? What's up with that?"

I give her a questioning look. There's no way that information leaked to the press already. "Where did you hear that?"

"Around," Jana answers in a way that's far too suspicious, and I immediately know that Barbie's the one who told her. "So where are you two going?"

"Canada," I say flatly, and Jana pulls a face at me.

"I'm pretty sure Jules is banned from Canada after the time he got caught hooking up with his costar in the airport bathroom," she says, and this time *I* make a face at her.

"TMI," I say, shutting the door behind her.

"What's TMI?" Safi asks, already at the dining table, grabbing a handful of french fries and chicken nuggets.

"Too much information," I say, reaching over to tug one of Safi's pigtails. "Your Jana Apu doesn't know when to keep her mouth shut."

"That's true," Safi agrees, shoving a fry in her mouth. "Ma and Baba always say she talks back to them too much."

I falter, looking at Jana, who's suddenly looking anywhere but at me.

"Why have you been talking back to them?" I ask. "You know that only makes them more angry."

Jana huffs, chewing angrily on a chicken nugget.

"They keep being mean about you," Safi says with a frown. "I think Apu just wants to protect you."

"Jana," I say miserably. "Don't stick out your neck for me. Please."

"They shouldn't be so rude if they don't want me to say anything," Jana says sharply. "Like I'm going to sit there and let them call you ungrateful and selfish?"

"Jana," I say again, reaching out to pull her into my arms. Something between my ribs is trembling. "You have to look out for yourself."

Jana doesn't say anything, and Safi joins the hug a moment later, squeezing her tiny arms around us.

After a long moment of silence, Safi pulls away, looking up at us with big brown eyes. "Can we watch *World of Tweens*?"

It's a rather obvious attempt to change the subject but I appreciate it all the same. "Of course," I say, and give Jana one last squeeze. "I'll put it on now."

## CHAPTER TWENTY-FIVE

## SUMMER ALI AND JULES MORADI ENJOY A ROMANTIC WEEKEND TRIP AT MORADI FAMILY HOME

I've always been a city girl, so I'm a little taken aback when we finally get to the Moradi family home and there's not a single industrial building in sight.

I get out of the car, trying and failing not to gawk at the house in front of us. It's huge, which makes sense since we're in the middle of nowhere, but I didn't expect it to look like a *mansion*.

"How much do you get paid?" I ask, throwing aside niceties for the moment. "And how do *I* get paid that much?"

"What would you do with a house this big?" Jules asks with an amused smile, hoisting his duffle bag onto his shoulder. "Anyway, I didn't buy it. My parents are doctors, remember?"

I give the house a long, considering look. "Should we have gone into medicine?"

Jules snorts, pulling me down the driveway. Before we can ring the doorbell, someone shouts, "Out here, Juyan!" from behind the house.

I blink in surprise, but Jules lights up and immediately heads for the backyard. I follow him, mystified by the extensive garden that someone clearly pours a lot of love into. My strawberry plant would *thrive* here.

In the backyard, there are half a dozen people standing around what looks to be a bonfire in the works. There's a woman at the grill wearing a ridiculous white chef's hat, and when Jules pushes open the gate, she looks up with a wide grin.

"Honey!" she shouts, holding open her arms.

Jules immediately fits himself in between them, laughing loudly. "Hi, Maman."

She pinches his cheek affectionately before pushing him aside, her bright gaze locking in on me. "And you must be Summer. We've heard so much about you—come here!"

I'm surprised when she pulls me into a hug, enveloping me in the scent of honey and lemon. "It's nice to meet you, Mrs. Moradi," I say a little shyly.

"Oh, nonsense, call me Fatemeh," she says, giving me a squeeze for good measure before pulling away.

"Uh—call me Sumaira then," I offer, glancing back at Jules nervously.

"Sumaira," she says, warmth seeping into her voice. "What a beautiful name for a beautiful girl." She turns to Jules, pointing a finger at him. "Don't mess this up, Juyan."

"I don't intend to," he says, rolling his eyes, but leans over to kiss his mother's cheek.

A surge of affection runs through me at the sight of them. Sometimes when faced with happy families, I find myself feeling sad without meaning to, but in the face of the obvious love between Jules and his mother, I feel only delight. He deserves to have this.

"Oh, you're here!" someone else calls, and as soon as I see her, I know it's Laila. She looks like Jules, with the same dimpled smile and twinkling brown eyes. "I've been waiting ages to do this," she says, and pulls me into a hug, completely sidelining Jules.

I startle a little but hug her back, a pleased flush climbing up my neck to my cheeks. "Giving good hugs must run in the family," I say when she leans back, and she grins at me.

"I'm here too, you know," Jules says behind her. Any traces of nervousness he had earlier have faded, replaced with an ease that clearly comes from being around his family.

"I see you all the time," Laila says, waving him off. "It's my first time meeting Summer. I can't believe he's been hiding you away for this long!"

"It hasn't been that long, in his defense," I say.

"Well over half a year is far too long," Laila says, turning to face Jules with a glare. "The next time you lecture me about one of my boyfriends, I swear—"

I lose track of the conversation, a little overwhelmed by Laila saying over half a year. Has it really been eight months? It feels like I just met Jules the other day.

But I look over at him as he bickers with his older sister, rolling his eyes and pouting in equal measure, and I realize it feels like I've known him my entire life, not eight months, and that terrifies me.

"You're stressing her out," Laila says, turning back to me. "Don't worry, no one here's going to give out your location or anything. Everyone knows to keep it on the down low when Jules is here."

"Oh, I wasn't—" I don't finish the sentence, realizing it's a good out. It's not like I want to explain what I'm actually worried about. "Thank you."

Laila nods, offering me a smaller smile. I remember that once upon a time, Jules told me she has anxiety too, and I can see hints of it in her expression, but it's obvious this is her safe place, where she feels most comfortable. "I think Dad went out to get some firewood, but he'll be back soon. He's excited to meet you, too."

"Wood . . . from the forest?" I ask, glancing behind them toward the wide expanse of trees farther down the backyard. Jules smothers a laugh, and I glare at him. "What?"

"You're too used to the city life," he says, reaching over to tug my ponytail. "Come on, I'll introduce you to everyone else."

A part of me wants to stay here, because whatever his mother is making smells delicious, but the rest of me is curious as to who all these other people are and what Jules' relationship is to them. Eventually, my curiosity wins out and I nod.

Jules throws a casual arm around my shoulders, which may or may not make my heart skip a beat. "Let's go."

It doesn't take long to meet everyone, most of them neighbors of the Moradi family or extended family members. One of Jules' aunts spends five minutes lecturing him for not using coconut oil in his hair more often, and I have to look away to keep from bursting into giggles.

Eventually, Jules leads me over to a large wooden log, gesturing for me to sit next to him. I raise an eyebrow but crouch down beside him anyway, scooting a little closer for the comfort of his side pressed against mine. "Why are we all the way back here?"

He gives me a crooked smile. "Why not?"

"I think you're trying to let the forest eat me," I say, glancing back warily.

"You caught me," he deadpans, and I swat his side half-heartedly. He captures my hand in his and pulls it into his lap, holding it hostage.

I roll my eyes. "I have Barbie and Zach on Find My Friends. They'll avenge me if this is all an elaborate scheme to murder me."

"Not everyone is trying to kill you, princess," he says, tracing the lines of my palm absently.

I know he's right, but there's a sense of paranoia in my every action lately, my brain still haunted by the photos of my nip slip. Being here, away from all that, is a nice reprieve. Jules must have known it would be.

"Your family is really nice," I say when the silence stretches.

"But?"

"There's no but," I say, glancing down at our hands. "I'm glad you have them, even if you don't get to see them all that often."

"Everything comes with a price, doesn't it?" he asks. "Our fame has to cost us something."

The words settle heavily across my shoulders. "Yeah. I suppose that's true."

Jules looks up at me, studying the expression on my face. "Do you need anything from me right now? You promised me you'd ask if you did."

"Not right now," I say, but I move closer, leaning my head on his shoulder. "This is enough."

When Jules' father, a large man with an even larger smile, finally comes back they all get together for a game of soccer that I opt out of immediately.

Jules' mother does the same, offering me a kebab skewer as I sit to the side and watch all of them divide into two teams. It's strange, seeing people with normal lives do normal things. Is this what it was like for Jules growing up? In between filming *World of Tweens*, he would come back here and be a part of this? Or did he miss out on this back then too and now only gets to steal glimpses of a life he could have had?

Fatemeh sits down next to me, excitement scrawled all over her face as she watches them run a soccer ball up and down the field. I don't expect to get invested, but when Jules makes his first goal, I jump to my feet, whooping loudly.

His mother stands up with me, joining in the cheering. Jules grins at us before passing the ball to his father and focusing on the game instead.

"He never brings anyone home," Fatemeh says, tearing me away from the game, my attention flitting to her. She doesn't look away from the makeshift soccer field as she adds, "You must mean a lot to him."

The news isn't surprising, since Jules hinted as much earlier, but the absurdity of the situation hits somewhere deep in my chest.

This isn't real. None of this is real. Jules and I are putting on a charade for the sake of furthering our careers, and it doesn't mean anything.

But I want Fatemeh's words to be true. I want this to matter.

Does Jules look at me and see only a business arrangement? Is fake dating all this will ever be?

I wish I had the answer.

"He means a lot to me too," I say, more honest than I should be.

Fatemeh smiles. "I know. I can tell. Mothers have a way of seeing these things."

"I don't know that my mother would agree with you," I say, and some of the bitterness slips into my voice. Fatemeh glances at me, her brows knitting together. "Sorry, I shouldn't have—it's just really, really nice to see that Jules has a family that loves him this much."

Something in Fatemeh's face softens. "You're always welcome to join him when he visits, Sumaira."

It's obvious she means the words, but she doesn't know that they ring false, like this entire situation. This might be the one and only time I ever meet Jules' family. "Thank you for having me," I say softly.

Fatemeh reaches over, smoothing a hand down my hair. The touch is gentle and caring, and makes me want to simultaneously cry and hug her. "Of course. We're glad you're here, Sumaira."

I give her a smile—or as much as I can manage—and turn back to the game in time to see Jules peel off his shirt. I make a choked noise of surprise and his mother doesn't even bother to hide her laughter.

When Fatemeh takes out her phone to commemorate the moment, I try not to melt into the ground. It's good that she's taking pictures and videos. It'll make for authentic content. I only wish it weren't of me gawking at Jules' back muscles.

Jules notices my stare and he winks at me before scrambling off to steal the ball from the opposite team. I scowl at him, but there's no heat behind it.

Laila finally swaps out of the game, tapping in one of her cousins so she can come to stand by us, swallowing down half a bottle of water. "Do you wanna play, Summer?" she asks me once she catches her breath.

"Absolutely not," I say, shaking my head. "But they're doing really well, I almost can't believe it. That's, what, the second goal Jules has made?"

"The rest of us were scoring too," Laila teases.

I flush and adamantly turn my attention back to the game. With Laila alongside us, it's even easier to get invested. At one point the two of us start jumping up and down, moving our arms side to side in an excited cheer, while Fatemeh films us with a fond look on her face. I consider regretting my actions, but I can't really find it in myself to when it seems to help Jules' morale.

He passes by us at one point to grab an extra bottle of water, and I pull him into a sweaty hug, whispering, "You're doing really great."

He beams at me before running back toward the field. Eventually, his team wins, four to three, and I grin so hard my cheeks ache with the effort.

Later, I scroll through the stories his mother uploads and the news articles that follow, all detailing how I'm Jules' biggest fan.

Jules reads one of the articles over my shoulder at the dinner table and says, "But you left your cheerleading outfit at home!" in false outrage, and I shove him lightly. He feigns falling off his chair, but none of his family members even look in his direction, apparently used to his dramatics.

I think I'm starting to get used to them too.

## CHAPTER TWENTY-SIX

# JULES MORADI'S MOTHER POSTS VIDEO OF GIRLFRIEND SUMMER ALI AS HIS PERSONAL CHEERLEADER AT SOCCER GAME

After the barbecue wraps up, Jules' mother pointedly offers me a guest bedroom before Jules and I have to engage in an awkward conversation about sharing a bed, and I consider kneeling at her feet in gratitude. Fatemeh digs through Jules' closet for a spare blanket while I sit at his desk and he watches her from where he's lying on his bed.

"I'll leave it in the guest room," Fatemeh says when she finally finds it. She gives me a smile and then turns a warning look on Jules, pointing a finger at him. "Keep this door open."

"I'm nineteen, Maman," Jules says, rolling his eyes.

"Notice how that has *teen* in it," Fatemeh says without missing a beat. "And I don't care how old you are. You're still my son. Leave this door open."

Jules grumbles for show, but the moment his mother leaves, he flops back onto the bed, melting into the sheets. "Home sweet home."

I spin in the chair until I finally face him. "How come you've never been in a serious relationship before?"

His head snaps toward me. "Excuse me?"

"They keep mentioning how happy they are that I'm here," I say, lifting my sock-clad feet and setting them down on the bed, within reaching distance of his legs. "Don't you think they deserve to meet a real girlfriend?"

"I'm too busy for a real girlfriend," he says dismissively, turning his head toward the ceiling.

"No, you're not," I say, exasperated. "You spend half your days with me doing nothing."

"Yeah, but I'm not actively filming right now," he points out, nudging his foot against mine. "Why haven't *you* had a real partner?"

"My parents thought it was a distraction," I say, and the honesty of my answer seems to surprise him, because he rolls over to face me.

With his searching gaze on me, I open the cracks in my walls a little more, offering him the truth. "They were really controlling. I never really took people seriously when they talked about having stage parents, but that's what mine were. Everything in my life was decided by them. What I sang, what I wore, what I ate. Even who I spent time with. If Barbie and Zach weren't under my record label, I probably would've never met them." I make an airy gesture to cover up how heavy the words feel. "They've always been that way, even when I was younger, but I think once I was on *Stars of America*, they took it to the extreme. I don't know. I haven't been my own person long enough to give dating any real consideration."

Jules considers me for a long moment, and then shifts to one side of his bed, patting the space beside him. "Come here?"

I move without really thinking about it, lying down opposite him. "Couldn't hear me over there?"

"This doesn't feel like a conversation we should have across a room," he says, his voice quieter. "I didn't realize it was that bad with your parents. I knew you didn't get along but that sounds . . ."

"Like emotional abuse?" I supply, and Jules grimaces. "I know. When I first fired them as my managers, Barbie had to sit down with me and have a talk about cutting them off. I knew if I gave them even an inch, they'd worm their way back into my life, and I'm . . . I'm so bad at saying no, especially to them. But I can't—I can't be under their thumb anymore, it's so suffocating, and sometimes, I feel like I can't breathe—"

I cut off, biting my lip.

"You don't have to talk about it if you don't want to," he whispers into the charged space between us.

I shake my head. "I feel like without this PR stunt as a distraction, I would've lost my mind a little these last few months, worrying about them. But this kept me busy and preoccupied so I didn't sit around asking myself *what if* over and over. I mean, I still do that, but less than I would've otherwise."

Then I make a face. "Sorry. That wasn't even the question. The point is, having a partner hasn't really been a priority for me. But you're different from me. You told me yourself you crave connection, Jules."

"First of all, don't apologize to me for this," he says, his eyes serious. He waits for me to nod before continuing, "Second, yeah, but I . . ."

"But you . . . ?"

Jules presses his lips together, clearly conflicted about something. I wait him out, staring at his Adam's apple so he doesn't feel pressured by my stare on his face.

"I guess I have trust issues," he finally says, and my eyes dart up to meet his. "I haven't told you about Alex, and I think a part of me was hoping I could avoid ever having this conversation, but . . . if you can tell me your hard truths, I should be able to do the same."

"This isn't a transaction," I say, reaching over to place a hand on his chest. Beneath my fingers, his heart beats steadily. "You don't owe me a truth because I gave you one."

"I know," he says, and his arm reaches across us, settling on my waist, squeezing lightly. "But I'm tired of keeping this from you. I want to tell you."

I nod slowly. "If you're sure."

"I'm sure." Jules takes a deep breath, bracing himself for the conversation. "Alex was my best friend. We met on the set of *World of Tweens*. Even though we started in similar places in our careers, he always got better roles than me, and for a long time, I didn't understand why. Then I realized it was because he was white, and when I brought it up to him, he said I was white-passing so I didn't have room to complain."

My jaw tightens in irritation, but Jules doesn't seem to notice, his gaze far away.

"I told Alex I was frustrated about being typecast and he said it could be worse. I think I kind of gaslighted myself into believing it for a while, but then Raj shook some sense into me. He was actually the one that suggested changing my name might help. Juyan and Jules don't sound that different from each other, so it wasn't that hard to adjust, and it *did* end up making a difference when it came to landing roles."

I sigh. "Of course it did. This industry is so . . ."

Jules gives me a thin smile. "I know. Honestly, I would've lost all hope in the industry altogether if it hadn't been for Yuri Fujisaki. He was the director for *Aftershocks,* and he believed in me enough to cast me in the lead role when most people would've tossed me aside for being a child star on *World of Tweens.* For all intents and purposes, I should've never been cast in a serious thriller, but Yuri saw something in me, and I'm grateful for it every day."

"I'm guessing Alex didn't take that well," I say, already noticing the downward turn of his mouth.

"Yeah . . . yeah. He was pissed that I hadn't told him about the role sooner so he could've also auditioned. Even more so when the film started getting acclaim." He closes his eyes as a full-body tremor runs through him. "Alex and I both got nominated for Best Lead Actor at some MTV award show. I honestly was happy I was even considered. I didn't expect to win, but even then, I told Alex I didn't want the award to come between us either way. He promised it wouldn't. When I won, I think it took us both by surprise, but I didn't think he'd be *angry.* I thought we cared about each other at the end of the day, even if there was some friendly competition between us. But he was so mad, Summer."

I move closer, pressing my legs against his. Jules opens his eyes to look at me, and I want to scream at how glassy they are.

"At the after-party, he told me—*loudly*—that I shouldn't have won and it was only for a diversity quota, and that I'd never be taken seriously or considered for bigger, more important roles. *This is the only victory you'll ever get in your mediocre acting career."*

My hand curls into a fist against Jules' chest. I didn't know I could feel so angry on behalf of someone else. "He said that? *In public?* I'll kill him, I swear to God."

He shakes his head, but he looks so miserable. I've never wanted to burn down the world so badly. If I ever meet Alex, I'm going to wring his fucking neck.

"It was disheartening, to say the least. That's when I went to my film agent and asked about auditioning for big roles in Hollywood, and the whole typecast conversation happened. Since then, I haven't really . . . I thought he was my friend. He meant so much to me, and he only ever saw me as competition. Barely even that."

"He never deserved you," I say sharply. "You have to know that. You deserve the world, Jules."

"It's not that easy," he says softly. "I've tried to make friends, to meet people, to date. But part of me is always so scared to really let new people in. And I hate it, Summer. I know it's my own fault for isolating myself, but I—I feel so fucking lonely sometimes and it breaks my heart."

"You're not alone," I whisper.

His hand shifts from my waist to my neck, touching the *J* necklace that I haven't taken off since he bought it for me. "What you were saying earlier, about how this PR stunt helped you. It's done the same for me. If it wasn't for this, I would've spent yet another year with no one but Raj to turn to, and he's off at law school most of the time. I'm . . . I'm glad I met you, Summer."

I shift forward, finally fitting myself against him, tucking my head under his chin. "I'm glad I met you too, Jules."

We lie like that for a long time, until his mother comes back and knocks on the door to say good night.

Reluctantly, I peel myself away from Jules and go downstairs to the guest room his family set up for me. Alone in my bed, I miss the warmth of him and wonder when it became so habitual to always seek him out in an empty room.

# CHAPTER TWENTY-SEVEN

## SUMMER ALI'S SECOND ALBUM: EVERYTHING WE KNOW SO FAR

Returning to New York feels like stepping out of a fever dream. It doesn't quite feel real until Jana and Safi come over for a movie night. Seeing them is like a shock to the system, forcing me back to reality, but even still, I can't stop thinking about everything Jules told me, everything I told him.

"Let's watch *Julie and the Phantoms*!" Safi says, getting comfortable on the couch.

I shake my head, fiddling with a file on my laptop. "We're going to watch a rough cut of Jules' new film tonight. It's super confidential and doesn't come out for another three months, so you can't tell anyone anything about it, okay?"

Safi widens her eyes. "What does *confidential* mean?"

"It means it's a secret," Jana says, sitting down beside her with a bowl of popcorn. "Like how coming to Summy Apu's apartment is a secret?"

"So we can't tell Ma and Baba," Safi says, nodding her head.

"You can't tell *anyone*," I correct. "Not until Jules says you can."

Safi looks around, stretching her neck to see over the couch. "Is Jules here?"

"No, Jules isn't here," I say, ruffling her hair.

"Well, why not?" she asks, placing her hands on her hips, and I don't have an answer for that.

I've spent so much time with him lately that the lines between real and fake are blurring more and more by the day, and I can't afford to fuck this up.

Scarier is the fact that this morning, for the first time in months, I finished writing a song I actually like.

"Hurry up already," Jana says, kicking me with a socked foot.

"Bossy," I mutter, but manage to get the film up and running on my laptop, broadcasting it onto the television. "Budge over."

Safi moves slightly so I can fit between her and Jana, squeezing both of them tightly before turning to my attention to the movie.

In the hour that follows, I learn what the film is about. A girl desperate to leave her hometown, to make something of herself. A boy who falls in love with her and has to learn to somehow let her go. The inevitable realization that, while they might dream of a future together, they can never have it—that even as strong as their love is, the only way for her to survive is to finally leave him and their town behind.

I'm so drawn in by the story that I nearly fall off the couch when Safi taps my ankle insistently. "Gotta pee," she says by way of explanation.

I reach over to pause the movie and nod for her to go to the bathroom. She runs off and Jana turns a knowing look on me.

"What?" I ask, already defensive.

"You keep making faces every time Jules has to interact with Angelina," she says with a shit-eating grin. "You're *jealous*."

"What?" I shake my head. "I'm not—"

But the words die on my tongue as I consider that the strange feeling in my chest *is* jealousy. Seeing Jules touch someone else, seeing Jules hold someone else, seeing Jules *kiss* someone else, it all feels wrong.

I glance back at the screen, paused on the two of them sitting on the swings on a playground. Jules is staring at her like the sun rises and sets with her smile.

Has he ever smiled at me like that? Is it silly of me to want that? This thing between us is entirely made up, just like his on-screen romance with Angelina.

I consider her for a moment, lingering on her high cheekbones and the playful curve to her mouth. She's beautiful beyond measure. I've always known that. Hell, *I* had a crush on her at one point.

If Jules had a choice, would he rather be with her? He's been with costars before, and it's probably easier, *and* better promotion for the movie, and she probably doesn't have half the baggage I come with—

"Hey, stop it," Jana says, flicking my forehead. "Don't start spiraling."

"I wasn't spiraling," I immediately say, and then my cheeks flush with the realization that I'm falling into the same trap as the media, linking Jules to a girl just because he breathed near her.

Safi skips back into the room. "Ready!"

"Thank God, Apu was about to lose her shit," Jana says, reaching over to hit play while I say, "Hey! Language!"

But the moment the movie starts, I'm pulled back in by the

arresting sight of Jules' smile and the way he effortlessly slips into character like it's a second skin. I had no idea he was this good at acting. The most I've seen of his filmography is the rare episode of *World of Tweens* when trying to pester him, but maybe I should have been watching Yuri Fujisaki's movie.

He's so talented. He's so *unbelievably* talented.

And I can't believe Hollywood tried to stick him in a box and leave him there to rot. Jules is more than his reputation, more than what the media says about him, but how many people can actually *see* that?

Unprompted, more lyrics pop into my head, and I reach for my journal, scribbling them down without looking away from the TV screen.

For the first time in a year, I write a song in a night. As soon as the movie ends, I type up the lyrics in an email and send them to Ariana, for her to pass along to the *Right as Rain* team. It's a rough draft, but it feels *right*. Hopefully they think so too.

Maybe my slump is finally over.

An hour after I send Jana and Safi home, my phone starts ringing. I glance at it and blanch when I see Ma's name plastered across the screen.

I force myself to take a deep breath and look away. I'm not allowed to pick up her calls. I'm not allowed, I'm not allowed, I'm not allowed. Everything will fall apart if I answer.

Instead, I wait for the phone to stop ringing before grabbing it and checking Find My Friends to make sure Jana and Safi got home safely. As I do, a notification pops up at the top of my screen. *One new voicemail.*

Despite knowing I shouldn't, I click on the voicemail, letting it play into the silence of my living room.

"How many times will you ignore our calls, Sumaira?" says my mother, her voice sharp, piercing straight through my chest. "You are an unbelievable disappointment. What did I do to deserve a child who is so disrespectful and cruel? And now you're rubbing off on your sisters too. I *know* they went out to see you. How dare you send them home so late at night? If you want to be irresponsible with your own life and choices, fine, but to treat your younger sisters with the same disregard is unbelievable. You know how much they look up to you, and you choose to be a terrible influence on them. It's shameful, Sumaira. Call me back when you've come to your senses and remember your place. You are *my daughter* and you should never forget that."

The line cuts out.

I set my phone down, pulling my knees to my chest in an attempt to curl into a ball and disappear. My breathing comes ragged and unsteady, not a full-on anxiety attack, but enough to make me lightheaded.

I rest my forehead against my knees and force myself to breathe through the ache in my chest.

Is this what it's always going to be like? No matter what I do, they're always going to be disappointed in me? No matter how much I succeed, it won't matter if they didn't have a say in it?

It's been five years of putting up with their constant need to control me, to make my decisions for me, and eighteen years of never being enough.

When I was thirteen, I secretly applied to be a contestant on *Stars of America* through an online audition. Once I was admitted through to the next level, I had no choice but to tell my parents, who were so *angry* at me, but in the same breath saw the opportunity for what it was—a way to show off their success to everyone, to show that they were the best parents on the block, that they had done better than everyone else, that all their sacrifices coming here from Bangladesh were worth it. It's too much pressure to put on any child, but even more so when I had to do it on *national television*.

I made it all the way to fifth place on the show, which I thought was amazing for a thirteen-year-old, but my parents found to be lackluster. If a record label hadn't approached me anyway, my parents probably would've written me off as a complete and utter failure. Instead, they negotiated a deal and let me launch my singing career.

They uprooted us from New Jersey to New York, forcing me into homeschooling so I'd have a more fluid schedule. I flashback to Jules talking about how empty and isolated he felt, and think that I know exactly what he meant, because those first few years were so *achingly lonely*. It took so long to record my debut album, piecing together all of the songs one by one, that I nearly gave up on actually making it several times in the process. If it hadn't been for my commitment to this dream, I would've broken down long ago.

Meeting Barbie and Zach was a stroke of luck that I'm infinitely grateful for. Without them, it would've just been me and my parents facing off against the world, and most of the time it felt like it was me and my parents against *each other*.

I think of Ma telling me to watch what I eat. I think of Baba telling me to be careful what I wear. I think of Ma deciding which events I was allowed to go to. I think of Baba refusing to let me spend my own money. I think of both of them looking at me time and time again, but never seeing me.

Even without my parents existing in my life, I feel the weight of them in every decision I make. I think about them every day, even if I don't want to. Even with all these months apart, I'm still struggling to figure out who I am without them.

Who *is* Summer Ali?

Does anyone know?

I cover my face with my hands, tired and exhausted. I'm sick of my parents controlling every aspect of my life, even now, and more than that, I'm sick of myself.

# PART FOUR: FALL

## SUMMER ALI'S FALL-ISH PLAYLIST
### October to March—*falling for and falling despite*

1. "my future" —Billie Eilish
2. "You Are In Love" —Taylor Swift
3. "Electric (feat. Khalid)" —Alina Baraz
4. "Greenlight" —Tate McRae
5. "Here With Me" —d4vd
6. "Honeymoon Fades" —Sabrina Carpenter
7. "Shout About It" —The Vamps
8. "Graceland Too" —Phoebe Bridgers
9. "Cover Me" —Stray Kids

## CHAPTER TWENTY-EIGHT

## ROTTEN TOMATOES REVEALS "RIGHT AS RAIN" TO BE ONE OF THE MOST-ANTICIPATED FILMS OF THE YEAR: ANGELINA RODRIGUEZ AND JULES MORADI IN TALKS FOR OSCAR NOMINATIONS

The next few days blend into weeks. Despite my frustration with myself, there are more pressing concerns.

Even though my sophomore album isn't officially due until two months from now, I can tell the record label is getting antsy, wanting an update on how it's all coming together. When Ariana calls to ask me how my writing process is going, I don't have to lie to her about my progress. I owe a lot of things to *Right as Rain*, and getting my flow back is one of them.

I've written dozens of drafts of dozens of songs for my second album. Some are going to be scrapped, but some are *finally* going to stay, and it's so relieving to be able to put words to paper again.

But as I write, I'm intimately aware that I'm drawing on more personal aspects of my life than I ever have before. None of the songs are *fully* me, but they're slowly inching in that direction, and it terrifies me. I already give so much of myself to the world—giving them this too feels like a step too far.

I don't tell anyone any of this, though Jules curiously asks about my songs every now and then, seeing me with my journal out in front of me every other day. He gives me an open offer to show him my lyrics if I ever want to. So far, I haven't been able to muster up the courage.

Even more than the songs on my album, I'm nervous about his reception of "Show Me," the song I wrote for *Right as Rain*. It was approved within days of me sending it along, and I've been in and out of the studio recording vocals for it.

I haven't mentioned it to Jules, partially out of payback for withholding the script from me for so long and partially because it feels like laying myself bare at his feet.

I have no idea how it happened, but I've come to consider him one of my closest friends. I go to him as often as I go to Barbie and Zach, and I spend more time with him than almost anyone else in the world. I'm so used to having him as a constant presence in my life that when he goes to California for two weeks to film press junkets for *Right as Rain*, I'm *bored* and I have no idea what to do about it.

I fill that time with Jana and Safi, and flying out to Atlanta for a weekend to catch one of Barbie's concerts. When I get back, I write two more songs, and resist the urge to FaceTime Jules just to tell him about it.

There's something strange growing inside me, and I'm afraid to put it into words. The bigger this grows, the more I have to lose, and I don't know if I can *handle* losing this on top of everything else. Everything feels so delicate, as if one wrong breath might topple it all over.

Over and over, I touch the *J* at the base of my throat and wonder when something fake started feeling so real.

Of course, everything falls apart the next month, in a way I should have expected but had hoped would never come to pass.

I return to my apartment after a recording session, mindlessly sorting through my mail, and then I belatedly realize there are four people standing in front of my doorway.

Jana looks up at me with guilty eyes and Safi is crying quietly while Ma and Baba glare at me from down the hall.

Shit.

"You're not supposed to be here," I say, taking an uncertain step back, toward the staircase. This is my worst fear come to life, and all I want is to be anywhere but here.

"Come here right this instant," Baba says in a low voice. "And open this door, Sumaira."

I shake my head, reaching out to place my hand against the wall to steady myself. "How did you—I never told you where—"

But Jana's guilty expression says it all.

"You made them tell you," I say, and my voice goes flat with the realization.

"You should've told us yourself," Ma says sharply. "How dare you screen our calls for months? You're our *daughter*."

"I am not your daughter," I say, trying to keep my voice from shaking. "You're both strangers to me."

"I can't believe how selfish and ungrateful you are," Baba says, his expression ripe with disgust. "How could we raise someone so unfeeling, so *evil*? To turn your back on your family? To leave us out in the cold?"

"Family doesn't treat each other like this," I say, shaking my head. "The way you talk to me, the way you act around me, that's not—that's not *right*. You treated me like a show pony, not your child."

"Do you hear yourself? You sound insane!" Ma says, and starts to stalk toward me. I scramble backward, reaching for the fire alarm. She falters, looking between my hand and my face. "You wouldn't."

"I would," I insist, though I don't know if it's true. "Don't come near me."

"Stop this childish nonsense at *once*, Sumaira," Baba orders. "Come over here and speak to us like the adult you claim to be."

"I don't want to," I say petulantly, even though I know it's only proving their point. "You can't control my life anymore. It's *mine*. I get to decide, not you."

"You miserable excuse of a child," Ma hisses, and I cower despite myself. "I wish I never gave birth to you."

My heart seems to stutter inside my chest. "Leave," I say hoarsely. "I want you to leave. *Now*."

"You think we don't know that Sanjana and Safina have been sneaking off to see you all these months?" Ma asks with a sneer. "Send us away, and you're sending them with us. I will not allow you to see my children if you refuse to acknowledge you're one of them."

Everything inside me comes to a standstill. "Excuse me?"

"If you don't want to be a part of this family, then you aren't part of this family," Baba says, eerily calm. "It's that simple."

Safi whimpers loudly, and my heartbeat is thunderous against my eardrums.

"When you come to your senses, you can see your sisters," Ma says, a cruel glint in her eyes. "And if I find out you've seen them without my permission, you will not like the consequences."

She grabs Jana by the back of her collar, pulling her toward the elevator, and my sister follows clumsily behind her. Baba picks Safi up, taking her away while she beats on his chest, giving me a desperate look over his shoulder.

I stand there, frozen in place by their words. They're *threatening* me? They're using my sisters as *leverage*?

I raise a hand to my mouth, pressing my fingers hard against my lips to keep from throwing up all over the floor.

I close my eyes, willing the bile to climb back down my throat. I can't—I can't believe—

I pull my phone out of my bag, calling an Uber. I stumble down the stairs dizzily, and by the time I get outside, the car is already there. I don't say anything, sliding into the back seat and ignoring the flood of saliva in my mouth that makes me want to hurl.

"Barbie," I gasp into the receiver once I arrive at my destination. "Let me up. Please."

The door buzzes me in, and I waste no time making my way upstairs. By the time the elevator doors open, Barbie is standing in the doorway of her apartment, eyes wide.

"What happened?" she asks, and I fall into her arms without saying anything.

Barbie curses under her breath, pulling me inside and shutting the door behind me.

What little remains of my control shatters and I finally let myself burst into sobs.

It takes ages for me to calm down enough to explain the situation. Barbie rubs circles into my back and reminds me to breathe, and I try not to cry all over again.

"They can threaten you all they want, but it's not as if they're with Jana and Safi every second of the day," Barbie says, running a comforting hand down my hair. "Jana can always come see you after school. She can pick up Safi on her way. Your parents don't have to know."

I shake my head. "No, they'll—they'll start picking up the girls from school if they have to. They're serious about this, I can tell."

"We'll find a way to get around that," Barbie insists.

I bury my face in one of her couch pillows. "It's not that easy. You know how controlling they are, Babs. If they put their mind to it, they—" I try to ignore the nausea swirling in my stomach. "Ma and Baba were so focused on me before, but now . . . This is all my fault."

"It's not your fault," Barbie says sharply. "Your parents are being shitty. That's out of your control."

"It's not though. They're going to punish my sisters because of my mistakes," I whimper. "I should've never changed managers. What was I thinking? I was being selfish. I should've known it would come back to bite me in the ass."

"Summer," Barbie says firmly, pulling the pillow away from me. "Look me in the eyes. It's *not* selfish to want control over your own life."

"It is selfish to leave my sisters alone in that house with them," I insist, and feel worse and worse by the minute. I should've thought this through better. I should've been more vigilant, more aware.

"Come on, Summer," Barbie says, lightly hitting me with the pillow. "I'm proud of you. No, I'm being serious. You stood up to them and that takes so much courage. I know how hard this is for you and

I know you're worried about your sisters, but you can't backtrack on this. We talked about this before. If you give them an inch—"

I shake my head stubbornly. "That was before they banned me from seeing my sisters. I'm so fucking stupid, Babs."

"Why are you stupid?" Barbie demands, looking close to shaking me. "Summer, they can only control your sisters to a certain degree. Hell, we'll hire family lawyers if we need to, but you *can't* let them win."

"I can't hire family *lawyers*," I say, aghast. "Can you imagine what the media would say?"

"Fuck the media," she says, exasperated. "You love your sisters, don't you?"

"What the fuck kind of question is that? Of course I do. You know I do."

"Then you have to know that the best thing you can do to protect them is stay away from your parents," Barbie says, whacking me with a pillow again. "You have to lead by example."

"Barbie," I say. "I can't do this."

This time the pillow hits me in the face.

"Stop that," I say, snatching it from her, but she only grabs another couch pillow and raises a threatening eyebrow.

"Do you want me to call Zach?" she asks. "I'll bring him in for reinforcement. How would you feel knowing you pulled him out of what's probably an extremely important recording session?"

I scowl at her. "You're a horrible person."

"It keeps me awake at night, it really does," is Barbie's dry response before she finally tosses both pillows aside. "Listen, I think you need to sleep on this. You can't make any rash decisions. I know you're worried about your sisters, but you have to think about yourself, too, okay? I love you and I want you to be okay."

"I don't know if I'll ever be okay," I say quietly.

Barbie pulls me into a hug, resting her chin on my shoulder. "You will be. I promise."

## CHAPTER TWENTY-NINE

## JULES MORADI AND SUMMER ALI CEMENT THEIR STATUS AS HOLLYWOOD'S NEW A-LIST POWER COUPLE AS THEY MAKE THEIR GOTHAM AWARDS DEBUT

I forget that Jules and I are supposed to attend the Gotham Awards until he sends me a picture of his outfit with a text that says, **wanna go to prom with me?**

Despite the fact everything else is falling apart, this makes me smile. He's been good about cheering me up the last few weeks, ever since I gave him a brief rundown over the phone about what happened with my parents.

**only if you get me a corsage**, I send back.

He replies with a salute emoji, and I sit back in my chair, looking around the recording studio. I've been spending more and more time in here, unable to stomach being in my apartment for too long. It feels so much emptier without my sisters popping in and out of it.

On Halloween, Jana sent me pictures of Safi's Rapunzel costume using a burner account on Instagram, and I nearly cried. I miss them more than I thought physically possible.

Thankfully Jana's been doing her best to update me, taking every precaution in case Ma and Baba check her phone. So far, it's been all right—not great, but all right. I was right that my parents would be much more controlling about both my sisters' schedules now, leaving no room for gaps when they could sneak off to see me.

I tell her to keep me updated if it gets really bad, and Jana promises she will. Safi uses her iPad to FaceTime me in secret and then deletes her call logs as soon as she's done. I feel awful making my little sisters sneak around like this, but I don't know what other option I have right now.

I pick up my pen, absently clicking it as I stare down at my journal. It's the first time I've written a song about my family, and it feels wrong to put something so personal on the page, but a part of me is relieved at letting it loose somewhere outside my mind.

"Not a Home" is the tentative title, and I find myself drawing tiny houses in the margins of the page as I try to come up with the next line.

On the page before this is another song, one that I'm afraid to look at too closely, all too aware of the *she* and *her* pronouns in it. It blurs the line between wanting to *be* the other girl and wanting to be *with* the other girl, and it feels like stripping down to my most naked self.

It'll never make it into the album. Not if I want any kind of peace of mind. I can't imagine how my parents would react, and how it would affect my sisters. I never thought my sexuality would have any impact on them, but I'm starting to realize *everything* I do has a ripple effect.

I drop my head to the desk and resist the urge to start banging it against the wood.

Even when I finally overcome my writer's block, there's another hurdle to jump over. Why is everything so *hard*?

Despite my text, I'm still surprised when Jules shows up in front of my apartment building with a beautiful red corsage that matches the strapless dress Versace sent for me to wear to the award show.

"You didn't have to," I say, but I can't hide my genuine delight as I hold out my wrist.

He slips it on, his fingers gentle. "Of course I did. Did you ever get to have a prom?"

I shake my head. "Homeschooled."

Jules gives me a rueful smile. "Me too. So I thought we should have a little fun with it. God knows these award shows can get tiring as it is. At least you guys get performances at yours."

I raise my brows as I follow him into the limo. "No one's gonna perform? How do you pass the time?"

"Exactly," he says grimly.

"Well, misery loves company," I say, patting his leg and settling back into my seat.

Jules glances at me at those words. "How are you holding up?"

We haven't been seeing each other as often lately. Jules' schedule has been jam-packed with movie promotions, though we've made a point to have dinner at least once a week, and Ariana sends us on a pap walk every now and then. He hasn't pushed for more details about the situation with my parents, despite the fact that I can tell he's been curious about it—but I don't want to add more to his plate. He's busy as it is.

"I've been better," I admit. "But the girls say they're all right."

He nods, reaching for my hand. I let him, taking comfort in the way his thumb brushes along my knuckles. "Do you miss them a lot?"

"More than anything," I say quietly before shaking my head. "I don't wanna be sad tonight. Let's talk about something else. How is movie promo going?"

Jules frowns for a moment, but then relents. "They sent me to *Hot Ones*. I almost died, Summer. I knew it was going to be spicy, but my mouth was actually on *fire*."

A genuine smile blooms to life on my face as I imagine him choking on the chicken wings. "Did you make it to the end?"

"I did, but at what cost," he says mournfully. "I don't think I can eat wings again for a year."

"How ever will you live?" I ask dryly.

"This may very well be the end," he agrees seriously, before nudging my foot with his. "How's songwriting going? Your deadline is soon, right?"

"I got a small extension, but it's due in the next two weeks," I say with a wince. "I have to send them a tentative track list with lyrics attached so they can approve it before I start recording."

He hums. "Are you near done?"

"I mean, I have twenty-five songs written so far," I hedge. "But I'm not confident about over half of them."

"I don't know shit about songwriting, but can't you have Barbie or Zach look it over? Or one of your producers?"

"I could, but do I *want* to?"

Jules raises an eyebrow at me. "All right. What about the song for the movie soundtrack?"

"Oh, I already turned that in," I say, waving a dismissive hand.

His mouth falls open. "*What?* Why didn't you tell me?"

"It's a surprise," I say sweetly. "Like how you didn't tell me what the movie was about for . . . eight months?"

"Oh, you're evil," he says, but there's delight underlining his words. "When did you get this evil?"

"I learned from my fake boyfriend," I say, and mimic shooting him.

Like the actor he is, he immediately slumps against the seat, holding a hand to his chest and gasping for breath. "How could you?"

I roll my eyes and shove him lightly. He shoves me back and then settles for holding my hand again. Can he tell I'm slightly nervous? Lately, he's been initiating physical contact more and more often. I try not to let on how much I've genuinely grown attached to it, but it's more natural to be touching him than not nowadays.

A chill runs down my spine at the thought I might lose this one of these days, whenever this PR stunt runs its course. I have no idea when that'll be—when the movie debuts? When Jules wins his Oscar? When Jules lands his next role?

I push the thought away and focus on the feeling of his rings pressing into the spaces between my fingers instead. There's never a time or place for thoughts like these, but right now *really* isn't the time or place.

It's actually bizarre how different film and TV award shows are from music award shows. I try not to feel intimidated by the lack of fans inside the venue. Everywhere I look, there are either celebrities or film critics and reporters. There's nothing to distract from the fact that we're *famous* and we're being perceived, and I have no idea how Jules deals with this regularly.

Slowly but surely, the tension in my body begins to grow,

until I'm as taut as a bowstring.

"I can't sit next to these people and be normal," I hiss to Jules when I see the rest of the people assigned to the table. They're A-listers that I have no business *breathing* around.

"Summer, you're literally famous," he whispers to me.

"Not *this* famous," I say back urgently. "What if I hide in the bathroom?"

"You can't hide in the bathroom," he says, pulling me toward the table even though I drag my feet. "Come on, it'll be okay. I'll field any questions."

"Oh my God, you're going to *speak* to these people?" I ask.

Jules shakes his head at me before leaning in to press a kiss to my temple. "I've got you. Do you trust me?"

My bottom lip juts out stubbornly even as I nod. "Yes."

"Then believe me when I say I'll take care of everything," he says quietly. "I'm right here with you."

"If I see Ryan Reynolds, I *will* pass out," I warn him, but ease up on my grip, allowing him to lead me to our designated table.

"Baby, if *I* see Ryan Reynolds, I'll pass out," he says as we take our seats, already turning a smile on the rest of the table. "Hey! It's been too long. How are you?"

I leave him to his greetings, too busy blinking to myself at the endearment *baby*. Where did that come from? I've heard *darling* countless times and *princess* once or twice, but this is a first.

"This is my girlfriend, Summer," Jules says, drawing me back into the conversation. I give everyone a shy smile and wave, hoping I don't look too much like a lovestruck fool.

I can't ask him about the pet name in front of all of these people, but even if I could, I don't know what I'd say. Would he even have an answer? Do I want to *know* his answer?

Before I can spiral too much, Jules' hand settles on my thigh, squeezing lightly. I blow out a breath and let the touch center me, turning my attention forward as more and more people filter into the room, taking their seats.

*Right as Rain* doesn't release for another week, so it isn't nominated for any of the categories, but *Bumblebees* is. Jules played a side character and is up for Outstanding Supporting Performance. He doesn't seem too worried about whether he'll win—he said he's proud of his contribution either way—but *I* want him to win. Knowing how hard Jules works and how much talent he has, I want every single accolade in the world for him.

All of a sudden, Jules' entire body goes stiff beside me, his fingers clenching against my skin. I immediately follow his gaze, and swallow back a gasp when I see a red-haired boy settling into a chair on the opposite side of the room. Alex Robinson.

Fuck.

I didn't even think about the fact that Jules might have to see him here. Have they seen each other since everything fell apart between them? Surely they must have if they both regularly attend events like this. Is he nominated for the same award as Jules tonight? God, I hope not.

I reach down, placing my hand on top of Jules'. His grip loosens on my thigh, but he doesn't stop looking at Alex, vaguely horrified.

"Hey," I whisper. "Jules."

It takes a moment, but Jules eventually turns his head to meet my gaze. "What?"

"Don't let him get to you," I say, quiet but firm. "Anytime you want to look at him, look at me instead."

Jules' mouth twitches in the corner, but he nods. "All right."

It's a lot easier said than done. Over the next four hours, Jules' head keeps minutely turning in Alex's direction before he pointedly makes himself look at me instead. I've taken to making silly faces to distract him and praying that I don't get caught on camera being ridiculous. Even if I did though, it would be worth it for the small smiles Jules manages to give me.

It's the first time I've seen Jules so unsettled, as if he might vibrate out of his skin at any moment. It's not quite anxiety so much as it is tension, coiled and waiting to spring.

On my end, I do my best not to glare at Alex too much. I don't want to give Jules any reason to turn his attention in that direction, but it's hard not to scowl every time his red hair enters the edge of my vision. He doesn't deserve to sit there and make small talk and laugh alongside some of the most talented actors in the industry after what he did to Jules. I want to tattoo the word *TRAITOR* across his forehead, so everyone who comes across him knows to turn and run in the other direction.

I start counting down the minutes until the award ceremony is over and the two of us can leave, freeing ourselves from this awful situation.

I nearly forget the reason we're even here until the Outstanding Supporting Performance nominations are flashing across the screen, including *Jules Moradi as Demetrius King in* Bumblebees.

I clutch Jules' arm with both hands, anxiously waiting for the actor presenting the award to say the winner's name.

"Jules Moradi!" he says after pulling an index card out of a golden envelope.

My mouth falls open. "Jules! That's you!"

Jules looks startled, turning left and right to look for his cast members as if he can't believe it.

"Congratulations," I say brightly, throwing my arms around him. He catches me, staggering a little before he laughs incredulously in my ear.

There are a dozen cameras on us and it gives me the courage I need to turn my head and press my mouth against his for one second, two seconds, three seconds, before pulling away.

He looks at me with wide eyes but there's a grin stretching across his face. "I—"

"Jules!" one of his cast members says, reaching out to grab his arm. "Come on!"

"Coming," he says, and gives my waist one last squeeze before hurrying to go up onstage, cast members left and right pulling him into hugs as he goes.

I sit back in my seat, clutching my hands to my chest in absolute pride and excitement.

"Wow," Jules says, and he takes the award, looking down at it with his jaw dropped open. "I wasn't expecting . . ." He huffs out a breathless sort of laugh. "Every time I win an award, I feel like I must be dreaming. I'd say pinch me, but I wouldn't believe it even then. Thank you so much for this award. Thank you to Maheen Rassell for giving me the opportunity to be in this movie, thank you to all the cast and crew for everything, I'm so honored to be surrounded by all your talent, thank you. Ariana, Penny, Yuri, Jacob, Ayesha, I wouldn't be here without any of you. Thank you to my family for always supporting my dreams. Especially my sister, Laila, who insists on watching the first cut of every film I'm in. Thank you to my best friend, Raj, for rooting for me, even when I struggle to root for myself." When Jules' gaze turns to me, I don't expect it. My breath catches as he says, "Thank you to my girlfriend, for standing by my side." He looks back around the room, beaming. "I'm grateful beyond words. I don't know if I'm the type of person who deserves an honor like this, but I'm going to spend the rest of my life trying to be."

My eyes prickle with tears, and I dab a napkin lightly at my waterline. He deserves this and so much more. Knowing how hard the people around him tried to box him in, seeing him break out like this sets a fire alight in my soul.

Jules files off the stage, clutching the award with a dazed look on his face. Someone takes it from him off-camera—if this is anything like music award shows, they'll inscribe it and give it to him later. When Jules comes back to the table, the people around us shower him with praise and congratulations, which he accepts with a gracious smile.

He finally turns to me and he looks almost surprised. "Have you been crying?"

I wrinkle my nose. "Did I ruin my makeup?"

"What *happened*?" he asks, immediately scanning our surroundings for clues.

I lightly hit him. "*You* happened. I'm so proud of you, I feel like I could burst."

His lips part. "You're crying because of me?"

"Of course I am, silly," I say, and sniffle for dramatic effect. "No one deserves this more than you."

"I can think of one person," someone mutters behind me.

I swivel in my seat and my eyes narrow at the sight of Alex standing there, a thin smile on his face.

Jules pales. "What are you doing here?"

"I wanted to congratulate you, of course," Alex says, louder this time. Most of the people around us have turned back to the stage as Outstanding Lead Performance is announced, but one or two onlookers smile at us, like Alex congratulating his childhood best friend is a heartwarming sight. There are a few people watching the interaction with sharp eyes, though, and I wonder if they've heard about Alex's horrendous behavior—and are they on Alex's side or Jules'?

"Thank you," Jules says blankly.

Alex opens his arms, as if waiting for an embrace. I resist the urge to stand up and punch him in the face.

"You don't have to—" I start to whisper, but Jules is slowly standing up anyway, leaning over to hug Alex.

Even though I'm right next to them, I can't hear what Alex whispers into Jules' ear, but whatever it is makes Jules' entire expression go flat. He lets go of Alex immediately and sits back down in his seat, turning to face forward.

I look back at Alex to see a smug smile on his face before he turns on his heel and heads back to his own table.

"What did he say?" I ask sharply.

Jules shakes his head, gaze lowering to the table. So it's not something he's willing to repeat. I grind my teeth, glaring after Alex's back.

"You know what?" I say. "No."

I start to stand but Jules immediately grabs my hand, pulling me back into the seat. I blink in surprise, looking down at the fingers wrapped around my wrist.

"Don't," he whispers. "We're going to look like the aggressors.

You know how they stereotype us. He's going to walk away from this without a scratch, but we won't."

I sit down, but my anger only grows tenfold and I have to clench my hands at my sides to keep from throwing something at Alex's head.

It's not fair. It's not fair that Jules can win an award and Alex can undo all of his happiness with a single sentence. It's not *fair*.

The rest of the award show passes by without incident, not for lack of trying, since I glare at the back of Alex's head like it might catch on fire if I stare hard enough.

As soon as the cameras stop rolling, Jules places a hand on the small of my back and escorts me out without meeting anyone's gaze. My jaw clenches at how uncomfortable he looks as he tries to maneuver us out of the room without running into that imbecile again.

It's not *fair*.

Jules doesn't look like he takes a single breath until we're sitting in a limo, finally on our way out. Only then does he let his head drop, his dark hair falling forward as he places his hands on his face, hiding his expression from view.

"I want a hug," I say, because it's the only way I know how to bring Jules back.

He looks up at me, face crumpled, but opens his arms anyway. I slip myself into them, then squeeze him as tightly as I can.

The world narrows down to just the two of us. Jules' fingers flex against my back, crumpling the fabric of my dress.

"What did he say?" I ask softly.

Jules buries his face in my neck and mumbles something.

I run my fingers through his hair, holding him close. "I can't hear you, sweetheart."

He moves back slightly, his nose still brushing my collarbone, then says, slightly clearer, "That at the end of the day, I'm a second-rate actor who relies on pity votes and nothing I ever do will make me deserving of this award."

A wave of fury rushes over me and I shove it down inch by inch. Jules sounds so miserable, every word aching inside of me like a throbbing bruise, but my anger isn't going to fix anything here.

"He's wrong," I say, squeezing the back of Jules' neck. "He doesn't know anything."

"He's known me for my entire career," Jules whispers.

"Well, he doesn't know you anymore," I say. "And it's obvious he's clouded by jealousy. He thinks he's entitled to your success, but he's not. Please don't listen to him."

"I can't—I don't know how to let go of him," Jules says in an awful voice.

And suddenly, I feel so hopeless. I'm so tired of sitting by and watching the people I care about suffer at the hands of other people. All I want is to be able to protect them from all this bullshit, and I *can't*. It's out of my hands.

"I'm so sorry he said that to you," I murmur. "But please don't let him ruin your night. You won this award, fair and square. He can say whatever he wants, but it doesn't change the fact that so many people believe you're talented and believe you deserve this, including me."

Jules sighs against my skin. "Your confidence in me is unearned."

"No, it's not," I say, lightly smacking the back of his head. "I'm never wrong, Jules. Name one time I've been wrong."

He leans back and opens his mouth to speak, but I raise an eyebrow. "Consider your answer very carefully."

When he smiles, small but *there*, I feel some relief chip away at the weight on my shoulders. "You're never wrong, darling." Then he pauses, looking at me with a clearer gaze. "You called me sweetheart before."

"Well, you called me baby before," I say instinctively, though I regret it a moment later, a flush climbing up my throat into my cheeks.

I wait, hoping Jules will take the joke route and write this entire exchange off, but instead, he keeps staring at me, something strange in his gaze.

"Summer," he says carefully, "do you want to end our PR stunt?"

I startle at the words. "What? No. Why would you assume—?"

He shakes his head. "I'm not assuming anything. I'm asking you, because I know how much I'm asking of you, and you have enough on your plate, and I . . . I don't deserve your kindness."

"Oh my God, shut up," I say, settling back in my seat now, crossing my arms. My heart is beating a little too fast, but I'm determined to ignore it. I didn't realize until this very moment how much I *don't* want our PR stunt to ever end, but I can hardly say that. "You don't get to decide that. Anyway, I don't give up on things halfway to the finish line. I'm seeing this through until the end, as long as you are."

Jules watches me with hooded eyes and then nods. "All right," he says, but his voice is much, much quieter than before. "As you wish."

We don't talk for the rest of the drive home.

## CHAPTER THIRTY

## CHILDHOOD BEST FRIENDS JULES MORADI AND ALEX ROBINSON REUNITE AT GOTHAM AWARDS AFTER JULES WINS OUTSTANDING SUPPORTING PERFORMANCE

I'm in the middle of tweaking the lyrics to the bridge of a song when my doorbell rings. I accidentally draw a line across the page, and I let out a groan, setting down my pencil.

It's been days of me hacking away at this song. It's the last one I'm stuck on, debating back and forth on whether to even include it on the album.

My eyes fall on the words *she* and *her* before I shut my journal and reluctantly get to my feet, wondering who it could be. I check the peephole first, wary now that my parents know my address, but Jules is on the other side, holding up a brown paper bag of takeout as if he knew I would check to see who was out there.

I open the door, lifting my brows. "Do we have plans I forgot about?"

"No, but I need your help," he says, and then hands me the paper bag, brushing past me to get inside my apartment.

I roll my eyes and follow after him. "Help with what?"

Instead of answering, he sets up camp on my living room floor, swinging his bag off his shoulder and unzipping it to take out five bound copies of . . . what?

I crouch beside him, glancing at the front page of the one closest to me. *Daydream*.

"Are these scripts?" I ask.

Jules nods, leaning back against the side of the couch. "I need your help choosing my next project."

I blink once, then twice. *"Me?"*

"I trust your opinion," he says simply before grabbing one of the scripts. "Ariana sent these over to me. Two of them are requests directly from the directors, and the other three are projects she thinks I'd be a good fit for. I'm not sure which one fits the direction I want to go in, so I thought I'd bribe you with Chinese food to help me. I don't have to decide for a few weeks, but I wanted to get a head start."

"You don't need to bribe me," I say, but my brain is on autopilot from shock. It seems unfathomable that Jules would come to me—or anyone—for help with his career when he detests having other people dictate what he can or cannot be. "Jules, I have no idea how to help you."

"Read through them," he says, handing me one. "Let me know your thoughts, and then we can talk through the pros and cons of doing each one. There weren't really any Iranian-specific roles when I went looking, since Hollywood isn't really looking for our stories, but . . . I asked Ariana to make sure all of *these* roles would allow me to play my own ethnicity anyway, rather than pretend to be white."

I sit back, a little stunned. "Really?"

"Yeah," he says with a small smile. "So you have to help me, all right?"

I take the script slowly, trying to communicate with my gaze that I'm hardly the right person to help him. But he only gives me a challenging look in return as he reaches for the takeout bag, pulling out a carton of lo mein.

I shake my head, a smile playing at my lips. "Pass the chopsticks," I say, and he does with a smug grin on his face.

Hours later, I'm flipping through the last script in my pile while Jules does the same, half lying in my lap as he skims over the words. My phone starts ringing, jarring both of us.

I glance at it, and then raise my brows when I see who it is. "Let me up, I gotta take this. It's Zach."

Jules nods, shifting to the side so I can stand and stretch my limbs out. "Take your time."

I slide my thumb across the screen, accepting the call as I step out onto the balcony, nearly running into my strawberry plant. "Hey, what's up?"

"Do you have a minute?" Zach asks, his voice quieter than usual.

"Of course," I say. "Is something wrong?"

He sighs heavily, and I immediately wish I could give him a hug. "I'm in Seattle and I'm . . . I'm with the guy I've been seeing. He's asleep upstairs and I needed to talk to someone because I—I don't know what to do."

My brows rise further up my forehead as I lean against the railing. "About what?"

"He's not like us," Zach says, though that's hardly an answer to my question. "He's normal, Summer. He's going to college, studying computer science, and I'm . . ."

"Zachary, I love you so much, but I need you to spit it out," I say as gently as possible.

"I don't know whether to go public with our relationship," he says in one quick swoop, and my breath catches. "He's out to his friends and family, but it's not the same. You know it's not the same. I'd be opening him up to public scrutiny, and I know first-hand how cruel people can be, and I don't—I don't know. At the same time, I hate that he has to sit by and watch me deny the truth of our relationship. I don't want him to think I'm hiding him away or that I'm embarrassed of him, but I'm worried that if I tell everyone the truth, he'll have to deal with a lot worse."

"Jesus, Zach," I say, rubbing my forehead. "I've told you a million times, but you're one of the bravest people I know. This is a shit position to be in. I don't have the answer for what you should do one way or the other, but I think the first thing is probably to talk to your boyfriend. I know you're scared of him dealing with bullshit from the media and the public, but I don't think you can decide for him whether or not he's equipped to deal with it. You have to let him have a say in it too."

"He's going to say it'll be fine," Zach says wearily. "But he doesn't know how bad it can be. I just—I want to protect him, but I don't want to keep hurting him, either."

"You have to talk to him," I say quietly. "You can't make decisions for the both of you. You know that, otherwise you wouldn't have called me."

"Maybe I was hoping you'd offer to airlift me out of here and take me to a remote cabin in the woods where we could raise alpacas together," he says. "Barbie can visit once a year."

"First of all, I would *never* live in the wilderness," I say. "I'm a city girl through and through."

"I know, but it was worth a try." Zach sighs. "Okay, I'll talk to him."

"*Good*," I say. "I'm proud of you."

"You'd like Alejandro," he says quietly. "He's as stubborn as you are."

"Sounds like we'll be best friends in no time," I agree. "Maybe I'll meet him sometime soon?"

"Yeah, I hope so." A long beat of silence. "Have you given any more thought to coming out?"

I wince, thinking about the song I was working on earlier. "I was hoping you wouldn't ask me that."

"So yes and no, I take it?"

"That sounds about right." I run a hand through my hair, suddenly antsy. "I—I wish I were as brave as you. I really do. But every time I think about it, I feel like a live wire. I keep thinking about how if my parents were still my managers, I wouldn't even be considering it."

"But they're *not* your managers," he says. "You left them for a reason."

"I know. But that doesn't make it any easier."

Zach makes a low noise on the other end of the line. "I don't think you give yourself enough credit. You left your abusive parents behind in favor of making a new path for yourself. You don't think that's brave as hell?"

"I don't know about all that. I'm still sitting here, letting them inadvertently decide what I do or don't do, and I don't know how to stop. I just—how are you supposed to know if you're ready?" I ask

Zach, picking at a loose string in my sweater.

"You'll just know," he says, voice gentle. "There isn't one specific thing that decides it either way. But I think the fact that you're asking me this means you're closer to being ready than you think, Summer."

My shoulders tense. "Yeah, well."

"Yeah, well. I love you, okay? I hope you know I called you about this and not anyone else in the world for a reason."

I press my lips together and nod even though I know he can't see me. "I love you too."

Zach says his goodbyes, and once I hang up the phone, I sit down beside my strawberry plant and watch the stars, convincing myself to breathe.

That's how Jules finds me. He's clearly more prepared than I am because when he sits down next to me, he offers half a blanket for me to burrow into.

"Is everything all right with Zach? Are you okay?" he asks, eyes clouded with concern.

I press against his side, happy to find that Jules is very warm. "Yeah, he's okay. Or he will be," I say vaguely. "And I'm fine, just thinking."

"About what?" Jules asks, resting his hand on my thigh. It's obvious that he's doing it to steady me, to anchor me. I wonder when he became able to pick up on all of my strange moods.

Instead of answering, I look back up at the sky. "Do you ever think about what life would be like if you hadn't done that one thing? If you could, would you change that thing?"

Jules doesn't reply for a long time, and when I look over, it's obvious he's in deep thought, clearly giving the question importance.

"I think . . ." Jules says, his gaze focused somewhere above the Manhattan skyline. "I think there are infinite universes and for every decision you never made, another universe was created. A universe where you did make that decision. And maybe it's a small decision like forgetting a pencil at school or a huge decision like getting married, but for each decision no matter how big or small there's another universe. Every decision you've ever made is what led you to this point in life. They're what made you who you are. I think that no one should ever regret who they are. So, no, I wouldn't change anything."

I stare at him, a little stunned by the sincerity of his answer. Then I shake my head, clearing my thoughts a little. "What if it was for the better?"

Jules shrugs, nonplussed. "No, not even then. We shouldn't focus on things in the past. If we want things to be better, we should work on changing things in the future. It's the decisions we make now that matter."

We're both quiet for a while before I break the silence. "Do you think the stars are universes?"

In response, Jules smiles. "Let's catch the stars and find out."

I don't know if it's the words themselves or the warmth in his voice when he says them or the way he looks at me, like the stars already exist in my eyes, but suddenly, all at once, I realize I'm in love with him.

"Oh," I breathe.

"What?" he asks.

I could answer. I could tell him the truth. *Oh*, I think. *Oh no.*

"What I was saying before," I say instead, lowering to a whisper to hide the tremble in my voice. "I was thinking about my parents.

Do you think there's a universe where I did everything right and my parents love me unconditionally?"

"What does doing everything right mean, though?" he asks, equally hushed. "Does it mean giving up who you are? Your core values?"

"I don't know," I say, though I do. The question we're skirting around is *what if I was straight?* "I feel like I don't know who I am without them."

"I do," Jules says easily.

I laugh half-heartedly. "Oh? Who am I?"

He shakes his head. "I can't tell you that, Summer. It doesn't mean anything coming from me."

I sigh, setting my chin on my folded arms. "Do you ever feel like we're playing an endless game of pretend? The person they talk about in the media . . . that's not us. The person I am in front of my fans . . . that's not me. Even the person I am in my songs isn't really me. So what's real? What's fake?"

It's a little too close to addressing the elephant in the room, our PR stunt, but I purposefully refrain from saying anything about it.

Jules exhales a cold puff of air. "I get it. Sometimes I wish I could just be a normal person and that I had a regular childhood instead of . . . whatever this media circus is. I don't have an easy answer."

"I think I'd have these problems even if I weren't famous," I say, feeling the weight of the words as I say them. "Maybe good things aren't in the cards for me. Maybe I'll never have peace."

"You don't believe that," Jules whispers. "You can't believe that."

"I don't know what to believe," I admit. "There's no handbook on how to get a happy ending."

Jules reaches over, brushing a thumb over my cheekbone. "No, but . . ." Then he pauses, seems to consider his words, and changes the direction of the conversation. "I meant what I said earlier, about not wanting to change who I am. I might want to be normal sometimes, but I would still choose this life every time. If there are alternate universes though, I hope I meet you in every single one. Even if we're regular kids who never set foot on a film set or a stage, I want you there with me. The same way I know who you are, you know who *I* am, and that means something, don't you think?"

I nod slowly. "Yeah. We see each other past all the bullshit."

"Exactly," he says, before turning my chin toward the sky with a gentle nudge. "Pick a universe and make a wish. Maybe it'll come true."

I consider the sky before pointing at one of the few stars visible, all the way at the edge of my vision. "That one."

Jules nods and closes his eyes, holding his hands to his chest as he makes his wish. I do the same, shutting my eyes and trying to settle on the one wish that might make things okay.

*I wish for happiness*, I tell the stars, *in whatever form it might be.*

And then I blow out a breath and hope for the best.

# CHAPTER THIRTY-ONE

## "RIGHT AS RAIN" REVIEW: ANGELINA RODRIGUEZ AND JULES MORADI'S LOVE DEFINES HOME AND LETTING GO

I'm surprised to see Ariana in the car when I finally climb inside, grabbing a handful of my dress so I don't trip over it. A team of stylists frets behind me and I wave them off before pulling the car door shut. I finally turn to my manager with a raised eyebrow. "I didn't know you were coming!"

"I've spent a *year* working to make this film premiere happen successfully," Ariana reminds me, leaning over to shift my necklace so the *J* settles nicely between my collarbones. "As if I'd miss it. I was on the first flight out to LA this morning."

I snort, adjusting my dress. It's an off-the-shoulder black piece with a cinched waist that Versace sent over last week with an official letter asking me to be one of their global ambassadors. Barbie and I popped cheap champagne bottles in celebration, and then got so drunk that we both fell asleep in my living room.

I try to imagine what the celebration would have been like if I were still living with my parents—and then realize there would be nothing to celebrate, because my parents never let me work with fashion brands, in fear they might ask me to wear something they deemed inappropriate.

Ariana must see me admiring the dress because she grins at me. "We'll work on a jewelry ambassadorship next," she says, touching my necklace again. "You won't need to wear this much longer."

My entire body goes still. "What do you mean?"

"Well, Oscar shortlist goes live in two weeks," she says, glancing back at her phone and tapping something out. "And the award show is in the early spring."

"So?" I ask.

"So after that you're a free bird," Ariana says, like it's obvious. "Honestly, maybe even before that. Ideally 'Show Me' will get nominated for Best Original Song, but if it doesn't, then I'm sure Jules would understand if you want to end the stunt early. It *would* be nice for you two to attend the Oscars together, if you're willing to hold out that long. But after that, we can release a press statement saying you both amicably parted ways."

I stare at her, the words going in one ear and out the other, because I can't fathom what she's saying to me. "So, what? In a few weeks, this is all over?"

Ariana nods. "Exactly. Not too long now," she says, offering me a comforting smile that does little to soothe me. "I was actually thinking we could add a few songs to the track list for your second album before it all gets finalized. Do you think you could make up something about Jules? Obviously, we don't want anything that'll damage his reputation, but something that would allude to him could be great to keep the momentum of the stunt going after the fact."

"Make up something about Jules," I say blankly.

Ariana continues tapping on her phone, not looking up at me. "Didn't you say most of your songs are fictionalized? This shouldn't be too hard, right?"

"Right," I say, and the word feels rotten in my mouth.

When we arrive at the film premiere for *Right as Rain*, I forcibly shove the entire conversation with Ariana out of my head and put on the brightest smile I can manage. I'm not going to ruin Jules' big day because my feelings are too big for me to contain in my chest.

Jules is already farther down the red carpet, taking photos with the rest of the cast members. My breath catches when I see him, my eyes going past the lapels of his black suit to the silk shirt underneath, the neckline so deep that it nearly reaches his abdomen.

Everything else seems to blur, with Jules as the only thing in focus, before Ariana lightly taps my arm. I turn to her, blinking in confusion, and she gestures for me to walk ahead of her, onto the red carpet.

I nod, making sure my smile is still in place before moving forward, Ariana two paces behind me. The lights of the cameras are blinding, but I've grown mostly used to them. At the start of my career, I'd blink constantly, and my parents would yell at me for ruining all my press photos.

What I'm less prepared for is an interviewer approaching me the moment I step to the side, away from the camera crew.

"Hello, Summer!" she greets me, eyes bright. "I'm Daphne from the *Hollywood Reporter*. Are you okay to do an interview?"

I glance questioningly at Ariana, who nods, reaching forward to fix the front strands of my hair before stepping back.

"Go for it," I say to the interviewer, and try not to visibly brace myself for what's going to be asked. So far, I've managed to avoid directly answering any questions about Jules, since I haven't done a press run aside from the one I did before tour. Ariana had blacklisted questions about Jules back then, to allow for mystery and intrigue.

I don't think the same thing is going to apply at Jules' movie premiere, but I hope Ariana is able to make them cut anything embarrassing that might slip out.

"First of all, congratulations! We heard you wrote an original song for *Right as Rain*? What was that like?"

Okay, easy enough.

"It was really fun," I say as I smile into the camera. "I've never written for a movie soundtrack before, so it was definitely a unique experience. Honestly, though, as soon as I finished watching the movie, there were already lyrics in my mind. The themes of identity and finding your place in the world really spoke to me. The song's called 'Show Me' and it'll be out on all platforms Friday night once the movie releases in theaters. It was really, truly, genuinely an honor to write a song for *Right as Rain*, and I'm excited for everyone to hear it!"

The interviewer nods and flips to her next cue card, which makes me a little lightheaded. So she was *expecting* to interview me then.

"Can you share any of the lyrics with us?" she asks.

I nod. "Of course. Do you want me to sing them?"

"If you'd like!" Daphne says eagerly.

I clear my throat and sing quietly, *"And I'm standing here in the rain and I don't know what to do. I didn't know I could need someone the way that I need you."*

"Oh my God, that's gorgeous," she gushes. "I can't wait to hear the full thing."

I grin and duck my head a little bashfully. "Thank you."

Daphne returns the smile before flipping to her next card. "So your boyfriend, Jules Moradi, is the star of the film! Did he help at all with your creative process when writing the song?"

My heart races a little faster at Jules' name before quieting again when I realize it's a normal enough question. Maybe I'll get through this in one piece.

"He brought me a *lot* of food," I say with a laugh. "I tend to get into a writing cave when I'm working on music, so it was nice to have someone remind me to eat and drink water."

Daphne flips to the next question even faster. "How did the two of you meet? Was it because of the movie?"

My smile turns a little stiff as I shake my head. "No, we met through a mutual friend," I say, which is the lie we came up with ages ago on the off chance someone asked us.

"How long have you been together now?" she asks.

"About a year," I say, glancing at Ariana, but she doesn't seem bothered by the fact the questions have turned away from the movie and entirely toward my relationship with Jules.

"Do you think your relationship influenced the writing of 'Show Me'? Do you anticipate writing songs about Jules in the future?"

I force a polite laugh. This conversation is eerily reminiscent of the one I had in the car with Ariana, and it's making me antsy, unable to stand still. "No, 'Show Me' wasn't impacted by my relationship. As for future songs, who knows? I guess you'll have to listen to them and decide for yourself."

Daphne's gaze turns a little shrewd even as her smile remains wide. "What did you think of Jules' acting in the film?"

It's obvious she wants me to reveal something headline-worthy about Jules, but I don't know what to say that won't give away the true extent of my feelings.

"I thought he was fantastic," I say finally. "When Jules is on camera, he has complete command of the screen. I've never seen someone so passionate before. I'm frequently in awe of him, and I genuinely believe he's one of the most talented actors of our generation."

"Is his acting part of why you fell for him?" Daphne presses.

I look at Ariana again and she nods for me to go on, and I want to *scream*. This isn't a question I should be answering for an audience. This isn't something for the whole world.

Then my brain stops and restarts as I realize that's exactly what it is. What Jules and I have isn't a secret, isn't something for me to keep to myself. I can pretend he's mine, but at the end of the day, he doesn't belong to me any more than I belong to him.

I swallow past the lump in my throat. "Jules is the best person I know," I say. "Of course he's talented and ambitious and deserving of every accolade in the world, but that's not *why* I fell for him. Sure, it's part of it, but I don't think the world truly knows how kind and sweet Jules is or how hard he tries to be the best version of himself. I'm a better person just for knowing him. He always looks out for the people around him and lends them a shoulder for them to lean on if they need it. For a long period of time, I felt unbalanced, and no one's ever steadied me the way he does. I can't imagine knowing him and not falling for him. To know Jules is to love him."

The interviewer blinks at me, surprised, and I hand my microphone back to her. "Thank you for the interview," I say with a small bow, and walk away, my fingers curling into my palms almost painfully.

Ariana hurries after me, eyes wide. "Summer, what was that?"

"An answer," I say tightly. It was too much, too real, too *honest*. "I'd like to go inside the theater now."

She looks bewildered but nods, maneuvering our way inside the building, out of view of the cameras. Across the room, Jules sees me and waves with a wide smile that makes my knees weak for all the wrong reasons.

I wave back and then turn away, toward the wall. I force myself to take a deep breath, drawing my shoulders in, before releasing it.

I can't afford to break down in public like this. I'm a professional and this is a business arrangement.

More than that, tonight is about celebrating Jules and I refuse to ruin it with all my sticky feelings. For his sake, I have to pull it together.

When I turn back around, my smile is back in place like it never left, and my manager is looking at me like I've grown a second head, but that can't be helped.

# CHAPTER THIRTY-TWO

## SUMMER ALI REVEALS JULES MORADI "STEADIES" HER AND SHE FELT "UNBALANCED" BEFORE A MUTUAL FRIEND INTRODUCED THEM

I don't have a moment alone with Jules until he grabs my hand at the end of the premiere and says, "Come back to mine to celebrate?"

I nod and I'm whisked away into a car with him. He refuses to let the driver play anything but "Show Me" on repeat, even as I protest, my cheeks flushed.

"It's a masterpiece," he insists.

"You're ridiculous," I say, unable to hide my smile. "If it's a masterpiece, it's only because you set the standard impossibly high with your incredible acting."

"Don't start," he says, wagging a finger at me, I half-heartedly throw one of my heels at him and he dramatically dodges it.

Before I know it, we're pulling up to Jules' place in LA. I've been to his apartment in New York a few times—though we usually spend most of our time at mine—but I've never been here before, and I'm surprised to find that he lives in a large house that feels far too empty.

I'm reminded of him asking me what I'd do if I had one of my own, and turn the question on him when we get inside. "What do you do with all this space?"

"Alex and I used to throw parties," he says, before looking around with a wrinkled nose. "Obviously, that no longer happens."

I tilt my head. "Why don't you sell it?"

Jules shrugs, going to the kitchen and opening the fridge, digging around for some wine. I follow him, still taking in all the decor. Like his New York apartment, it's mostly minimalist, with a few pictures of his family hung here and there. The biggest difference is that in the living room, there are huge framed posters of different movies.

My eyes trace over the various titles. *Moonlight, Eternal Sunshine of the Spotless Mind, Dead Poets Society, Howl's Moving Castle, The Usual Suspects, I Saw the TV Glow, Black Swan, Memento, Get Out, Lady Bird, The Social Network, Pulp Fiction, Goodfellas, Everything Everywhere All at Once.* There are more, but I can't see that far from the kitchen.

"Why didn't you go to the after-party?" I ask after a moment, glancing back at Jules as he unscrews the cork on the wine bottle. "I overheard Angelina inviting you."

"You don't like crowds," he says offhandedly, and something splinters in my chest.

"It's your movie premiere," I say hopelessly.

He shakes his head, finally getting the bottle open and pouring us each a glass of red wine. "I wanted to celebrate with you." Then he makes a face and adds, "I heard Alex might be there too. I don't want him to ruin this for me."

My brows pull together. "You shouldn't let him take this experience from you, Jules. He's taken enough without—"

"It's okay," he says softly, handing me a glass. "Trust me, I'd rather be here with you anyway. Cheers?"

I sigh and clink my glass with his, tabling the conversation for another time. I hate the idea of Alex having this kind of hold on Jules so long after the fact, but maybe this isn't the night to get into it.

After one sip of the wine, I grimace and hand it back to him. "Do you have coffee?"

He gives me an amused look. "You want coffee at midnight?"

"I didn't realize red wine tastes so bitter," I say with a pout. "Do you have coffee or not?"

Jules chuckles and gestures to the coffee machine in the corner. "Help yourself."

I stick my tongue out before moving past him, our shoulders brushing.

By the time I finish making it, Jules has disappeared, and I scowl at the empty room. "This house is too big for me to hunt you down," I say loudly.

"I'm upstairs," comes Jules' voice, tinged with laughter. "First bedroom on the right!"

With a sigh, I trudge upstairs, taking care to hold my dress with the hand that's not holding the coffee so I don't trip.

When I enter his room, he holds out a pair of shorts and an oversized T-shirt. "I thought you might want to change," he says, eyes dropping to the way the fabric of the dress is bunched up in my fist.

"Oh, thank God," I say, immediately grabbing them from him. "Bathroom?"

He gestures down the hall and takes my coffee from me with an amused shake of his head. When I come back, he's dressed in his own pajamas, sitting on his bed, cross-legged.

I hang my dress on the back of his chair before joining him, grabbing my coffee off the bedside table and drinking half of it in one go.

He looks up at me with a warm smile. "Hi."

"Hi," I say. "How did you want to celebrate?"

"I want to listen to your song," he says, his eyes glittering so brightly that it's hard to look at him.

I groan, shoving at him uselessly. "We've listened to it like twenty times already."

"Not that one, though believe me when I say it's going to top my Spotify Wrapped next year," he says, squeezing my ankle. "I mean the one I've seen you working on the last few weeks. Don't say you don't know what I'm talking about, because I've *seen* you hide your journal every time I've looked your way this last month."

My mouth dries. "It's not ready."

"I don't care," he says without missing a beat. "I want to hear it."

I grimace. "It's bad right now."

"There's no way it's bad," he says with a dismissive flick of his hand. "Come on, what is it?"

I groan, burying my head in my hands. "Jules, don't make me do this."

He reaches forward, gently pulling my fingers away from my face one by one. "Why not?"

I sigh, sensing a losing battle. "I'm not going to sing it for you," I say, and kick him lightly when he goes to protest. "But I'll show you the lyrics. If you say you hate it though, I *will* lose my shit, so you need to know that ahead of time."

"As if I'd ever have a bad word to say about your work," he says, rolling his eyes. "Show me."

Reluctantly, I pull out my phone and open to the Notes app. "Here."

I bury my face in his pillows as soon as I hand it to him, not wanting to see his reaction. "Pink" isn't about anyone specific, but it *is* about me. About all the crushes I've had on girls in the past, littered with *she* and *her* pronouns, and the push-and-pull of different desires. Jealousy, heartache, yearning, and confusion.

When he's finished reading, I feel rather than see Jules lie down beside me. Gently, he starts running his hands through my hair, ruining the curls that my stylists spent so long coiling to perfection.

"Summer," he says.

"No," I say.

He sighs and keeps petting my hair. After several long minutes, I finally roll over to face him. "Do you hate it?"

"Why would I hate it?" he asks softly. "Of course I don't."

I bite my bottom lip. "Do you think it'll ruin my career?"

"No, I don't," he says, reaching out to brush a strand of hair off my forehead. "Is this your way of coming out?"

"I don't know. Do you think people will realize I'm . . . ?" I can't bring myself to say *pansexual* in the space between us, suddenly terrified of the word.

"I think some people might, yes," he says, watching me with careful eyes. "But are you asking about them or are you asking about your parents?"

I groan, burying my face in his shoulder. He sighs, pressing a kiss to the side of my head.

"Summer."

"No."

Again, long minutes of silence go by.

Then, he says, "Darling, you might be able to hide from the world, but you can't hide from me."

I bite his shoulder in response.

"Ow," he deadpans, and I grumble before pulling away from him.

"I'm tired," I say, a clear excuse, and he knows it too by the way he levels a look at me. "Do you have a guest bedroom?"

"We're going to talk about this," he says, a promise and a warning, before sitting up. "Come on, you can use Laila's room. It should be made up from the last time she visited."

I tear myself away from him and get to my feet, and I try not to wilt underneath his knowing stare. Half of me sings in response to being perceived so deeply, while the rest of me wants to book the next flight back to New York City just to get away from this feeling.

I can't decide which part is winning out.

In the middle of the night, I sit up abruptly, tangled in the sheets. I heave for air, blinking over and over until I'm sure the room in front of me is real and the vision of my parents calling me *a disgusting abomination* was just a dream.

"Ugh," I say to myself, running a hand through my sweat-soaked hair.

I sit there for a long time, trying to force my brain to come back to itself. It takes me longer than it should to remember this isn't my room, and it belongs to Jules' sister.

As if on instinct, the moment Jules comes to mind, I stand up and start padding down the hall. I can't see myself falling back asleep anytime soon and being around Jules always puts me at ease. I hesitate before I knock on the door quietly, and when there's no answer, I try the doorknob.

To my surprise, it opens easily, and I step inside the dark room. It's dimly lit by the moonlight coming in through the window. In bed, Jules is lying on his side, breathing quietly.

I wince, almost certain that Jules is sleeping. I know I should turn around and go back to Laila's room, but instead, I take a few steps forward until I reach Jules' bed.

I stand there for a moment, unsure, and then finally give in to the urge to whisper Jules' name.

He stirs slightly before blinking his eyes open. "Summer?" he asks groggily.

Immediately, I feel bad. I know how busy Jules is this week with the release of the movie and how hard he's been working, yet here I am, waking him up in the middle of the night because I'm afraid to go back to sleep.

"I'm so—I'm sorry, I shouldn't have—I was—I'm sorry, I'll go back to—sorry," I stammer, making a move to leave, but Jules' fingers wrap around my wrist, keeping me in place.

"What's wrong, baby?" he mumbles, pulling on my wrist until I turn back toward him. "Are you all right?"

I nod, a flush rising high in my cheeks. "I'm fine. I'm sorry, I shouldn't have—" I start to say, gnawing on my bottom lip, and Jules tugs sharply on my hand until I stumble into the bed.

"Stop apologizing, all right? Lie down with me," he says, letting go of my wrist only to intertwine our fingers instead.

I hesitate briefly before deciding I might as well if I'm already here, and I lie down beside him. "Are you sure this is okay?"

Jules shushes me, moving closer until his head is against my shoulder. The *J* of my necklace sits next to his cheek, reflecting the moonlight faintly. "Go back to sleep."

It's then that I realize Jules smells like rain, as if he came straight out of the movie he starred in.

> *Like a drizzle on a summer afternoon*
> *A storm in the dead of the night*
> *Early morning dew*
> *Rain will always remind me of you*

"I'm sorry," I say quietly. "I shouldn't be here."

"Yes, you should," he says sleepily. "You're my best friend. Where else would you be?"

I inhale sharply, but he doesn't seem to notice, pressing his lips against my collarbone before settling in, his hair tickling the skin underneath my chin.

*You're my best friend.*

I look down at him, already fast asleep against me, and wonder for the first time if maybe he's in love with me too.

## CHAPTER THIRTY-THREE

### "RIGHT AS RAIN" TO SWEEP OSCARS: FIRST TIMERS MINA RAHMAN AND JULES MORADI PREDICTED TO BE NOMINATED FOR BEST DIRECTOR AND BEST ACTOR AMONG OTHERS

In the weeks leading up to the Oscar nominations, I have approximately three mental breakdowns. I deal with two by myself, and Barbie unexpectedly has to deal with the third when she asks me how Jules is and I burst into ugly sobs.

"Oh dear God," she says, and pulls me into her arms and attempts to distract me with updates about how her not-romance is going with Spencer.

For the most part though, I hold it together. I go to my vocal lessons and try not to feel guilt over making my fans wait so long for new music. I go to the studio and record half the album. I hire an accountant and finally take some classes on budgeting. Jules and I go for two pap walks, once to get brunch and once to the studio. During the latter, Jules spends the entire time poking around, asking me what all the equipment does. I answer with faked exasperation and he grins at me like he knows.

The rest of the time, Jules comes over to mine and goes through scripts, or I go over to his and rewrite songs. I see him more than I see anyone else in my life, and I'm fatally aware of the fact that I'm going to lose this soon.

Unless I get the courage to say something to him.

I write a song called "Bravery" five different times, crumpling each attempt into a ball and throwing it in my trash can.

In December, the shortlist is revealed, and I nearly heave when I find out both Jules and I are under consideration. Zach demands we throw a party to celebrate, but Jules refuses, not wanting to jinx it until the official nominations are released.

When my phone starts ringing near the end of January with my ringtone for Jules, every muscle in my body tightens in anticipation and I pick up the FaceTime call, hoping, *praying* that it's good news.

"Well?"

Jules grins at me, so wide and bright and beautiful that my heart cracks. "We're nominated! It's official!"

I whoop loudly, beaming back at him. My nomination pales in comparison to his since I don't expect to win. Being nominated is already a huge win in and of itself, and I'm content with it. For Jules, though, this is his first nomination and it's for *Best Actor*, of all things. If he wins, he'll be the youngest person to ever take it. It's absolutely insane to think about and I'm glowing with pride for him.

"I'm so proud of you," I say sincerely. "You deserve this more than anything."

Jules' gaze softens. "Celebrate with me tonight? I'll make dinner."

I nod. "It's a date," I say, but even over the phone, the word seems to change the air between us.

"It's a date," he agrees softly, and hangs up.

I think about dressing up fancy for tonight, but then realize that it wouldn't feel true to what we've become. And I don't want to sit around and pretend with him, not anymore.

I settle for a band T-shirt and a pair of sweatpants, which upon further inspection I realize might belong to him.

When I show up to his apartment, I don't bring anything but myself and a lone sunflower I bought from the market on my way here.

Jules opens the door and smiles warmly at the sight of me. "You brought me flowers."

"A flower," I correct, stepping inside when he holds the door open. His apartment is much cozier than the empty house in LA, and I immediately feel relaxed when I step inside. My mouth waters at the smell of fresh spices drifting through the space. "What did you make for dinner?"

"Zereshk polo," he says, gesturing for me to follow him into the kitchen. "I called my mom and she sent over a recipe. Have you tried it before?"

I shake my head, eyes wide at his setup. "How long have you been at this?"

He takes a dish towel off his shoulder, wiping down the counter. "Don't worry about it. I wanted to celebrate and I haven't had home-cooked food in a while."

I reach out, hugging him from behind, pressing my face against the side of his arm. "Thank you for inviting me over. I really am so proud of you."

He presses a kiss to the top of my head. "Of course, Summer."

I smile up at him and go to set up the dining table while he brings the food over. There's already a lit candle, and I breathe in the calming scent of vanilla.

A lyric tugs at my mind, and I open my Notes app, writing it down.

*Vanilla fog, burning candles*
*This is too delicate to handle*

Then I put my phone away, setting it to do not disturb. Texts have been coming in from my parents all morning, asking me to reconsider being under their management, and Jana called me earlier saying they're incensed that I somehow got an Oscar nomination without any help from them.

I try not to think about any of that, focusing on Jules as he carefully ladles food onto my plate, his brows furrowed with concentration. He's so handsome, almost ethereal in the candlelight, and I'm so incredibly in love with him that it's a little hard to breathe.

"Thank you for this," I say again.

Jules shrugs, but there's a flush on his cheeks. "It was nothing."

All through the meal, I make a point of telling him how delicious it is, pestering him into agreeing to cook for me again, but it feels different from before.

The weight of this thing between us is palpable and heavy in the air. I wonder if Jules can feel it too.

As we're washing our dishes, I quietly say, "The other night you said I was your best friend."

Jules falters for half a beat but then continues scrubbing the plate in his hand. "Is that a surprise?"

"No," I say, tilting my head. "But I . . ." I don't know what to say, how to say it.

"But you . . . ?" he prods.

I shake my head. "Nothing. You're my best friend too."

He gives me a soft smile. "I know, Summer."

And for now, it's enough. But will that still be true weeks from now, when the Academy Awards are done, and there's no more professional obligation left? What do we do then?

I'm not brave enough to ask, but I wish I were.

# CHAPTER THIRTY-FOUR

## ANGELINA RODRIQUEZ THROWING PRE-OSCARS EXTRAVAGANZA FOR THE NEW GENERATION: A TRADITION FOR YEARS TO COME?

I'm surprised when I get a personal invite from Angelina Rodriguez to attend her pre-Oscars party, and even more surprised when she tells me to extend the invitation to Barbie and Zach.

I tell Jules about it and he smiles a little shyly. "I talk about you a lot. I guess I must've mentioned Barbie and Zach at some point."

I try to pretend that doesn't make my stomach flutter, but I suspect I do a terrible job of it. Even though Jules and I haven't spoken about what we're going to do once the Oscars are over, it sits there between us, waiting to be brought up.

Barbie insists I tell him the extent of my feelings, but quickly shuts up when I say she should do the same for Spencer.

Despite myself, I notice Jules looking at me sometimes, a strange expression on his face that I don't dare try to put into words.

The night of Angelina's party, I catch him staring at me with that look on his face more than once while we're all getting ready. Zach notices it at one point and raises an eyebrow at me, but I give him a minute shake of my head, not wanting to get into it.

My phone buzzes and I glance at it, grimacing when I see a string of texts.

> **Father Figure:** Sumaira, this has gone on long enough. You can't be mad at us forever.

> **Mother Figure:** we're sorry ok? but it's time for you to be mature and do the right thing

> **Father Figure:** How long are you going to act like a little kid? This temper tantrum is beneath you.

> **Mother Figure:** come home sumaira

"Summer," Barbie warns, and I set down my phone far away from me.

The texts leave a bitter taste in my mouth for the next hour, even as I try to focus on getting hyped up for the party. Jules has been watching me with concern ever since I picked up my phone. Eventually, instead of asking about it, he holds his arms out for me in a quiet offer.

I slip into them eagerly, closing my eyes and letting him hold me until I can focus on something other than the words *come home, Sumaira*.

It's fine. The party will be a good distraction. It'll make things better. It has to.

At first, the party *is* a good distraction. It *does* make things better.

I stuff myself into a photo booth with Jules, Barbie, and Zach and make silly faces into the camera, laughing uproariously when Barbie nearly whacks her head on the top of the booth.

Jules insists I play beer pong with his cast members, and I'm helpless to do anything but agree when he pouts at me like that. In turn, I finally pay him back and drag him to do karaoke with me in front of everyone.

After one drink too many, I leave to find a bathroom. In the mirror, I look at myself, wearing the red corset Jules bought—or rather *I* bought—all those months ago, which I never thought I would have use for. I look the same, but also different somehow. Something has changed, visible in the curve of my mouth, the glint in my eyes.

I smile and wonder if this is what it looks like to finally be myself.

I step back outside, ready to poke at Jules until he agrees to do another song with me. Then I realize the entire room has gone quiet, save for two people: Jules and Alex.

Alex is standing in front of Jules with an almost feral sort of smile on his face. "At the end of the day, you don't deserve this nomination. You know it as well as I do."

Jules doesn't say anything, his jaw tight with silent fury.

I push my way through the crowd, ready to strangle Alex with my bare hands, but Barbie catches me, holding me back from stepping in the middle.

"I think he's going to hit him," she whispers to me, her eyes darting back and forth between them. "Stay here. You'll get hurt."

"Hit—?" I give her an incredulous look. Jules would never . . .

I falter when I notice the lazy way Alex is cracking his knuckles. There's a hazy look on his face that makes me think he's been drinking, and a *lot* at that.

"You might be able to scam the rest of these idiots, but I know the truth," Alex says, giving Jules a mocking little shove. "You've been coasting by on diversity your entire career, and for what? Your skin color is barely any different from mine, even if you decided to change up your makeup routine. What makes you deserving of an Oscar and not the rest of us? You're an untalented waste of space."

Still, Jules is silent.

*Say something*, I want to yell. *Tell him what an asshole he is.*

But Jules only stands there, taking it without a word.

"You won't even deny it," Alex says, shaking his head ruefully. "It's a shame, Jules."

Then he takes a swing, and the impact snaps Jules' head to the side.

I gasp in disbelief and shake Barbie off me. "Hey, asshole, touch him again and I'll *kill* you," I say, shoving my way in between them. "Leave him the fuck alone."

"Oh, look at that," Alex coos. "He's got a knight in shining armor, is that it?"

I smile at him, wide and sharp. "Do you want to hit me too, then? Go ahead. I'll sue you so fast you'll never see a fucking dime of your residuals again."

Alex blinks at me, clearly taken aback.

"I'm going to count to three," I say sweetly. "And by the time I'm finished, you're going to leave, or I'm going to ruin your life. Do we understand each other?"

"Don't bother counting," Alex scoffs, shoving past me to go to the kitchen. He makes a point to ram his side against Jules as he leaves, and I audibly hiss with irritation. Fucking dickhead.

"Come on," I say, grabbing Jules' arm, and pulling him in the opposite direction. "Let's leave."

He doesn't say anything, his head bowed low, but he follows me. I glance back at Barbie, giving her an apologetic look. "Sorry, I think I need to take him home. I—"

She shakes her head. "No, go, go. I'll explain to Angelina if she asks. Dear God." Then she glares at the person next to her, who's holding out their phone, recording us. "What the hell is wrong with you? Zach! Can you come here?"

I leave her to deal with that, lifting my phone to my ear to call our driver. Once I have confirmation they're pulling up, I finally look at Jules.

"Let me see," I say, touching his jaw, and he flinches away from me. I hesitate, considering him more thoroughly. "How bad is it?"

He lets out a weak laugh, and it sends chills down my spine. I open my mouth to ask another question when our car pulls up on the curb.

I blow a strand of hair out of my face in frustration, and wait for Jules to get inside before I reach for him again.

"Let me see," I repeat, and Jules finally lets his head loll to the side, revealing a red mark on his cheekbone. I grimace, certain it's going to bruise. "Does it hurt?"

When he doesn't respond, I narrow my eyes at him. "Are you ignoring me?"

"No," he says, his voice rough. "I'm listening."

"Then why won't you answer me?" I ask, tugging on his shirt sleeve until he looks at me. "What the hell happened back there? Why didn't you say anything to him? How could you let him hit you?"

Jules sinks lower in his seat. "What was I supposed to do?"

"Stand up for yourself," I say incredulously. "You can't let him push you around like that."

"He was drunk," Jules says, his voice quiet.

"So what? You can't—Jules, you have to see how he's holding you back. Why are you letting him do this? Why would you stand there and take a punch instead of calling him out on his stupid, racist bullshit?"

Jules presses his lips together tightly, which only further highlights the redness of his cheek.

"Jules," I say in disbelief. "What is this? Some kind of misplaced loyalty? He doesn't deserve that from you. You know that."

"I don't know anything, okay?" he snaps. "He was my best friend, Summer."

"*Was* being the operative word!" I say, throwing my hands up. "This is ridiculous, Jules. You have to let go of him. You can't keep holding on to the person he was! It's hurting you. It's *been* hurting you. Why are you letting this happen?"

"The same reason you refuse to set firm boundaries with your parents," he says, and the words feel like having my head plunged into ice water.

"*Excuse* me? That has nothing to do with this!"

"It has everything to do with this," Jules says, and his words finally have some strength in them, but for all the wrong reasons. "Maybe they don't manage your life anymore, but they have more of a say in it than anyone else does. Everything you do, it's like you're waiting for the other shoe to drop, to see what they'll say. You let them control you to this day, and I *see* how much it hurts you. Even earlier, your entire mood shifted after reading their texts. Tell me I'm wrong, Summer."

"That's not—" I splutter uselessly. "They're my parents!"

"And all they ever do is hurt you, but you won't let go," he says. "I see Alex maybe four, five times a year. Your parents call you *every day*. I've heard you listening to their voicemails. They're awful to you, so why do you deal with it? Back there, you stood up for me, but why can't you do the same thing for yourself?"

"It's not the *same*," I say, and I hate the way my voice cracks.

Jules winces, but it doesn't stop him from saying, "Yes, it is. Pot, kettle, and all that jazz."

"My parents have never hit me," I say, lifting my chin defiantly, ignoring the way it trembles slightly.

"I don't think they needed to," Jules whispers, and it's worse than anything else he could've said.

My mouth closes, my teeth clacking together almost painfully.

Jules sits back in his seat, looking tired. "Are you going to deny it?"

I look away from him and lean forward, speaking to the driver. "Please drop Mr. Moradi off at his apartment first."

"Summer," Jules says.

"Fuck off," I say tightly. "I don't want to speak to you right now."

His jaw clenches but he nods. "Okay."

When we pull up to Jules' building, he looks at me again. "Summer."

"Get out of the car, Jules," I say quietly. "I have nothing to say to you."

After a beat of silence, Jules nods again and opens the door. "Okay. I'm sorry for—everything, I guess," he mutters, eyes on the ground. "I'll leave you alone."

I watch on in silence as he turns his back on me, exiting the car and disappearing into his building.

And then I'm alone, as promised.

The car begins to move again. I can't swallow past the lump in my throat anymore—it hurts to try. It takes a second for everything to sink in, but then the gravity of the whole situation hits me. I start to sob quietly, hot tears streaming down my face as I wonder how my life turned out to be such a nightmare.

## CHAPTER THIRTY-FIVE

# WHAT LED TO THE PUNCH: THE HISTORY BEHIND ALEX ROBINSON AND JULES MORADI'S RELATIONSHIP

For the next few weeks, I barely look at my phone. I don't want to see any of the calls or text messages piling in. If anyone really needs to talk to me, they can show up at my apartment and say what they want to me in person.

The only exception I make is for my sisters, and I regret even that when I pick up their call and see twin disappointed faces.

"Are you out of your mind?" Safi asks bluntly. "Why would you do that?"

"I have my reasons," I say, keeping my face blank. I don't bother asking what they're talking about or who told them. The only way they could know about the situation with Jules is if Barbie told them. She and Zach are the only people I've allowed in my space these last few weeks, and while Zach likes my sisters well enough, he doesn't keep up with them regularly the way Barbie does.

"I'm sure you do," Jana mutters before sitting up straighter. "If the reason you won't cut off Ma and Baba is because of me and Safi, you need to tell us right now, Apu. Because if that's what it is, we'll talk to Ma and Baba ourselves and find a way to fix this. You can't *do this*—I don't care. It's not worth losing Jules over, and you deserve better than making yourself miserable over *us*."

I gape at them. "*What?* No, don't talk to Ma and Baba. I'll handle this my own way. The last thing I want is for you two to get involved."

"Don't say you're going to handle it if you're not actually going to handle it," Jana all but shouts, and Safi nods in agreement.

"You have to talk to Ma and Baba," Safi says, resolute. "Or we will."

I consider banging my head against the wall.

"It's not that simple, Safi. Don't you understand I'm looking out for you two? I can't—I can't protect you from here, and if I don't have access to Ma and Baba, then anything could happen to you and I'd have no idea."

Jana glowers at me, looking like she wants to shake me through the phone. "We don't need you to protect us, not if it means you're going to lose the things that matter to you. Don't you understand that we love you and want you to be happy?"

"You're being stupid, Summy Apu," Safi adds.

"Language," I say automatically, and both my sisters huff.

"Enough, Apu!" Jana says, exasperated. "You're a kid, too. You deserve to have your own life. You don't have to sacrifice your happiness for us!"

"You don't get to decide that," I say sharply.

"I think we do," Jana says. "How are you going to stop us if we decide to ignore you?"

I narrow my eyes at them. "You wouldn't."

"We would," Safi says, and then reaches forward and hangs up right in my face.

I stare at my phone in disbelief. Then I grab a pillow and scream into it until my voice is hoarse. God. *Fuck.*

This isn't how this is supposed to go. I'm the older sister, I'm the one who's supposed to look out for *them*. Since when do they get to turn the tables on me?

I can't lose my sisters on top of everything else. I'm not strong enough to survive that. Already, I barely feel like I can function. My body instinctually looks for Jules when I enter a room, and my mouth opens, turning to say something to him before I remember he's not there, and it's my own fault.

Everything happening to me is a hell of my own making.

Later, in the middle of the night, I send an SOS text and Barbie lets herself in using the extra key I gave her months ago. She sighs when she finds me sitting on the cold kitchen tile with my phone held tightly in my hand.

"You need to call them," she says, hands heavy when they come to rest on my shoulders.

"Call who, Babs?" I ask, and my voice is so far from steady it's laughable.

Barbie shakes her head, squeezing my shoulders. "You know who. It's time to break the cardinal rule, Summer. You need to talk to them. We both know what the problem is here, and it isn't Jules."

"I know," I whisper, and shut my eyes, wishing I could rid myself of my treacherous heart. "I know."

But knowing doesn't mean doing. I pull up Ma's contact several times over the next week, my thumb hovering over the call button, but I can never make myself hit it.

What am I supposed to say to them? *Leave me alone?* It's not that easy, and even if I say it, it doesn't mean they'll listen to me. They never have before.

But I can't let my sisters keep being collateral between us. It's not *fair*, to me or them.

I open my lyric journal and carefully scrawl "Cardinal" at the top. On the page before, I can see the bleed over from "Bravery," and it makes me want to put my head in a blender.

While Jules hasn't shown up at my apartment, he has reached out through text several times, mostly variations of **Summer, can we talk?** and **I hope you're all right.**

But I don't know how to face him now, knowing that he was right. I already faked sick to get out of the Oscar Nominees Luncheon earlier this week. How can I tell Jules to cut his losses with Alex when I won't do the same? When I let my parents haunt my every move, whether or not they're physically present in my life?

I hate the idea that no matter what I do, no matter how much agency I gain, it won't matter because my mind will keep coming back to what my parents will think about me.

I flip through my journal until I finally come across "Pink" and stare at it, long and hard. Am I strong enough for this? Am I brave enough for this?

Slowly, I reach for my phone, and instead of calling my parents, I call my PR team. It's late enough in the evening that they might not pick up, but I wait and hope anyway.

The line rings and rings. Then there's a pleasant and familiar voice on the other end. "This is Rory speaking, how may I help you?"

"It's Summer," I say, worrying my bottom lip in between my teeth.

There's a beat of silence and then Rory starts shouting, "Oh my God, *Summer*? Guys, Summer is on the line!" and suddenly three other people are on the line with us.

"Summer, honey, how are you?" Tina asks, but it's overshadowed by Charlie cursing at me in what may or may not be three different languages.

It takes a while for all of the commotion to settle down, but once it does, Zoey is the one to ask, "No, really, how are you? Are you holding up well?"

"I'm all right," I say before sighing. I haven't spoken to them since Angelina's party, mostly out of embarrassment. "How much of a mess did I make?"

"Nothing we can't handle," Rory says. "You hired us for a reason, and that's because we're good at our jobs. Don't you dare forget it."

I smile faintly. "Wouldn't dream of it."

The girls spend ten minutes catching me up on what's happening in the media, and how a video leaked but the backlash has been mostly against Alex. Jules' reps haven't said anything, but my team put out a blanket statement saying that the situation is being handled privately. There's an almost protective edge in Charlie's voice as she explains that they've been stonewalling Alex's reps, and it causes a pang in my chest. Undoubtedly, this is how I sound when I talk about my sisters.

It takes a lot of work to build up the courage to open my mouth after that, but when there's a brief silence, I say, "So . . . some things have changed for me, perspective-wise. About my sexuality," so quietly that I almost hope they don't hear me.

"If you say you've been dating a girl in secret all this time, I might actually start screaming," Charlie says, too cheery. "You're supposed to tell us these things, Summer."

"I'm not dating a girl in secret," I say in exasperation, but then I falter, considering my next words. "But . . . I guess since I have you here, I *am* in love with someone."

"With a girl?" Tina asks softly.

"With Jules," I say, and it feels like I can finally breathe easy again. The entire line bursts into noise, half of them whispering excitedly while Charlie says, "Oh my God, *finally*."

"Have you two talked about it?" Rory asks, and as much as she's trying to be professional, I can hear the delight in her voice.

"Not in any way that matters," I say, sighing as I lean back in my chair. "But I—I'm calling because I want to be brave. I mean, I guess dating a guy takes away some of the bravery, but I was thinking . . . do you think it would be all right to release a song with *she* and *her* pronouns? I don't want to do an official coming out or anything, and I don't want to answer any questions or put out a press statement, but . . . yeah, I don't know. What do you think?"

"First of all, it does not take away any of the bravery," Tina says firmly. "It doesn't matter if you're in a relationship with a boy. You're still pansexual, regardless of who you're dating."

"I guess that's true," I say in a small voice.

"Second of all," Zoey says. "We think it's a great idea, but don't worry about what we think—frankly, I think half of us have been hoping you'd call about this eventually."

"Waiting for me to ruin my own career?" I say, trying to make a joke, but it falls flat.

"It's not going to ruin your career," Rory says without missing a beat. "It might be difficult at times, yes, but we'll work through it together."

"Are you sure this isn't a problem for you guys?" I ask, biting the inside of my cheek, ignoring the taste of blood in my mouth.

"This is our job," Tina says, her voice soothing. "Summer, you could kill someone and we'd spin it into something good."

"Don't kill anyone, though," Charlie threatens, but then softer, she says, "We'll help you through this, Summer. It'll be okay. Send us the song when you have a chance, and we'll get to work, all right?"

I blow out a breath and nod even though they can't see it. "Thank you. Really."

"Of course," they all say before Zoey adds, "But *don't* disappear off the face of the planet next time."

I laugh, and there's a well of relief inside my chest, small but present amidst all the fear and apprehension. "I'll do my best."

The day before the Oscars, I sit down in my bedroom with my phone out in front of me. I look around my room, at this home I made for myself, at this space I carved out even when my parents argued against it, and try to find courage.

And I finally press the call button.

My mother picks up on the second ring. "I see you've finally come to your senses, Sumaira."

"No," I say softly. "I'm calling to tell you to stop."

"To stop?" Ma repeats, and then I hear her say, "Sumaira's Abbu, come here! To stop what?"

"To stop this," I say. "To stop all of it. Can't we put an end to this? Just let me go. Let me live my life. Why is that so hard?"

My mother scoffs. "You finally call us and you *still* insist on being disrespectful? Sumaira, *you* need to stop. Come home already. Enough is enough."

"I am home, Ma," I say, curling my fingers into my blankets and sheets. "Please, just . . . just stop, okay? Stop calling me, stop texting me, stop yelling at me and lecturing me. Stop trying to make me feel guilty for choosing myself."

"If you feel guilty, you should think about why," Baba says as he joins the call, his voice cold and unyielding. "You know you did something wrong. You know your behavior has been inappropriate. Give it a rest. Your career was so much better off with us managing it. We've only ever looked out for you; can't you see that?"

"Maybe you believe that, but it's not true. You took my sisters from me. Even if I forgave you for everything else, I will *never* forgive you for that," I say, and my voice finally starts to gain some strength. I sit up straighter, the thought of my sisters bringing forth a tangle of emotions. "You both *have to stop*. Do you understand? I'm not going to deal with this anymore."

"What are you going to do if we don't?" Ma asks, her voice mocking. "What *can* you do? You're a child, Summer. You're *our* child. We know you better than anyone, and there's nothing—"

"I'll cut you off," I say, braver than I've ever been. "I'll completely cut both of you out of my life, block your numbers, and get a restraining order. Then I'll hire a family lawyer and sue for custody of Sanjana and Safina."

"Excuse me?" Baba demands, his voice rising. "How *dare* you? You can't speak to us like that!"

"You think I won't do it? I will. And I'll *win*. Who do you think the court is going to believe? You're the ones who made me into

America's 'innocent and pure' sweetheart. Not to mention all the texts and voicemails of you both yelling at me, threatening me using Sanjana and Safina."

"Sumaira Ali, don't you *dare*—" Ma starts shouting.

"I won't have to, if you stop behaving like *children*. The two of you love to accuse me of acting immature, yet you insist on acting like this!" I blow out a breath and try to remember the language my lawyer coached me on. "From now on, you will *only* contact me as it pertains to my sisters unless I reach out first. And I'll see them whenever I want to see them, as long as it doesn't interfere with their schooling. If I hear from either of them that you're mistreating them, I will engage in legal action."

"Sumaira," Baba hisses. "You can't do this."

"I can," I say. "I should've done it a long time ago, but better late than never, I guess. Do you guys accept my terms or should I invest in a family lawyer?"

They don't reply for a long time, though I can hear muffled whispers through the speaker. I sit there and wait, my heart racing so hard I feel dizzy.

Ma comes back to the phone, and her voice is so icy it makes me recoil. "Fine. I hope you're happy, Sumaira."

And then the line cuts off.

I stare at my phone incredulously, trying and failing to process the words. Did . . . did I win?

Is it finally over?

My phone buzzes and I pick it up, expecting a scathing text from my parents, but instead it's a text from Jana's number with a selfie attached of both of my sisters grinning at the camera, their ears pressed up against the door of my parents' bedroom.

**Sanjana Ali:** sleepover next week when ur back from the oscars??

I laugh breathlessly.

**Me:** wouldn't miss it for the world <3

## CHAPTER THIRTY-SIX

## JULES MORADI ARRIVES AT THE ACADEMY AWARDS WITHOUT SUMMER ALI ON HIS ARM: TROUBLE IN PARADISE?

It's hard not to regret the series of decisions that lead to me standing by myself on the red carpet of the Academy Awards. I offer the cameras a bright grin just as another round of flashes goes off, people yelling at me from all sides. It makes my head pound with the beginnings of a headache, but I don't dare wipe the smile off my face.

"Summer! Summer, are you excited to attend the Oscars for the first time?"

"Summer, do you care to comment on the fallout between Jules Moradi and Alex Robinson?"

"Why didn't you arrive with Jules, Summer?"

"Smile pretty for me over here, would you?"

"Do you think you'll take home a win tonight, Summer? You're up against some huge stars!"

"Over here, Summer! Come on!"

I offer a wave and then keep moving along the red carpet, letting the next person have their turn being yelled at.

One of my publicists, Tina, is with me tonight along with my bodyguard, Damon. She offers me my purse when I get off camera and I smile gratefully. The two of us adjust the folds of the ostentatious red dress Versace sent me to wear, sheer lace built into the bodice and a slit down the left side, revealing a sliver of skin from my leg up to my thigh. It's snug enough that I find it a little difficult to breathe, but it's not as if I anticipated having perfect control of my lungs tonight anyway.

More importantly, I asked for red, and Versace delivered.

As far as I know, Ariana is with Jules tonight, wherever he is. I can't help that my eyes skip past all the other celebrities around me as I search for him in the crowd. I need to talk to him, to apologize for everything that happened.

I only stop for a brief moment when I see the director of *Right as Rain*, Mina Rahman. She's talking animatedly to an interviewer, gesturing at her boyfriend, Emmitt Ramos, while he waves her off with a fond smile. I'm pretty sure he's also nominated for Best Actor, and all of the predictions I've seen say he's most likely to win.

I don't think it would crush Jules to lose to Emmitt, not when it's his first time even being nominated, but I still *want* Jules to win. After everything, he deserves this.

I rise on my tiptoes to check if any of the other members of the *Right as Rain* cast are near Mina, but I don't see any of them. I try not to frown, conscious of all the cameras around, but it's hard.

When an interviewer approaches me, I'm kind of startled. I didn't think I was important enough for anyone to seek me out specifically, but I guess with all the recent headlines about Jules and

Alex, and the lack of response from either of them, I'm the best shot anyone is going to have at shedding light on the situation.

"We can decline," Tina murmurs in my ear, side-eyeing the interviewer. "It's up to you."

"Will you blacklist questions about Alex?" I whisper back.

Tina immediately leans over to tell the interviewer our stipulations. As predicted, the interviewer looks disgruntled, but eventually nods.

"Hello, Summer," she says with a thin smile. "I'm Reem from *Entertainment Weekly*. Do you mind if I ask you a few questions?"

"Of course," I say smoothly, and force myself to keep my gaze focused on her despite the urge to keep searching the crowd for Jules.

"Starting off, congratulations on your first Oscar nomination! How does it feel?"

"I'm still in shock," I say truthfully. "I never in my wildest dreams thought I'd end up at the Academy Awards. It's an honor to be up against such talented songwriters, and I feel really lucky to be here."

Reem nods. "Will you tell us more about the song?"

"Yeah, of course," I say, and feel comfortable for the first time since I stepped onto the red carpet. "So, I wrote 'Show Me' after watching *Right as Rain*. I felt so moved after I finished it, and part of it was how incredible the actors are"—I pretend not to notice when Reem's eyes light up and she opens her mouth to interject, refusing to falter for a second in my own sentence—"but part of it was how raw the themes of the story are. This idea that you're running from your hometown, desperate to get away from it, but there are things that still tie you back to it, and you're somehow supposed to balance all of that while staying true to your heart. I think my thought process when it came to writing the song was, *What would I want if I were in the main character's shoes?* And the answer was that I would want the people around me to show me they love me, whether they were the person I was in love with or the cousins I grew up with or the friends who saw me through it all. To show me that they understand why I'm leaving and won't love me any less for it. To show me that they see who I am. *I'm begging you to show me, to give me something to hold on to, to remind me of the strength I know I have.*"

The reminder of my own lyrics settles something in me, and I know, as soon as this interview is over, I need to find Jules.

The interviewer looks a little taken aback by my ramble but recovers quickly. "Wow, thank you for sharing some of your songwriting process."

I give her a genuine smile. "Of course."

Reem's expression shifts slightly, less sharky and more like a normal person. "Maybe next year you'll be invited to perform. Wouldn't that be incredible?"

My eyes widen. "Are there musical performances at the Oscars? Oh my God, that'll be so fun. Who's performing tonight?"

Reem blinks at me, and I wonder if I look stupid for not already knowing there are performances. Then I realize her bemusement is because she doesn't have the answer to my question.

"Uh." She looks behind her, and someone off camera says, "Toma Ozan!"

"Oh, that's so exciting!" I say brightly. "He's always great onstage."

Reem nods, gaining back her bearings. "Absolutely. How are your nerves tonight? Are you feeling good?"

"I mean, I'm definitely nervous, but it's really, truly an honor to even be nominated. I'll be satisfied with myself no matter who wins, *but* I won't say no to taking one of those little golden dudes home," I say with a light laugh. "I'm more nervous for the movie as a whole, honestly. I got to visit set at one point and I saw how hard everyone in the cast and crew was working on it, so I really hope they get all the wins they deserve."

"Speaking of the cast," Reem says, and I barely refrain from rolling my eyes, "I noticed you're here without your boyfriend, Jules Moradi."

*Is there a question there?* I want to ask.

Instead I say, "Yes! I wanted him to have his own moment in the spotlight. This is the first time he's been nominated, you know? I'm really excited for him and I'm keeping all my fingers crossed." I pointedly hold up my hand up to the camera.

Reem deflates a little, clearly hoping for some morsel of gossip. "That's lovely. And who are you wearing tonight?"

"I'm wearing Versace," I say brightly, taking a step back so more of my outfit is in view. "Isn't it beautiful?"

There are the customary *oohs* and *ahhs* as they take in my dress before Reem's eyes lock in on my necklace. Despite my styling team insisting I wear something to match the dress, I couldn't bring myself to take off the *J*, too used to it sitting in the hollow of my neck.

"And what about your jewelry?" she asks.

I touch the necklace, my fingers brushing over the ruby. "It was a gift," I say softly, a little wistful, "from the boy I'm in love with."

The interviewer finally smiles, pleased. "Well, thank you, Summer. I hope you have a great time tonight!"

I don't catch sight of Jules until I'm inside the theater, and then it's too late to *really* talk to him. There's so much to talk about, between our unresolved fight and my feelings for him, but the Academy Awards is hardly the place to start that conversation.

Jules is in the middle of saying something to Angelina, his expression serious, when our eyes meet across the room. I feel the painful distance between us so keenly that I'm surprised there isn't a knife to my chest.

For once, his hair isn't slicked back but loose and wavy around his face, and he's wearing a two-piece suit that's the pale pink of sunrise with a ruffled white shirt underneath. I wonder if he also asked YSL for pink, the way I asked Versace for red.

I start walking toward him without thinking, and Jules immediately breaks away from his conversation with Angelina to do the same. Before I can get to him though, Alex cuts in between us, and I nearly gape at the audacity of him. He's going to cause a scene at the *Oscars*?

But Jules only gives him a brief glance before skirting around him, walking over to me.

He's almost to me when Alex jogs after him, reaching out to grab the sleeve of his suit jacket. "Jules, wait. We need to talk."

"Don't touch me," Jules says, his voice low and flat. "I told you already, I never want to speak to you again."

My eyes widen, and Alex scoffs in disbelief, but Jules doesn't seem to notice or care as he shakes him off and continues toward me.

"You—what—?" I ask, my mouth opening and closing stupidly. "I thought—"

"You were right," he says softly, holding his palm out toward me, a peace offering. "I'm sorry."

"No, I—you were right," I say, taking his hand in mine. "I called my parents, and . . . Let's talk after?"

He nods, and then hesitates before slowly leaning forward to kiss the top of my head. Without meaning to, I make a low noise in the back of my throat and throw my arms around his neck, hugging him tightly.

Jules exhales, wrapping his arms around my waist and burying his nose in my hair. I don't know how long we stand there like that—it can't be long, since there *are* cameras around and the award show starts soon, but it's enough for me to feel a little more hopeful about the world.

I pull away first, dabbing my fingers to the corners of my eyes to make sure I don't mess up my makeup. Jules kisses my head again before pulling me toward our designated seats, squeezing my hand in his.

Moments after we sit down, the cameras start rolling, launching into this year's Academy Awards.

Somehow, the next few hours feel like the fastest and slowest in my entire life. My leg starts bouncing ten minutes in, and I only manage to stop when Jules places his hand on my thigh.

"Aren't you nervous?" I whisper to him during Toma Ozan's performance.

"Yeah, but I don't need to win to *win*," Jules says quietly. "There's always next year, right? And the year after that and the year after that."

I study his face, trying to see if he really means it, and he meets my gaze evenly. While there is a bit of tension to the set of his brows, his brown eyes are calm, steady.

"I still hope you win," I say, turning back to the stage, but nudging my knee against his.

Jules smiles, nudging me back. "I hope so too."

When Best Original Song comes up, the presenters read out the nominees, and it feels surreal to see my name up on the screen, to hear my voice playing softly through the room.

"Show Me"

From Right as Rain

Music and Lyrics by

Summer Ali

When the winner is announced, and it isn't me, I hardly care. I stand up, clapping for them with a wide smile before sitting back down next to Jules, a little more at peace now that the stress of my award is out of the way.

"You're all right?" he checks.

"Right as rain," I say with jazz hands, and he snorts.

The closer we get to Best Actor though, the more nervous I get. I bite my bottom lip, glancing at Jules out of the corner of my eye, and it finally looks like the stress has gotten to him. He's absently tapping his rings against arm of his seat, watching the screen with intense eyes. For Best Director, Mina wins and nearly passes out, Emmitt catching her when she swoons and kissing her amidst uproarious laughter.

It helps ease some of Jules' nerves, and he and the rest of his cast members whoop and holler for her excitedly.

But before we can bask too long in that victory, the time comes for Best Actor. The two presenters onstage are saying words, but it all feels like white noise in my head.

"... here are the nominees for best performance by an actor in a leading role! Jules Moradi, *Right as Rain*; Emmitt Ramos, *Dare to Love*—"

I lean forward in my seat, holding my breath in anticipation.

"And the Oscar goes to . . . Emmitt Ramos!"

At my side, Jules starts clapping, a smile on his face, and I stand up to join him, but I don't bother looking at the screen, my eyes only for Jules.

He sees me looking and gives a small shake of his head. "I'm all right, darling."

I try not to sigh, aware of the cameras on us, and turn my attention to Emmitt Ramos as he says, ". . . Mina told me I wasn't allowed to thank her first this time, so I guess I'll start by saying thank you to my mother, for being my first fan. Love you, Mum! And *now*, I'll say thank you to the love of my life, Oscar Award–winning director, Mina Rahman. You are my light and my muse. Thank you for being my home. Another huge thank you to the cast and crew of *Dare to Love*—"

I allow myself a smile. I guess if someone other than Jules had to win, Emmitt Ramos will do.

I almost forget that *Right as Rain* is nominated for Best Picture until Jules grabs my hand, holding it tightly as he watches the screen intently, the nominees flashing across it.

"And the Oscar goes to . . . *Right as Rain*!"

I blink, astonished, and then the entire room bursts into chaos.

"Oh my God," Jules says in my ear. "Oh my God."

"Oh my *God*," I repeat in disbelief. Then Jules is leaning in to kiss me and everything is right in the world, loud applause thundering in my ears.

He pulls away, tugging me into a hug that soon consists of four or five people as different cast members throw themselves at Jules and vice versa. I let out an incredulous laugh, and Jules slips his fingers around my wrist, tugging me toward the stage along with everyone else.

I don't process any of it, too in shock. Mina goes up front to give a speech with tears in her eyes and everyone crowds around her to hug her. Jules keeps whispering, "Holy shit," into my hair, and I understand the sentiment. "Oh my God."

Between one blink and the next, we're being escorted offstage and into the press room, people shoving mics and cameras in our faces.

I keep staring around in disbelief, and Jules *is holding an Oscar*, laughing brightly as he talks to the interviewer in front of him.

I barely hear anything Jules says until he looks over at me and declares, "The role was actually a lot harder than I thought it would be. I'd never been in love the way my character was in the film. I didn't even think love like that existed in real life until I fell for Summer."

My breath catches in my throat, and the interviewer turns their camera on me, as if expecting me to say something coherent. When I'm silent, they turn the camera back toward Jules, who continues on to talk about what a massive honor it is to be in an Oscar Award–winning movie.

All I can do is stare at him and wonder if he means it, if this means as much to him as it means to me.

If, in between all the pretenses, we accidentally stumbled upon something true.

## CHAPTER THIRTY-SEVEN

## "RIGHT AS RAIN" SWEEPS THE OSCARS WITH SEVEN WINS!

The after-party passes by in a blur. I mostly hang on to Jules' arm and try not to gawk when someone a little too famous comes into my line of vision.

But for once, I don't feel out of place. When people introduce themselves to me, I smile and offer them my hand. When someone insists I record a song for their upcoming film too, I nod like a bobblehead and somehow manage to give them my contact information. When someone asks me what my plans are after the party, I look at Jules drawn into conversation with a director, and say, "I go where he goes."

At one point, Angelina corners me and says, "Summer is going to sing for us!" and everyone cheers.

I give her a wide-eyed look of confusion and she grins, dragging me away from Jules and to the front of the room. "What am I supposed to sing?" I protest.

"The song from the movie!" comes a chorus of answers, but Angelina shakes her head.

"No, I want to hear the song about Jules," she says, a bright and mischievous glint in her eyes. "Please, Summer?"

And maybe, if it were a few months ago, I'd decline.

But I think about Jules and the interview he did earlier, and I want to be brave. *I want to be brave.*

I nod. "All right."

Somehow, a guitar ends up in my hands, passed through the crowd within seconds. Jules is near the front now, looking bemused, and I offer him a shaky smile.

"This song is called 'Bravery,'" I say, and begin to strum the basic chords to it.

Through the entire song, I only look at Jules, and his expression slowly grows more and more slack with disbelief with each line.

Finally, I reach the outro, and sing over and over:

*I'm afraid of losing you*
*I'm afraid of bruising you*
*I'm afraid of choosing you*

And then I end with: *But I'm learning to be brave.*

Everyone cheers, clapping loudly, and I take a polite bow before slipping back into the crowd.

Jules is looking at me like there's no one else in the room, and when he says, "Come with me?" I put my hand in his.

After the driver drops us off at Jules' house, he leads me to the backyard. My heart races in my chest, so fast that it's a miracle I'm even breathing.

Jules grabs a blanket off a chaise and sets it down on the grass before motioning for me to join him. I toe off my heels and hope Versace won't be angry if stray blades of grass make their way onto this dress before lying down beside him, staring up at the sky.

What is bravery?

Is it leaving behind everything you've ever known to try to build a new path for yourself?

Is it continuously putting yourself in the limelight when it makes something inside your chest tremble with anxiety?

Is it holding your head high as people weave narratives about you, both true and untrue?

Is it facing off against the people who once had complete control over your life and taking it back from them?

Is it lying underneath the stars with a boy that is both a stranger and your best friend, and laying your heart at his feet?

"Jules," I say softly.

He turns his head toward me and as soon as our eyes meet, the entire world seems to change, charged with an invisible electric current.

"Summer," he says.

"What happened with Alex?" I ask, shifting so I'm on my side, facing him.

Jules reaches over, brushing a strand of hair away from my forehead. "I spoke to him. With my lawyer present."

I choke slightly. "With your *lawyer*?"

He gives me a sheepish smile. "Well. With Raj present."

"Ah," I say, huffing a breath of amusement. "That makes more sense."

"I basically told him I wasn't going to deal with his harassment anymore," Jules says, his nose wrinkled. "And that if he kept it up I would sue him for slander and libel. Taking a page out of your book, if you couldn't tell."

I burst into laughter. "You told him you'd *sue* him?"

"Raj wants to anyway," Jules admits with a faint smile. "But yeah, I . . . I guess I realized enough is enough. He made me feel less than for so long, and I doubted my place in Hollywood and in my *own* life because of him. He's always known exactly how to get in my head. And it fucking sucks, because a part of me still misses him and what we had before it all went downhill. But he's not the person I knew back then, and I think it's time I make peace with that."

"I'm sorry you had to lose him," I say softly. "I know it couldn't have been easy. But you deserve people who wholeheartedly cherish you and aren't threatened by your talent, and I'm glad you're starting to realize that."

"Getting punched in the face will do that to you," he jokes, and I roll my eyes, lightly shoving him away from me. "How did it go with your parents?"

"Funnily enough, in a way that is *not* funny at all, I went a similar route. I threatened to use lawyers to get custody of my sisters if they didn't cut this shit out." I smile thinly. "And pointed out the court was much more likely to side with me than them given my name, reputation, and the countless texts and voicemails from them I have on file."

Jules lifts his eyebrows. "*You* said all that to *them*? Holy shit."

"You can say that again," I say, blowing out a deep breath. "And I told them if they kept contacting me to yell at me, I'd block them once and for all and get a restraining order."

He lets out a low whistle. "How'd they take it?"

"Terribly," I say with a shake of my head. "But I got my way in the end, and I'm allowed to see my sisters again, so I guess that's what matters."

Jules reaches an arm out, snaking it around me and pulling me closer to his chest. "They're lucky to have you as their sister. I know you didn't have anyone in your corner fighting for you back then, but the fact you're still doing everything you can to ensure Sanjana and Safina's happiness and well-being probably makes a world of difference for them."

I blink, my eyes suddenly wet. That was the last thing I expected him to say. "I'm always going to fight for the people I love."

"I know," Jules says, and his expression is pained. "I'm sorry about everything, Summer. I shouldn't have thrown your parents in your face like that. You were just looking out for me."

I shake my head, my bottom lip trembling. "No, it's not your fault—I think I was projecting onto you a little bit, and I should've gone about the entire situation differently. I'm sorry too. I never meant to hurt you. Will you forgive me?"

"There's nothing to forgive," he says, stilling my head with two fingers pressed to my jaw. "Maybe both of us got a little caught up in all of this?"

"I think so," I say with an uncertain smile. "But it's all over now, isn't it? The Oscars are done. We don't have to keep pretending anymore."

"I suppose that's true," Jules says, and he sounds as unsure as I feel.

I take a breath and summon all the bravery I've hidden away in my heart, willing it to stay strong for my next words. "*Is* this pretend?"

Jules keeps staring at me, holding my gaze for what feels like an eternity before he quietly says, "It's not. I don't think it's been pretend for a long time."

"So what is it?" I ask.

There's a long stretch of quiet, both of us staring at each other. Neither of us says the words, but we can both hear them in the silence.

"It's love," Jules finally whispers, reaching up to touch my cheek. "Isn't it?"

"It's love," I agree softly.

Jules leans in, capturing my lips with his own. I exhale into the kiss and let myself go. For once, I don't have to worry whether this is real or not, because everything inside of me knows this is the most honest and true anything could ever be.

# EPILOGUE

**MEET THE COUPLE COINED "SUMMERJULES"—SINGER SUMMER ALI AND ACTOR JULES MORADI TAKE HOLLYWOOD BY STORM (OR RAIN)**

**JULES MORADI AND SUMMER ALI VACATIONING IN PARIS FOR VALENTINE'S DAY**

**JULES MORADI HAS THE SWEETEST NICKNAME FOR SUMMER ALI**

**SUMMER ALI AND JULES MORADI ARE "VERY IN LOVE"**

**SUMMER ALI "FITS IN SEAMLESSLY" WITH JULES MORADI'S LOVED ONES**

**JULES MORADI TELLS SUMMER ALI "I LOVE YOU SO MUCH" IN NEW VIDEO**

**BARBIE LI AND ZACH MURPHY STILL TEASE SUMMER ALI OVER COMMENT JULES MORADI MADE WHEN THEY FIRST STARTED DATING**

**SUMMER ALI & JULES MORADI'S DATING TIMELINE IS ACTUALLY SO SWEET**

**SPOTTED AT NYC PRIDE: SINGER SUMMER ALI CARRYING PANSEXUAL FLAG, BOYFRIEND JULES MORADI CARRYING HER VERSACE PURSE**

**IT'S SUMMER IN JULY: SUMMER ALI AND JULES MORADI POSE FOR ROMANTIC BEACH PHOTO**

**JULES MORADI DEDICATES OSCAR WIN TO GIRLFRIEND SUMMER ALI**

**SUMMER ALI BRINGS JULES MORADI OUT ONSTAGE FOR SURPRISE 21ST BIRTHDAY CELEBRATION**

**JULES MORADI SHARES HOW HE AND SUMMER ALI AVOID "OUTSIDE NOISE" SURROUNDING THEIR RELATIONSHIP**

**SUMMER ALI IS "INCREDIBLY HAPPY" WITH JULES MORADI YEARS INTO THEIR RELATIONSHIP**

**SUMMER ALI AND JULES MORADI SEEN HOUSE HUNTING IN MALIBU**

**ALL OF SUMMER ALI'S EIGHT SONGS ABOUT JULES MORADI: "BRAVERY," "THREADS," "STRAWBERRIES," AND MORE**

**SUMMER ALI DEDICATES GRAMMY WIN TO BOYFRIEND JULES MORADI**

**JULES MORADI ADMITS THAT HE FELL IN LOVE WITH SUMMER ALI AFTER SEEING HER PERFORM FOR THE FIRST TIME**

**INSIDE SUMMER ALI AND JULES MORADI'S VERY PUBLIC YET PRIVATE ROMANCE**

**JULES MORADI AND SUMMER ALI ADOPT PET CAT, "RAINY"**

**SUMMER ALI IS ENGAGED TO JULES MORADI AFTER "INTIMATE" PROPOSAL FIVE YEARS INTO THEIR RELATIONSHIP**

**SUMMER ALI SAYS SHE'S "STILL SPEECHLESS" AFTER JULES MORADI PROPOSES**

**JULES MORADI AND SUMMER ALI PUBLISH TELL-ALL ABOUT THEIR FAKE RELATIONSHIP TURNED REAL, "I'LL PRETEND YOU'RE MINE"**

# ACKNOWLEDGMENTS

I already did an Oscars acknowledgments bit in *A Show for Two*, so I'll spare you the theatrics this time around—well, mostly. I'm still going to get a little emotional. No matter how many times I write these, I never stop feeling immensely grateful for everyone who's ever touched my books in any way, shape, or form.

As always, I want to say a huge thank-you to all my readers for giving Summer's story a chance. She is so important to me, and I hope her journey brought you some warmth and comfort and hope.

Thank you to everyone in publishing who made this possible: JL Stermer, who sold this book and believed in it from the start. Stuti Telidevara and Peter Knapp, who treated this book like it was their own. Sara Schonfeld, who helped me dive deeper into the heart of Summer's story. Everyone at Harper, including Shannon Cox for marketing, Kelly Haberstroh for publicity, David DeWitt and Alison Donalty for design (and Guinevere for an amazing cover!), Erin DeSalvatore and Gweneth Morton for managing ed, and Danielle McClelland and Melissa Cicchitelli for production, all of whom put so much hard work and effort into making sure *I'll Pretend You're Mine* became a real, physical book that we can all now hold in our hands.